GET A FR

Click here to download The Watcher, a novella exclusive to Ty Patterson's newsletter subscribers

Check out Cordite here, the next Cutter Grogan thriller

Check out Moscow here, the previous Zeb Carter thriller

Join Ty Patterson's Facebook group of readers, here

ALSO BY TY PATTERSON

Zeb Carter Series

Ten books in the series and counting

Cutter Grogan Series (Zeb Carter Universe)

Six books in the series and counting

Zeb Carter Short Stories

Three books and counting

Warriors Series (Zeb Carter Universe)

Twelve books in the series

Gemini Series (Zeb Carter Universe)

Four thrillers in the series

Warriors Series Shorts (Zeb Carter Universe)

Six novellas in the series

Cade Stryker Series

Two military sci-fi thrillers

ACKNOWLEDGMENTS

They say it takes a village to produce a book. In my case, many continents have been involved. Sure, an author's job is a solitary one, but writing is just one part of putting out a book.

My beta readers, who are around the world, are my first responders. I owe a debt of gratitude to them for getting into shape all the words I write.

They are:

Dori Barrett, Laura Rachwalik, Jobins MJ, Simon Alphonso, Steve Panza, Maria Stine, Ann Finn, Don Waterman, Kimber Krahn, Robin Eide Steffensen, Blanca Nichols, Loz Yeung, Charlie Carrick, Martin Pingere, Terrill Carpenter, Kathryn Defranc, Dave Davis, Mike Duncan, Donna Young Hartridge, Shadine Mccallen, Shell Levy, Wanona Koeppler, Marion McNulty Hulse, Gerry Kenny, Rob Fox, Toni Osborne, Cathie M Jones, Debbie McNally, Sylvia Foster, Beth Perry, Mike Davis, Pat Barling, Mary Kauffman, John Spiller, Dave Campbell, Mark Campbell, Cathy Silveira, Franca Parente, Jan Fisher, Nancy Schmit, Claire Forgacs, Pete Bennett, Jimmy Smith, Suzanne Mickelson, Brad Werths, Allan Coulton, Paula Artlip, Pat Ellis, Linda Collins, Tricia Cullerton, Alun Humphreys, Jimmy Smith and Jennifer Anderson.

Donna Rich, my proofreader, and Merwie Garzon, my editor, have been invaluable in polishing the book.

Lastly, a special thanks to Debbie Gallant, Tom Gallant, Michelle Rose Dunn and Cheri Gerhardt, who have supported me since the beginning.

DEDICATIONS

To my wife and son for their sacrifices in supporting me

Leave the Devil alone and he might return the favor

CHAPTER 1

Mumbai

ZEB WANDERED THROUGH THE CRAWFORD MARKET, ONE OF the largest of its kind in Mumbai. Vegetables, poultry, fruits and fragrances, the market had them all.

It wasn't the city's most glamorous bazaar. It was untidy, it smelled, it was crowded, but it gave a glimpse of the real Mumbai.

He wasn't there to buy anything. He was following his team, who were browsing through various stalls. Meghan, negotiating with a vendor for a scarf; Bwana, trying on a turban; he took them in, enjoying the warmth, the sounds and smells of India's largest city, the capital of the state of Maharashtra.

They were vacationing in the country. They had been invited by his close friend, Vikram Kohli, Special Agent, Research and Analysis Wing, of the country's secretive foreign intelligence agency.

'Warm weather, very warm. Good food and the opportunity to get away from it all.'

That had been Kohli's spiel. Bwana and Roger were sold instantly. The twins agreed, too. Chloe arm-twisted Bear into accepting. Zeb looked at Broker, who had shrugged. 'We have nothing else to do.'

That had nailed it.

The sisters planned their visit, which was how they ended up in Mumbai, sampling the wares in the market.

It was the man's sudden turn that alerted Zeb.

He had noticed him behind them and thought nothing of it. The man looked like a Westerner in his patterned shirt and loose shorts, but there were thousands of tourists in the country and many in the market.

The man swiveled suddenly when Zeb looked back casually, which got his attention.

Is he following us?

Zeb fingered a shawl, asked its price, nodded politely at the storekeeper and moved to another shop.

The stalls were lined irregularly. Some shops ran straight, others angled out with different wares.

He cut to another row of shops and inhaled perfumes from display bottles. From an ornate plate's polished surface, he saw the man follow him.

Could be anyone. We don't have enemies here. India is our ally. None of its agencies are hostile.

He shrugged mentally and put the plate down. Sidestepped a young girl who was playing a flute.

'Put it down, Nisha,' her mom told her in Hindi.

Zeb didn't show that he understood her. It was standard operating practice for them. While visiting a new country, learn its language well enough to understand it.

Nisha blew harder on the instrument.

He stifled a smile as he went to the next stall, one that sold ceramic pottery. He inspected a bowl idly while he checked out his friends.

'Ma, I need to practise. You know I am in the school band.'

'Play at home. We bought you a new flute.'

Nisha pouted. Her pigtails bobbed when she returned the flute to the stall. She caught his eyes and grinned when he winked at her.

The man drew closer to them.

'Zeb!'

He looked up to see Kohli hustling up.

The RAW agent was beaming. He weaved through the crowd easily, using his height and presence to part the shoppers.

The man who'd been tailing them was between his friend and Nisha and her mom. The man raised his hand. A metallic shape in his grip.

Zeb recognized it.

'SHOOTER!' he yelled.

He made to dive at Nisha.

The explosion threw him back against a stall's counter. His ears rang. Smoke filled the market.

A second blast sounded, and he heard nothing else.

CHAPTER 2

'Papa!' a young girl screamed.

'PAPA, HELP ME!'

Zeb struggled through the fog that seemed to grip his body. He realized dimly his hands were secured behind his back. The child was a hazy shape as she yelled frantically. He struggled against his bindings, her screams growing louder.

'PAPA!'

'Zeb.'

'ZEB!'

His eyes flickered open.

Meghan and Beth bent over him, worry in their eyes. His friends hovering behind them. He propped himself on his elbow and blinked rapidly.

He wasn't tied down in any way. He was on the ground in Crawford market. No girl calling out his name. No fog, either. There was smoke and the smell of explosions and screaming and crying around them.

He knew the girl who had been calling him. He knew where the memory had come from. He shoved it back to the depths of his mind, where the boxes of images and sounds and remembrances of a different time were stored.

A time when he had a family. He let those memories surface rarely, and only when he was alone.

He cleared his mind, sat on the ground, and checked himself out quickly. No injuries. His head throbbed, but he couldn't feel any bleeding. His limbs worked. There was a large red patch on his shirt. It didn't hurt when he touched his chest.

'Saffron,' Beth said. 'From the stall behind you.'

'How long was I out?'

'About fifteen minutes. You were closest to the explosion. You jumped behind the stall and upturned it, and that might have saved you. See?' She pointed to the shrapnel stuck to the underside of the wooden shelf. 'It was a low-intensity bomb.'

He swigged water from the bottle Bwana thrust at him and wiped his mouth. Saw a pair of legs underneath another stall.

'Nisha!' he said hoarsely.

'Who?' Meghan frowned.

'There was a girl near me. She and her mom—'

Chloe pointed at two bodies who were being stretchered out of the market.

'Those two?'

Zeb got to his feet and hurried to them. He ignored the EMT staff's orders to keep away.

The mother was moaning softly, as she tried to reach for her daughter. Blood on her chest. Nisha had her eyes closed, a nasty wound on her forehead.

'Is she—'

'Behosh hai. Bahar se aur kuch nahin hua usko. Undar ki zakhm dekhna padega. Picche hat jao.'

She's unconscious. No other injuries on the outside, though we'll have to see if she's got any internal ones. Stand back.

The emergency worker brushed past him impatiently and followed the stretchers out.

'Thirteen dead.'

Zeb turned at Kohli's voice. The RAW agent had a forehead

gash, against which he jammed a gauze bandage, which was reddening slowly.

'There will be more fatalities,' he said grimly. 'At least thirty are injured, some of them seriously.'

'I am okay,' he replied at the Agency operatives' searching glances. 'I threw myself to the ground as soon as Zeb shouted. I hit my head against a stall's leg.'

Zeb scanned the market swiftly. Khaki-clad cops clearing the crowd and keeping spectators at bay. Blue-uniformed officers helping bomb-disposal units. SWAT personnel, alert, gripping their HKs, watching the scene.

Force One, he corrected himself absently. *That's what they are called.*

'The shooter didn't look Indian.' He searched the bodies being carried out and the injured being attended to. 'Light-skinned—'

'We have those complexions in India too.'

'Yeah, but it felt like he wasn't a citizen.'

No one argued. His team, even Kohli, knew of Zeb's gut feelings. They had proven more often right than wrong.

'He wasn't the bomber. He couldn't have been.' Roger frowned. 'Why would he draw a gun if he was planning to detonate?'

'He wouldn't,' Bear agreed. 'Were there any—'

'A few Western tourists,' Kohli said grimly. 'None of whom fit your description. Most of them were women. Two men.'

'Were?'

'Yes, some of them are dead.'

'Did you find a handgun?' Zeb asked him.

'Not yet. We are still searching, however. There were over a thousand people in the market today.' Kohli inspected the gauze, made a face and threw it in a litter bin.

'Cameras?' Beth asked sharply.

'There are a few. We'll go through the CCTV footage. We'll

also request people to share their mobile phone recordings if any of them were doing that.'

Zeb read his glance when the RAW agent's eyes swept over them.

'You want us out of the way.'

'It will help us. Besides,' Kohli said, smiling briefly, 'the police are wondering who you are.'

'You didn't pull your authority?'

'I did, that's why they didn't hustle you out.'

'You'll let us know if you find anything?'

'I will.'

Zeb led his team out of the market, aware of the curious glances of several Force One officers.

'What have you been holding back?' Beth demanded as soon as they climbed into their van, which was parked in a street bay next to Chhattrapati Shivaji Terminus, CST, station. It was Mumbai's best-known train terminal and one of the busiest ones in the country, from which several suburban as well as long-distance trains originated.

'That shooter.' Zeb got behind the wheel, the younger twin in the passenger seat beside him.

India drives on the left, he reminded himself, and waited for a red city bus to pass before merging into the traffic.

'I HAVE A FEELING HE WAS FOLLOWING ME.'

'If he was'—the younger sister worked it out quickly—'he knew who we were. We planned our India visit at the last moment. Only Clare knows where we are. How did the shooter find us?'

Zeb didn't respond. He was frowning at a van that was drawing close in the side-view mirror. It didn't slow as it neared.

'HOSTILES!' he yelled as it crashed into them.

CHAPTER 3

The van swerved. Zeb yanked the wheel hard to evade a cab parked at the side. He jammed the gas to speed down Sir Jamshedji Jeejeebhoy Road, a large street that went alongside the train terminus and joined several others in a crowded junction.

A bus honked angrily as he nearly swiped it.

Too much traffic!

He gritted his teeth as their attackers slammed into them again. He jammed his horn to clear the surrounding vehicles. Heard the splat of rounds striking their van. Saw a woman fall to the ground on the sidewalk to their left, red blossoming on her shoulder.

Traffic parted magically.

'They've heard the shooting.' He spoke aloud, thinking desperately as they raced down the street.

Can't lead the shooters to crowded areas. Neither can we escape, though. They're on our tail.

'Vikram, we're under attack. Permission to go hot?'

He snatched a glance in his rear-view mirror. Meghan, on her phone, talking as if she were discussing the weather. No inflection in her voice. Calm, composed, only her narrowed eyes indicating her concentration. His friends were in a similar state.

She put the call on speaker.

Kohli didn't ask questions.

'Under attack? GO!'

'You know what to do?'

Bwana squeezed his shoulder.

'I do.' Zeb nodded.

He coaxed their van to go faster, down the center of the street, which was free of buses, taxis, private cars and vehicles of any kind.

They've scattered. People are fleeing or are taking cover. Someone will call the cops and they might take us to be hostile, too.

He didn't have much time to act. He could sense the van slowing.

Must have lost rear tires.

The fuel gauge was emptying rapidly.

Must have taken a hit.

His right wing mirror splintered from a round. More bullets crashed into their ride.

It's plated, but how good is the protection?

Zeb clenched his jaw.

The CST junction with other streets was approaching swiftly. He snatched a glance behind, through the pock-marked rear window, to check if their pursuers had fallen behind, but they were gaining swiftly.

'Now,' he alerted his team and yanked the wheel hard to the right.

Tires squealed. Rubber burned. The van teetered precariously at the savage turn and came to a shuddering stop at a cross angle in the middle of the street to block oncoming traffic.

The right flank of the vehicle was facing the approaching shooters, its left shielded by the van's body.

Beth threw open her passenger door and dove out. The van

rocked when Bwana and Bear swung the sliding door on the left and his friends jumped out.

Zeb ducked when a round slammed into his window and crawled back, cursing in the narrow space, and then felt hands on him as his crew yanked him out.

They dropped to the ground, eight of them, with their Glocks, firing beneath the van at the approaching shooters.

'They're masked,' Broker said grimly.

Zeb nodded.

They had only their handguns. The shooters seemed to have automatic rifles which they thrust through the windows to fire at them.

The hostiles' ride slowed and stopped as it absorbed their shots. Its windshield cracked.

Zeb reloaded swiftly and got to his feet when the vehicle started backing away.

He dove into the van and got behind the wheel as his friends covered him, shooting at the retreating attackers.

He turned the key.

The engine didn't fire.

He swore and tried again.

'DROP YOUR WEAPONS. RAISE YOUR HANDS AND COME OUT.'

The cops had arrived.

CHAPTER 4

Zeb saw the bullhorn on the edge of a police SUV. The officer repeated the order in Hindi and then in English.

He glanced through the van behind him and saw more officers behind their rides. All of them armed, training their weapons on the Agency operatives.

He threw his Glock out of the window.

'I AM UNARMED. I AM COMING OUT.'

He raised his hands and stood non-threateningly.

His friends joined him at another command.

'I've never been arrested before,' Beth whispered.

'There's always a first time,' Roger said laconically.

A bunch of armed officers approached them cautiously, spread out, their HKs unwavering.

'Turn around and lean against the vehicle. Hands spread wide.'

They complied.

'I've never been handcuff—'

'We know.' Meghan cut her sister off.

Zeb felt a body come up behind him. His hands were yanked back roughly and steel bracelets encircled his wrists.

He was pushed sharply towards a command vehicle when a Range Rover raced up and squealed to a stop.

Kohli jumped out from the passenger side and hustled towards the commanding officer.

'CHOD DO UNKO. WOH MERE SAATH HAIN.'

Let them go. They're with me.

Zeb stopped on the street. His friends stopped too. Their cops didn't object as they all listened to the wrangling between the RAW agent and the police.

The command officer finally saw the light and ordered his men to release the Agency team.

'You came in time,' Beth said feelingly when Kohli joined them. 'I wasn't fancying my cell.'

'It wouldn't have been comfortable.' He grinned.

His smile faded.

'What happened?'

BETH BROKE IT DOWN SWIFTLY AS THEY GATHERED IN THE AIR-conditioned interior of a Force One van that Kohli had commandeered.

'We haven't found the attackers,' the RAW operative said grimly. 'Every officer in the city is looking out for a black Toyota filled with men.'

'They were masked.'

'Yes, we heard that.'

'You'll find it somewhere, abandoned.'

'Why were they targeting you?'

'We'd like to know that, too.'

'Who else knows you are in Mumbai?'

'Clare, you, no one else.'

'I didn't tell anyone. Even my boss doesn't know. Your calls come to my phone,' he said, holding it up, 'which is checked every day. It's clean.'

'We could have had a tail,' Zeb thought aloud, 'at the airport.

We didn't fly commercial. We came in our Lear. There are a few hostile agencies who know of it. They could have spotted it and had us tailed. We were careful, but'—he nodded at the bustle of the city—'we could have missed them.'

'There's something else you need to know. That shooter in Crawford Market ... he could have been coming for me.'

'You're sure of that?'

'No.' Zeb grimaced in frustration. 'He wasn't looking at me, but there wasn't anyone else around that I could see. You were behind him. Civilians around us. His gun was rising in my direction.'

'Why would they bomb the market? If whoever is behind these attacks sent shooters, why the explosions?'

Beth said it. 'The bombers and the shooters ... they could be two different parties.'

CHAPTER 5

'Yeah.' Zeb nodded at the digital sketch. 'That looks like the shooter.'

They were on the second floor of an office building in Nariman Point, a prominent business district in the south of the city.

Kohli had taken them there after the cops had taken their statements, and the RAW operative had then set Zeb up with an artist who had drawn a portrait of the shooter based on his recollection.

'You were close enough to see his eyes?' Meghan spoke over his shoulder.

'They stood out. I could make out their gray color even with the distance separating us.'

Brown hair, lean jaw, light stubble, no scars or tattoos that he could recollect.

'I don't recognize him.' The elder twin shook her head.

'Neither do I.' Beth handed the screen to the rest of the operatives, who shook their heads or shrugged their shoulders. 'We'll run him through Werner.'

'Werner?' Kohli asked, dismissing the artist with a nod. The man flushed at the twins' smiles, bobbed his head awkwardly and left the room.

'Our system.' She didn't elaborate that it was cutting-edge Artificial Intelligence software that was the heart of their outfit. It maintained databases, ran facial recognition algorithms, scanned newsfeeds and assessed threat levels based on public information and the covert intelligence it gathered.

'I'll get my team to run facial recognition on that sketch. If we're lucky, the cameras in Crawford Market might have captured him.'

'What is this place?' Broker looked around the room they were in. Large, polished wooden table which could seat over twenty people. A wall-mounted TV, overhead projectors, remote controls for the various devices, speakers.

Feels like a board room. Zeb went to the window blinds and raised one of them. His jaw dropped at the sight of Marine Drive, a stretch of road that ran along the Arabian Sea in the south of the city.

'Our Mumbai office.' the RAW agent grinned at his expression. 'We have several in the city, but this is like our state headquarters.'

'Those folks outside?' Chloe opened the door and peered out at the women and men working on their screens in open-plan seating. They had looked curiously at the Agency operatives as they had arrived on the floor and entered the room they were in.

'My team. Analysts, field agents, admin staff. I flew them from New Delhi since I was going to be based in Mumbai for the duration of your visit.'

He runs an outfit like ours within RAW, Zeb mused. *Counter-terrorism and overt operations in different countries.*

He knew Kohli had a wide remit. *He goes after any threat to India's national security, just like we do for our country.*

The agent was taller than the average man in his country. At five eleven, he was an inch shorter than Zeb, but had the similar lean, wiry build. Clean shaven, close-cropped hair and black eyes.

No tattoos or scars. Other than his height, nothing drew attention to him.

'This is prime real estate.' Bear joined Zeb at the window and looked out at the promenade—empty since the city was under a state of emergency for the day—and the sparkling waters beyond.

'We don't have many luxuries.' Kohli grinned. 'But this is one of them. Office space.'

His smile faded when he looked at Meghan. 'You didn't have to ask my permission to go hot.'

'We didn't want to complicate matters for you. We are your guests—'

'Defend yourself if under attack. Leave the bureaucracy to me. Glocks!' He chuckled. 'What happened to your HKs?'

'We're on vacation. We figured we didn't need the rest of our gear. Our handguns ... we don't go anywhere without them.'

'What's the toll?' Zeb asked.

'Twenty dead overall. The number of those injured has risen too,' Kohli said soberly. 'Over fifty, now.'

He paused a beat for the numbers to sink in and then resumed. 'We found the Toyota in a residential building's yard in Byculla.'

That's not far from the market. Zeb pictured the city in his head.

'It was empty. Nothing in it. No blood, no belongings. Police are interviewing residents, but I am not hopeful.'

'They were masked.' Bwana popped a knuckle. 'Their ride seemed to be armored.'

'It was. They weren't your ordinary spray-and-pray killers. They are pros.' Kohli drew his fingers through his hair. 'The last time Mumbai experienced—'

'About thirteen years ago. November 2008.' Meghan nodded. 'We know.'

Lashkar-e-Taiba, LET, an Islamist terrorist group from Pakistan, had carried out coordinated attacks in twelve locations over four days.

One-hundred-and-seventy-five dead, Zeb recalled grimly. *More than three hundred wounded.*

The city's landmarks had been targeted. CST Terminus, high-profile hotels, a popular tourist café, and many other locations had been attacked.

'New York, DC, Paris, London ... all the world's cities and hotels studied those attacks and changed their security systems.' Kohli continued bleakly. 'The city never forgot. And now this.'

He swore under his breath and then raised his hand apologetically at them.

'No need for that.' Bwana went over to him and squeezed his shoulder.

'The shooter and the bombings may not be connected,' Beth told the RAW agent.

'Yes, we are working on that angle as well.'

'We? You have the lead on this?' Zeb asked him.

'We are working with the National Intelligence Agency. I lead the Joint Task Force.'

NIA is the country's federal agency for counter-terrorism. Kohli's agency has a broader responsibility but is focused on foreign intelligence.

'Mumbai Police, other investigative units, they are all part of the JTF.' Kohli glanced at his watch. He straightened.

'Calls? Meetings?'

'Several of them. Briefings with the prime minister, defense minister, the state's chief minister, various other officials ... you know how it is.'

'No, we don't,' Chloe said dryly. 'Clare does that for us.'

Kohli nodded in understanding. He cocked his head at the room. 'Use this if you wish. It's secure. I have arranged passes for you. Or, if you wish to resume your vacation—'

'Holiday is over,' Meghan growled. She looked at the Agency operatives quickly and got confirming nods. 'We're here to help. We will run our own investigation ... we'll share whatever we find. Yeah, the optics, we'll make sure no one knows what we are doing.'

Kohli's face lightened. It seemed a weight had lifted off his shoulders. 'I was hoping to hear that. My team knows who you are. They will provide any help you need. Equipment, cars, you need to talk to anyone— they'll arrange it and run interference if needed.'

'Our identities?' Zeb asked him. 'Mumbai Police saw us. Many other visitors to the market would have seen us. The attack near CST—'

'A covert American unit in Mumbai on a joint training exercise with us. That's how I have explained your presence and your access to weapons. I haven't taken names. My team interviewed every witness in the market and at CST and got them to delete any cell phone recordings. Your identities are safe.'

He opened the door, then beckoned and made way for a woman to enter the room.

She was as tall as him, dressed casually in jeans and a white shirt whose sleeves were rolled to her elbows. Her black hair was tied back in a ponytail. No makeup. Short nails. Trainers on her feet.

She seems to be the same age as Beth and Meg.

'Meera Ranganathan, my deputy.' He made the introductions.

Her palm was hard when Zeb shook her hand.

'You were in the military, Ms. Ranga—'

'Meera will do.' Her teeth flashed. 'No. I was a civilian, like Beth and Meghan. Long story.'

'You know about us?' The younger twin smiled warmly at her.

'There isn't a day when Vikram doesn't talk about you.'

'I am offended.' Roger presented his profile. 'The most interesting person in this room is me and he doesn't mention me.'

'Yeah.' The deputy grinned. 'He said you would say that. You need weapons? A ride?'

'No.' Zeb shook his head and finger-waved at Kohli, who departed.

We'll get those from our CIA friends in the country.

'You'll need these.' She handed out plastic cards with their names, JTF, Mumbai Police, a holographic sign and a phone number on them. 'No one should stop you if you present those, but if they do, ask them to call that number. Our call center is briefed on your presence.'

'Break it down for us.' Meghan bobbed her head as she took the cards and handed them out. 'What's happened so far?'

Meera had only one additional detail to add that they weren't aware of. 'Prints. We found several of them in the Toyota. But they aren't in our system. We have sent their deets to Pakistan, China, FBI ... all our allied foreign agencies. We haven't heard from them.'

'Can you share them with us?' Beth asked.

'Sure.'

'If they're pros,' Chloe thought out aloud, 'and it feels like they are, then they left those prints behind knowing they wouldn't lead anywhere.'

'That's our thinking as well.' The RAW deputy nodded. 'But we have to chase down everything. I'll be with my team. Shout if you need anything.'

'Our vacation,' Zeb began when she left the room.

'We came to India for some R&R,' Bwana said with a glint in his eyes. 'But knocking out some badasses while we're here sounds even better.'

CHAPTER 6

'Werner has nothing on the prints.' Meghan rubbed her eyes. 'And that shooter could be European, North American or Central Asian. The probability of his being an Indian is low.'

Werner's algorithms could read photographs and not only compare them to others, but also worked out likely ethnicities based on facial features.

'The gray eyes could be contacts,' Roger interjected.

'Yeah.' Beth kicked at a trash can in frustration. 'Which means we have nothing.'

Zeb listened to them gripe for a few moments and then pulled out his phone. Meghan craned her neck to see who he was dialing and waved her hand to quiet the operatives.

'Ma'am,' he started when Clare came on the video call. 'We—'

'Are you okay?'

'Yes, ma'am. None of us are hurt.'

'You were in the market when the blasts occurred. You were attacked. Why do I have to hear this from others?'

'Who briefed you, ma'am?' Beth asked curiously.

'Bose. I called him when I couldn't reach your phones. I

knew Kohli was meeting you and figured his boss would know where you would be.'

Aditya Bose, RAW's chief, an ally of the Agency.

Zeb had met the austere-looking man a few times.

'We are unhurt, ma'am,' Zeb said.

'We really are,' Meghan said reassuringly and at that, the crease on their Director's forehead disappeared.

'Are you planning to return or go ahead with your vacation?'

'Neither, ma'am. We're staying here. We'll help out however we can.'

Clare nodded as if she were expecting such a response. 'President Morgan spoke to Prime Minister Mehta a short while ago and promised our full support. I'm greenlighting you. You are officially on mission.'

She smiled at Bear and Bwana's fistpumps in the background.

'Someone knows we're in Mumbai, ma'am.'

'Yes, I worked that out. Only I knew your vacation plans. But the Lear ... anyone could have spotted it. The Russians, Chinese, Iranians ... we have a long list of enemies.'

'That shooter in Crawford Market.' Zeb rubbed his jaw. 'That's not their style. The attack near CST ... that's not them either. These killers aren't from our usual suspects.'

He looked around at his team and read the understanding in their eyes.

'We have a new enemy, ma'am.'

CHAPTER 7

'Don't spread rumors,' Kohli addressed the journalists assembled in the Taj's ballroom.

He had deliberately selected the iconic hotel near the Gateway of India for the press conference. It had been the scene of a gruesome 2008 attack in which several of its guests and employees had been killed.

'False news and misinformation spreads panic. I urge every Mumbai citizen to be responsible on social media and at the same time to be vigilant.'

He took questions for an hour and then wrapped up the press conference.

'Sir?' He grimaced when he joined Bose in the director's car. 'Why did you make me the lead on this JTF? And why is RAW playing such a prominent role? Shouldn't it be the NIA?'

'There were the usual turf wars. Every agency jostling to be the lead. The prime minister had enough of it.'

'We'll be in the public eye.'

'Not any longer. This was the first press conference. From now on, get someone at NIA to handle them. You head the JTF, but for all public-facing events, let them take the credit. What about Carter?'

'They are staying in Mumbai, sir. They will help us.'

'Good. I spoke to Clare, and she too said her agency would do whatever it could.'

Kohli followed Bose's gaze out of the window, at the visible presence of police and army officers on the streets.

'Is Carter okay?' Bose asked.

'He is, sir. None of them are even scratched.'

'He and his team have nine lives.'

Kohli nodded. 'I have given them permission to weapon up.'

'I expected nothing else. These terrorists think they have struck a mighty blow on our country. They will now see RAW and the Agency's response.'

CHAPTER 8

Zeb and his team broke up in the evening after several hours of chasing down leads, making calls to the world's intelligence agencies.

They had nothing.

The shooter remained unidentified. The Toyota's prints, as well. No witnesses had come forward with anything actionable.

'It's been a long day.' Zeb drank from a water bottle, capped it and stretched. 'Let's gather tomorrow.'

As they went down the hallway, he nodded at Meera, who flashed a smile and continued speaking into her phone.

'They'll probably stay all night,' Meghan murmured, gesturing at folded beds stacked in a corner.

'They'll camp here for days,' Zeb agreed, 'until there's progress.'

They got inside the van that Meera had arranged and directed the driver to the US Consulate's office in mid-town Mumbai.

Traffic was thin. Police and military vehicles, a few government cars with red lights on their roofs. Very few private rides.

'This would have taken us close to an hour any other day.'

Roger brooded as they sped down Marine Drive and entered the upscale neighborhood of Worli.

Colonial-style buildings built during the British rule vied for attention with swanky, mirrored-glass ones. The country's burgeoning middle class demanding fancier homes.

'Even in this little traffic.' Beth grinned. 'I counted more Beemers and Audis than we would have seen in an hour back home.'

'There's a reason why every corporation wants to set up shop here.'

Small talk ended when they rolled up to the Consulate and passed through security. Zeb told the driver to return to the RAW base and nodded at the man who was waiting for them in the lobby.

'It's bad.' Eric Waller, CIA Station Chief, fist-bumped with them. 'The Ambassador and I flew down from our New Delhi office as soon as we heard the news. My entire team is here, liaising with RAW.'

'They know about you?' Chloe adjusted her shades.

'Not officially, but I'm sure they know the legal attaché cover I maintain in Delhi is just that. What about you folks? I heard you got into some trouble.'

'We didn't kill anyone,' Bwana growled.

'That bothers him more.' Meghan chuckled.

Waller was one of the few people who knew about them. He was former Delta, had been on several missions with Zeb during their special forces days.

'Your gear.' He led them down the side of the building and tossed them the keys to two black Range Rovers.

Broker opened the rear door to one vehicle and whistled at the array of weapons.

'You have these in the Consulate?'

'Someplace else. I loaded them myself and drove them here. Everyone thinks they're security vehicles.'

'They are.' Bear grunted.

They were on the road a few minutes later, Zeb at the wheel of the first Range Rover, Meghan beside him in the front, Beth and Broker in the back, the rest of them in Bear's vehicle.

A half-an-hour drive downtown to a building on the edge of Mumbai where land ended and the sea began.

Zeb and the twins climbed the stairs swiftly, unlocked the empty apartment, removed the false tiles from the floors and extracted two large shock-proof cases. They sealed the residence, turned its security back on and returned to their rides.

'It was clean?' Roger asked.

'Yeah,' Meghan nodded.

It was their safe house. They had many such caches around the world, in apartments or houses whose rents, taxes and bills were paid regularly.

The twins opened the cases, brought out light-weight armored vests, and distributed them. Chloe dug out the near-invisible comms kits and handed them out.

The last pieces of gear were the drones in the cases. The sisters assembled them swiftly and test-flew one of them.

'We're good,' Beth announced when the UAV responded to her screen control and returned to the Range Rover.

Zeb sensed their grimness as they were driving back to their hotel.

We're in mission mode.

But we don't know who our targets are.

CHAPTER 9

He went for a run after an early dinner. Shorts, tee, vest beneath it, Glock in a shoulder holster with a light jacket to cover it.

Down the sidewalk on Marine Drive, heading north. He wasn't alone. Many of the city's residents had come out of their homes. He overheard snatches of conversation as he ran past families and groups of friends. The bombing was all that they talked about.

A police vehicle drove down the promenade, bristling with armed officers. A long empty stretch of sidewalk. Zeb picked up his pace, feeling his body loosen up. A car went down the road, tunes playing loudly. Another police vehicle drew up and accelerated away.

He felt an engine rev behind him and half-turned to see an ambulance approach. He continued running as its lights splashed on the sidewalk.

He heard a door open.

His steps didn't falter.

Rushing feet behind him.

The moves came as naturally and instinctively as if he had been training all his life.

Which he had.

His body reacted like it was a lethal animal straining to be unleashed.

Which it was.

He pivoted on his heel smoothly.

Three masked men. Large, stocky, bearing down on him. Hands outstretched, reaching for him, no weapons in them.

He used his momentum to skip to the right.

The men followed. The distance between them widened.

He caught the closest man's forearm, spread out his legs to brace himself, grabbed the man's shirt with his second hand and using his core body strength and the attacker's forward motion to send him windmilling towards the concrete embankment that bordered the sidewalk.

The thug couldn't control himself. He toppled over it and fell onto the rocks with a shriek.

Zeb didn't stop moving. He crouched low and spin-kicked a second attacker to sweep his legs from beneath him. He straightened up to charge at the third man when a muzzle appeared in the ambulance's window.

He threw himself to the sidewalk, rolling desperately as rounds smacked into concrete.

I've got no cover, he thought desperately.

He snatched at his Glock and brought it out, but he had no target. The two thugs had jumped back into the vehicle, which was racing away. He fired at the ambulance. One of its rear windows shattered, but it didn't slow down. He cursed when it turned at a light and disappeared behind a building.

Zeb spun at another vehicle's approach. His heart sank at the sight of cops spilling out of it.

He dropped his gun, raised his hands and while doing so, pressed hard on the knob on his wristwatch.

That will ping Beth and Meg.

It also turned his customized Submariner into a surveillance device.

'You need to track that ambulance,' he told the cops in Hindi.

'Who are you? Why are you carrying a gun?'

'Usne kuch nahin kiya,' a voice yelled.

He didn't do anything.

An elderly woman walking her dog came up to them.

'I saw everything,' she told the officers. 'This ambulance came from behind and three men attacked him. One of them is still on the rocks.'

The senior officer nodded at his men. A cop approached the embankment and peered cautiously over it.

'Ek admi hai.'

There's a man.

'He's not moving.'

'Check him out. Carefully,' the officer ordered. 'No,' he snapped at Zeb, who was lowering his hands. 'Keep them up. Why do you have a gun?'

'I told you,' the woman said, irritated. 'They attacked him. They shot at—'

'Shot? We didn't hear anything.'

'Silenced guns,' Zeb offered.

'QUIET,' the officer thundered. He turned to the witness to question her and stopped when a command vehicle with a red light on its roof rolled up.

'Woh hamare saath hain,' Meera Ranganathan said authoritatively as she climbed out with two armed officers.

He's with us.

'Who are you?' The officer didn't budge.

'JTF.' She flashed her badge. 'Let him go. This scene is ours. I will take over.'

The cop inspected her credentials, spoke softly in his radio, hung up, nodded, returned to his ride and drove away with his men.

Meera Ranganathan placed her hands on her hips, surveyed him, and sighed.

'You are a—'

'Trouble magnet,' Beth supplied as she got out of the JTF vehicle along with her sister.

CHAPTER 10

Zeb briefed them quickly and repeated it again when the rest of his friends turned up in their Range Rover.

'That's correct.' The witness confirmed his account.

'I live in that building.' She pointed to the other side of Marine Drive. 'Socrates needed some fresh air.'

Socrates?

'Her dog, dumbass.' Beth read Zeb's expression and whispered in his earpiece.

'I crossed the road and saw it happen,' the woman continued.

'Did you see the vehicle's license plate, ma'am?' Zeb asked her.

'No. I was terrified when they started shooting. I was running back to my building. I returned when the police turned up.'

She whirled on Meera. 'Why didn't they go after those men?'

'I'll find out.' The RAW agent's lips twitched as she hid a smile.

'Do that.' The witness stormed. 'It is because of such officers that today's bombing happened. The police are corrupt, lazy, they are not fit for—'

'Ma'am, we need your details. We might need to interview you again.'

'Take them. But do something about those police officers, otherwise I will call the police commissioner myself.'

'Yes, ma'am.'

They watched her cross the road and disappear into her building.

'You need to recruit her,' Meghan said dryly to Meera.

Her expression turned serious when she regarded Zeb.

'You got lucky. Those men would have filled you with so many holes—'

'No,' he said bleakly. 'They weren't out to kill me.'

CHAPTER 11

Meera's forehead creased in a puzzled frown.

'Why do you say that?'

'They weren't shooting at me. Like you said, they could have riddled me with rounds if they wanted to. I had no cover—'

'You were shooting back. That might have caused them to miss.'

'I hadn't drawn my Glock then. They had me and deliberately missed.'

Meghan worked it out. Her eyes lit up. 'They wanted to snatch and question you.'

'Yeah—'

'But why?' the RAW agent asked, bewildered.

'These thugs were sent by the terrorists who—'

'They want to know who you are,' Meera completed excitedly. 'They heard about the shooting at CST and figured you have some value, which is why they sent goons to grab Zeb.'

'Correct.'

Which also means they know where we are staying. They have eyes on us. No other way they would have known I was out for a run.

Zeb didn't need to articulate his thoughts, however.

'They must have found out where we're staying,' Meghan said quickly. 'A watcher at the hotel must have seen Zeb go out.'

'Your faces aren't on any media. We made sure of that.'

'Those shooters at CST saw us. Our descriptions must have gotten around in the underworld.'

Meera nodded, but before she could speak, another vehicle drew up and Kohli climbed out.

'I heard about this.' He inspected Zeb swiftly, searching for injuries. His face hardened when Beth brought him up to speed.

'We'll check out the hotel to see who the watcher could be.'

'He would have left by now.' Zeb shook his head. 'The terrorists won't risk having him there anymore.'

'You need to move,' Kohli said.

'No.' Meghan said firmly. 'There's no point hiding. This isn't the first time we've been hunted. I doubt they'll attack us again. Their body count is increasing. They can't risk sending more goons at us.'

'Which reminds me,' Zeb said dryly. 'There's a thug on the rocks. I forgot to mention I threw him over the embankment.'

'Now you tell us!' Meera exclaimed. She signaled the RAW agents and approached the concrete barrier cautiously.

'He might be dead,' she called out as the two agents climbed onto the rocks.

'We know him,' Kohli said grimly when the men returned, confirmed that the attacker was dead and showed his photograph on their cell phones.

'That's Abbas Ismaili. He's with the Abu Mastan gang. They aren't the biggest in the city but are vicious.'

'We have an informer,' Meera began.

'Yes, let's talk to him right now before the gang goes to ground.'

'Go,' Zeb told him when Kohli looked their way. 'We'll get back to the hotel.'

'How?'

'We'll hitch a ride.' Zeb jerked his shoulder at a Range Rover that drove up. Bear at the wheel, Broker beside him, both hard-faced and ready for war.

ZEB WAS SILENT ON THEIR RIDE TO THEIR HOTEL. HE WAS jammed between the twins, who spoke softly to the rest of the operatives. He was aware of their soft conversation and Chloe's laugh.

He sat up straight abruptly when they neared a red light.

'We've got gear here? HKs, body armor...?'

'The works.' Bwana raised a 416. 'Why, what's up?'

'Kohli is in trouble.'

CHAPTER 12

'Why does Sharif Khan want to meet us there?' Meera thought aloud as Rahul, their driver, sped towards Lower Parel, a central Mumbai neighborhood. 'And why in an under-construction building? He meets us on the streets usually.'

'No idea.' Kohli shrugged. 'He was eager to meet as well. He needs a lot of convincing, normally.'

They fell silent as their ride navigated past city buses and a few other vehicles. Residential buildings on either side. Tall structures that soared into the sky. Mumbai was an island. Space was at a premium and there were limited options for new construction. Reclaim land from the sea, which was expensive and required government regulation. Demolish old buildings, construct new in their place and go high in the sky. The latter option was the most favored by developers, which was why the city had one of the highest densities of residential skyscrapers.

They went over the Senapati Flyover overpass and turned at the approach to Kamala Mills. Koli Chawl was on their left, a sprawling, five-story high construction that had multiple apartments on each floor. Each residence was a *kholi*, a room, though in reality many of them had more than one. Several chawls had shared bathrooms and toilets on each floor; those that had their own were more expensive. Chawls were where the city's underprivileged resided.

And then the builders and developers came along, bought them out and built swanky high-rises in their place for the rich, Kohli thought. It was how Mumbai worked. *The entire country*, he corrected himself. *The poor get pushed out of their spaces, the middle class and the wealthy take over.*

I live in such a place. He smiled bitterly at the irony. *Over a billion of us, in one of the densest countries in the world. All of us want to better ourselves.* It came at a cost, on the shoulders of the underprivileged, a fact many Indians were painfully aware of.

Their vehicle went past Koli Chawl and entered into the next property. An under-construction site which had once housed another low-income building.

Kohli got out of their vehicle and looked at the four in-progress residential towers being built. None of them were fully formed; they had skeletal outlines only, with every floor looking out into empty space.

'Fourteen stories high.' Meera joined him. 'Three-, four- and five-bedroom apartments. The top two floors of each tower have penthouses with sea views. All of them are already sold.'

'I did my research,' she said defensively when he raised an eyebrow. 'And yeah, I was curious how much they were going for.'

'How much?'

'More than we can afford on our RAW salaries, Vikram.'

'I can sell a kidney.'

'You can sell your entire family's and you still wouldn't be near the ballpark. Where's Khan?'

Kohli shrugged and went to the nearest tower. He looked around and saw no signs of security.

There should be a couple of guards. Every construction site has a few.

Concrete-mixers, sandbags, mounds of bricks, earth-moving

equipment, cranes and scaffolding. Floodlights on tall poles that provided ample illumination, but no human presence.

Kohli took the steps. Gravel crunched under his feet. Meera was behind him, with Rahul and Kishore, the second armed operative, bringing up the rear.

'Savdhan raho,' he whispered.

Be alert.

'I don't like this,' Meera murmured.

'Neither do I, but Khan was clear this is where he wanted to meet.'

Tube lights on each floor projected their shadows.

'Sharif?' Kohli called out softly.

'KHAN?' Meera yelled.

They stopped on the sixth floor. A light breeze wafting in from the Arabian Sea ruffled Meera's ponytail. Kohli went to the edge of an apartment and peered out into the night. A tower in front of him, another to its side, to his right, with the fourth one behind the two.

He pulled out his phone and made a face.

'No signal here. I checked,' Meera confirmed.

'Central Mumbai.' He straightened, looking intently at the neighboring tower. 'There's no way there can't be cell-phone coverage.'

Is that a sandbag? He narrowed his eyes at the shadow in the second building.

It moved.

'DOWN!' he roared and threw himself at Meera, bringing her down just as the first shot sailed over their heads.

CHAPTER 13

Without waiting for Zeb's explanation, Bear U-turned when the light turned green. Zeb briefed them while their ride sped down Marine Drive.

'Mastan would know his man was identified. He has no love for the Mumbai Police. His gang may or may not be the terrorists but—'

'He'll set a trap for Kohli.' Meghan snapped her fingers.

'Yeah.'

'What about the informer?' Broker objected.

'Doesn't matter,' Zeb replied tightly, holding on to the grab-handle as Bear tore through a red light without waiting for it to change. 'If I were Mastan, I would draw Kohli into my web. Think of the creds he'll gain in the underworld. Killing RAW agents on the same day as the bombing. That will make him the most wanted man in the country, but will establish his gang as the go-to for any criminal activity.'

He tried Kohli's number and swore when he got voicemail.

Watch your back, he sent a message. *You could be ambushed.*

'Aditya.' He called RAW's director and got him at the first ring. He didn't waste time on greetings and pleasantries. 'Zeb, here. Where's Vikram? He was going to meet an informer in Mastan's gang. He could be in trouble.'

Bose cottoned on to his tone. He didn't ask *why, what, how,* either.

'In Lower Parel. A building site. He messaged me when he was nearing it. I'll send you the address. I'll also send backup.'

'We might get there quicker.'

Twelve minutes, Beth mouthed.

'We're twelve minutes out,' he repeated. 'Tell your teams to be ready for anything.'

'They always are.'

KOHLI ROLLED DESPERATELY AS A FLURRY OF SHOTS SEARCHED for them. He felt a round tug his shirt and another blow past inches from his face. He dove behind a concrete pillar and caught his breath.

Meera snapped a look from another pillar and ducked back when a bullet whined in the night.

'Are you okay?'

'Yeah,' she drawled. 'See the world, protect the country ... that was your recruitment spiel. You never said anything about being shot at every second day.'

'That was a given.' He grinned. 'It didn't need to be told. Rahul, Kishore, are you hurt?'

'No, sir,' the former replied. 'We both are behind these concrete slabs, at your seven.'

Kohli snatched a look and caught his hand wave.

'We are surrounded, boss,' the second agent said. 'I saw movement on the ground. I counted at least three shooters.'

'Khan betrayed us,' Meera said savagely. 'He set us up.'

'Either that, or Mastan found out about him and forced him to call us.'

Kohli winced and ducked when a bullet ricocheted near him

and spattered him with stone chips. 'We can't last long here. Rahul, Kishore, can you slide one of those blocks down the steps? That should delay their approach.'

'That will leave us without cover, boss,' the second man said apologetically.

Kohli calculated rapidly. *These pillars and slabs protect us from the shooters in that building behind us, but our backs are exposed. We will be exposed to them if killers come up the stairs.*

'Shoot out the lights, in that case.'

Kohli lunged in the air, shot at the nearest light and rolled towards Meera's pillar. She caught his shirt and yanked him behind cover, simultaneously firing into the night.

'You know that won't help, don't you? They are hidden and beyond our shooting range.'

'I know.' She slapped in a new magazine. 'But it feels good.'

Another light went out from Kishore and Rahul's shots, and then a couple more, until their floor went dark.

The fusillade didn't abate, however.

'They have night vision.' Kohli cursed and drew his leg up sharply when a round tugged at his shoe heel.

'The neighboring residents might call the police.'

'They won't hear what's going down.' He shook his head. 'Mastan's men are using silencers. The sounds won't reach Koli Chawl and the road at the front ... there's hardly any traffic this time of the night. The rest of the buildings are office complexes. No one will be there at night.'

'You are saying we are screwed.'

'How many magazines do you have?'

'Two more.'

'Kishore, Rahul?'

'Same, sir.'

'Save your rounds until the killers come up.'

And then we go down fighting.

'I am proud to work with you—' he began.

'Save it.' Meera cut him off. She wiped perspiration off her forehead and gripped her Glock firmly. 'We aren't close to dying yet.'

We will be, soon.

CHAPTER 14

Bear took the exit on Senapati Flyover and parked their Range Rover behind a travel bus.

They climbed out swiftly and silently, bearing HKs, spare magazines, armored vests, and grim visages. Zeb helped Beth and Meghan open the drone cases and waited for them to assemble the UAVs and when they were done, led the way out.

'Police,' he said gruffly to a man who reared up from the handcart he was sleeping on to stare at them. The man didn't ask why Mumbai Police had white officers and an African-American. He yawned loudly, fell back into the cart, drew his blanket over his head and returned to sleep.

Zeb jogged swiftly, picking his way through the litter on the sidewalk, scanning the line of shuttered shops for signs of movement.

Mastan could have posted watchers.

Another shape on another handcart beneath a quilt. The person didn't stir as they passed.

'Birds are in the air,' Beth said softly in his earpiece.

He squinted at the cloudy sky, orange from the city's lights, but didn't spot the drones. *Stealth paint, active noise abatement ...*

they have the works. They'll be invisible to the naked eye unless they are up close.

He slowed as he approached the Koli Chawl's driveway. A few lights from within some of the rooms but no movement in the passageways. A dog barked somewhere in the distance. It quieted when someone yelled at it irritably.

'Boundary wall,' Meghan whispered as Zeb crossed the road to the opposite sidewalk. 'The construction site is like a large square. Shared wall with Koli Chawl, entrance on this road, undergrowth on all other sides.'

Zeb stopped behind a van and checked out his team. The twins crouched behind a handcart, their screens barely visible in their palms. The rest of the operatives ranged out in the shadows.

No street lights, here. *There never were or did the killers shoot them out?* He shrugged in the darkness. It didn't matter. Light from within the construction site spilled over onto the road but it was faint, cut off by overhanging trees and the line of buses, trucks and cars parked on the road.

He cocked his head at faint pops.

'Shooting,' Bwana guessed. 'Suppressed rifles would be my guess.'

Kohli and Meera are alive!

'Two sentries at the gate,' Beth commented.

Zeb peered beneath the van at the construction site. An opening in the wall which made up the entrance. A couple of barrels on either side.

A rope across them is the gate to such sites, manned by a guard.

'Four men going to the stairs in the first tower. Six men holed up in the building behind it, all of them on the eighth floor ... Kohli and Meera!' she burst out excitedly. 'I can see them on the sixth floor of the first tower, behind a pillar. Two men with them, ducked behind some slabs.'

Zeb looked at the trees on the sidewalk. Banyans, with branches that swept over the road and the walls of the buildings.

The city council had cut their branches and trimmed them to allow for traffic passage.

'Bwana, Roger, see that tree on your side of the gate? There are a few branches that go close to the wall. They look big enough from here. Can you get shooting positions on them?'

'On it,' the Texan drawled. Zeb looked down the sidewalk to see them detach from behind a car and disappear across the road.

'Beth—'

'I'll stay on the street, controlling the drones. Broker—'

'I'll be with you. Hostiles might come up the street. We'll cover the rest of you.'

'Those two guards aren't paying any attention to the road.' Meghan briefed them. 'They're looking at the shooters and the four men going to the tower. We'll have to hurry. They're on the steps.'

Zeb broke out from his cover. He walked casually across the road, his HK slung behind his back, his hands loose and empty, close to his waist.

He crossed the sidewalk and passed the barrels. Rope beneath his feet. The two guards, relaxed, their backs to him, what looked like AK-74s in their hands, dressed in loose pants and shirts and trainers.

Gravel crunched beneath his feet.

He cursed silently.

They started turning.

'Woh awaz kya aa raha hai?'

What's that noise?

It could have been his accent that made them hesitate. It gave him the window he wanted.

He lunged across the three meters that separated them, caught the nearest guard and sank a Yarborough blade into his neck. He felt movement behind him. Meghan, who darted past and knocked out the second guard with the butt of her Glock.

'This is faster,' she whispered as his victim thrashed and

lashed out with his dying breaths. Zeb twisted the blade savagely, and taking her cue, drew out the knife and smashed its hilt on his forehead.

'Go!' Beth said tautly. 'They're already on the first floor. The shooters haven't spotted you. Bwana, Roger?'

'Give us time,' the African-American operative complained. 'I'm big, these branches are small, besides we need to find—'

'Quit complaining.' The Texan cut him off. 'I've found a shooting spot.'

Zeb tuned out. He hurried across the open yard to the first tower, skirting construction equipment and piles of cement sacks.

Can't run. That might catch the shooters' attention.

Meghan, Chloe and Bear behind him.

No cover for us. If the snipers see us, they'll warn those four men, who will run up and kill Kohli, Meera and their men.

'You've got to hurry,' Beth urged. 'They're on the second floor. Those stairs aren't long.'

Zeb thew caution to the wind. He sprinted towards the building. Slowed to a stop when he reached it and motioned to his friends.

Concrete steps. We can't race up. Our pounding will be heard by the killers.

He started climbing carefully just as, from behind, he heard a phone ring.

CHAPTER 15

Zeb froze.

'It's one of those guards,' Chloe snapped. 'Keep going. The shooters will see their bodies. We didn't hide them.'

He took to the steps, two at a time, fast-climbing, still taking care to place his feet, picturing the layout in his mind.

The flights of stairs were bare concrete structures with no enclosing walls. Empty space and the ground below on either side. No protective rails.

They went up the first floor.

'They're on the third.' Beth updated them.

'I have a shooting position too,' Bwana whispered.

The snipers might have radio contact with these killers. If Bwana and Roger kill the shooters, these men might find out from the radio silence. They'll rush up to kill the RAW operatives. We can take them out from behind, but we might be late.

'You have them in your sights?'

'Yeah,' the African-American said confidently. 'They are on the floor, prone, their upper bodies are visible to us. They're higher than us, two hundred fifty meters, but there's very little wind. We can take these shots in our sleep.'

'Don't,' Beth retorted.

'Don't what?'

'Don't fall asleep.'

Zeb grinned inwardly.

It was a sign of his team's competence and experience that even in an intense moment, they found humor.

'Wait for my signal,' he radioed.

'Wait for what?' Roger asked, aggrieved. 'We can take the shots.'

'The killers we're tracking might know.' Meghan caught on instantly. 'Zeb is right.'

'They are on the fifth while you folks are dawdling,' Beth said urgently.

We are on the third!

Zeb climbed faster. His drew his Glock without conscious thought. *They won't rush shooting. They will check out the sixth floor carefully. That will give us a few moments.*

He could hear his team's breathing behind him. Even. No gasping. Climbing six flights of stairs wasn't any effort for them.

Fourth floor.

'They are on the landing beneath the sixth. Going up slowly.'

'RUKO!'

WAIT!

Zeb yelled and sprinted up the stairs.

He heard an exclamation from the higher floor.

He bounded up the steps, crossed the fifth floor and got onto the stairs leading to the next landing.

A bearded, scruffy man, looking down at him in confusion.

'TUM KAUN HO?'

WHO ARE YOU?

'Take them,' Zeb commanded.

He dropped onto the steps, wincing at the impact from the hard concrete. His Glock stretched out. Sight to target, eye to sight. Bottom of respiratory cycle.

He took the shot. A red, uneven flower bloomed on the

killer's forehead. His torso jerked back and fell to the floor. His AK-74 clanked to the floor.

Shouts from the landing. A head appeared. A rifle barrel followed. He dove to the other side of the steps, realized too late that there was no supporting wall, and braced himself for the fall to the ground when strong hands yanked him down and back as bullets showered gravel in his face and Glocks roared in his ears.

Bear and Meghan's faces, tight-lipped, over his shoulder as they triggered rapidly and drew him back.

'Cover me.' Zeb planted his palm on a step to regain his balance and lunged up the steps again.

He heard a woman shout.

Meera!

He didn't know if Bwana and Roger had taken out the snipers.

No time to ask them.

He burst through the landing and up the steps.

Two shooters running up. Meera and Kohli desperately scrambling for cover.

The killers heard him.

One of them turned and sprayed his AK-74.

Zeb dove over the last few steps, felt the rounds buzz over his head, felt a bullet nick his jacket and then he was landing hard, the nearest thug's body jerking from his rounds and those of his friends. The second man turned, but he was trapped between the RAW and Agency operatives and his rounds went wild, and theirs didn't, and he collapsed to the floor.

Motion from behind a slab.

Zeb reacted instinctively, bringing his Glock up to bear down on the head that appeared.

'NO!' Kohli stopped him. 'That's Rahul. And Kishore,' when another head appeared. 'Our team.'

'Sitrep?' Zeb rapped out.

'Snipers are dead,' Bwana replied. 'Like I said, in my sleep.'

Zeb got to his feet. Chloe and Meghan went past him to help Meera.

'You are—'

'Unhurt.' Kohli grinned at him. 'You came in time or else ...' he trailed away and went to the bodies, searched them and came up with their phones.

'How did you know we would be here?' Meera asked them.

'Bose told us,' Chloe replied.

'Yeah, but how did he know?'

'We figured it was a trap,' Bear growled. He picked up a fallen AK-74 and inspected it. 'PBS Suppressor. Looks like old stock.'

'Old can kill.' Chloe grunted as she collected the weapons and stacked them to the side.

'Sharif Khan?' Zeb asked Kohli and Meera.

'Never showed up,' the Special Agent replied. 'He either suckered us knowingly or Mastan made him do it.'

One of the dead men's phones, now in Meera's hand, rang.

She showed its screen to them.

Number withheld.

'Take it,' Zeb told her.

She accepted the call.

'Rafiq, unko khatam kiya kya?' a voice growled.

Rafiq, did you finish them?

'Mastan!' Kohli whispered. 'I recognize his voice.'

He took the phone from Meera, bit into his collar to distort his voice and growled. 'Haan.'

Yes.

'What happened to your voice?'

'A stone chip hit my mouth during the shooting.'

'Ustad phone kyon nahin utha raha hai? Sab ka phone band hai.'

Why isn't Ustad answering his phone? Everyone's phone is dead.

'Sab mere saath hain. Unke phones switched off hain, maine abhi mera chalu kiya.'

All of them are with me. Their phones are turned off. I turned on mine just now.

'Thik hai. RAW walon ka photo lelo aur udhar se niklo jaldi.'

Okay. Take the RAW agents' photographs and get out of there quickly.

'Kidhar milna hai?'

Where should we meet?

'Ville Parle mein. Pata nahin kya? Naye ho kya?'

In Ville Parle. Don't you know? Are you new?

Mastan hung up angrily.

'This is it!' Meera said excitedly. 'We can get him.'

'Ville Parle is a big neighborhood,' Beth objected. 'Do you know where he is specifically?'

'No, but our tech team could figure out where the call came from... we could tap our informers.'

'Not so fast,' Zeb cautioned her. 'You all need to die.'

CHAPTER 16

'What do you mean?' Kohli's eyes narrowed.

'Mastan isn't a fool,' Zeb explained. 'He bought your explanation, about your voice. He might keep trying the others' phones, however. He'll wonder why they are still turned off.'

'There needs to be an announcement that you are dead.' Meghan followed Zeb's reasoning. 'If he hears that, he'll feel assured. He might not change his location.'

'We can't risk that.' Meera looked at Kohli. 'This is our best chance to nab him. If he moves base, he'll disappear into the city.'

'I'll organize that.' The Special Agent brought out his phone. His brow cleared when he saw there was a signal. 'They must have been using jammers when we entered and turned them off when the shooting started.'

'We spoke to Bose while coming here. He's sending backup teams, but we can't hang around. We need to get going.'

Kohli stopped dialing at Zeb's words.

'What do you suggest? Y'all?' he exclaimed when it came to him. 'You'll go with us for the takedown?'

'You have no one else and we can't lose time.'

Kohli made his decision swiftly. He nodded and gestured at his two men. 'Rahul and Kishore. Two of our best operatives.'

He made the introductions and led the way down the steps with his phone to his ear.

'Bose has greenlighted it,' he said when they reached the entrance of the construction site. 'There will be a tweet from our official account saying senior agents were killed in a gang shooting in Lower Parel. No more information. The backup teams are more than ten minutes away. They are coming up from the port side of the city. Our tech team will locate Mastan and get back to us.'

They reached the Range Rover where Beth and Broker were stowing the drones away. Kohli took in the scene and looked up at Bwana and Roger, who joined them. His eyes lingered on their HKs and swept the surroundings.

'You took out the shooters? From where? There isn't a sniping—'

'The banyan tree,' Bear cocked his head towards it.

'The tree! You found shooting positions on it?'

'We make impossible things happen,' Bwana said, straight-faced. He raised an eyebrow when Meghan handed out comms units to the RAW operatives. 'We're going somewhere?'

'To get Mastan,' the elder twin replied. 'He's somewhere in Ville Parle. Vikram's team is working on identifying his location.'

Bwana's face split into a wide grin. He fist-bumped Bear and got into the Range Rover.

'We'll follow you,' Meghan told Kohli and got in beside Bear in the front. 'We'll use our comms channel for now. Once your team arrives, we can switch to yours.'

'Mastan will have more men. They will be heavily armed,' Kohli warned. 'They won't go down without a fight.'

'We are hoping for that,' the African-American replied.

'The odds are with them until my teams join.'

'We have grenade launchers and rockets with us.'

Kohli and Meera stopped in their tracks and looked at them in astonishment.

'You came prepared!' the latter exclaimed.

'We always are.' Bwana grinned.

CHAPTER 17

'It's a building on Park Road.' Meera briefed them when they drove away from the construction site. 'That's where his call came from. I am messaging you the address.'

'Have you re-routed your teams to get there?' Zeb asked.

'Yes. We have also arranged for a JTF team to secure the construction site. They should be reaching there any moment now. They will search the bodies and let us know if they find anything else.'

'How many people in the backup teams?'

'Eight.'

That's twenty of us, Zeb thought. *That should be enough.*

Bear overtook a lumbering truck and got onto Annie Besant Road. More traffic, which parted when Kohli's vehicle turned on its siren and red light.

'This many trucks and cars?' Broker whistled.

'The state government has relaxed the emergency for the night,' Beth explained, 'to allow for delivery vehicles to travel in the city and do their business.'

Police checkpoints, Zeb observed, all over the city. *They are randomly inspecting vehicles.*

'There's a bomb squad.' Chloe pointed to sniffer dogs examining a car.

'This country lives with terrorism,' Bear said grimly. 'Either domestic or foreign hostiles, there's always something happening someplace in India.'

Zeb nodded absently and leaned over Meghan's shoulder to watch her work on Werner.

'Any luck with shooter dude?'

'No.' She sighed in frustration. 'I have sent out his sketch to the CIA, Mossad, MI6, all our allied agencies. Let's see if any of them get back to us.'

Their system was hooked into several federal, national and international agencies' databases and, on top of that, the sisters had also hacked into many other systems. In the covert intelligence world, however, not every identity was recorded digitally.

Humint, Zeb mused. *Some case officer somewhere might have seen the shooter and might never have reported or logged him.*

He knew the chances were low, but they had to try.

Bwana lowered the window when their ride got onto the Bandra-Worli Sea Link, a bridge that connected midtown to its western suburbs. It jutted out from the coastline, over the Arabian Sea, and curved back to join the city. The construction had been a welcome relief for the city's commuters since it cut down drive time significantly on its congested roads.

'Mumbai,' Broker chuckled. 'Nowhere to go except up in the sky or onto the sea.'

Their tires hummed on concrete as the cable stays flashed past. Kohli's ride didn't slow at the toll booths. His arm came out of the window to show his badge and he pointed backwards at their Range Rover.

Bear didn't slow either and kept going when they joined West Express Highway, past the International Airport and down the service way to enter Ville Parle.

A suburb. Residential buildings around them. Commercial

complexes as well, shopping malls and offices, hospitals and colleges. All of them illuminated in the night. Some pedestrians, a stray dog which darted away in their lights.

Bear parked behind Kohli's vehicle on Ajmal Road and they climbed out.

'You have vests?' Zeb asked the RAW agents.

'No.' Meera shook her head. 'We came to rescue you from the cops on Marine Drive, remember?'

He grinned, reached into their shock-proof case and brought out four vests.

'We don't have many of these,' he said apologetically, raising his tee to show his lightweight armor.

'These will do.' Kohli strapped on his plated protection. 'The two teams are still ten-twelve minutes away.'

'Recon,' Zeb said.

They split up.

The twins, along with Meera, took the lead to go down Ajmal Road and turn onto Park Road.

Zeb, Bear, Bwana, and Roger climbed over the fence into a residential building's yard and sprinted towards its rear wall.

'Why are we doing this?' Bwana grunted when they vaulted over it and landed on the parking lot of another building.

'Because Park Road is a dead-end road, slowpoke,' Roger admonished. 'This way, we'll come up at its far end and can get to Mastan's building from the opposite side.'

'Pincer move! Gotcha.'

'It's your height.' Bear shook his head sadly at the African-American as they entered another building. 'Less blood reaches your brain. Slows your thinking.'

Zeb held his hand up when a khaki-clad guard got up from a chair and barred their way.

'Police ka kaam hai,' he said authoritatively and flashed the badge Meera had handed out to each of them.

Police work.

'Shor mat karo. Humme jaane do.'

Don't make noise. Let us go.

The sentry scratched his head. He tapped his wooden cane on the ground. He took in their HKs and their grim faces, opened his mouth and then decided what was going down was well over his pay grade.

He nodded and returned to his chair.

Zeb sprinted to the rear wall and vaulted it nimbly. He landed lightly on his feet and held his hand up for silence.

Sidewalk straight ahead.

Cars and vans parked on the road.

Two residential buildings to their side and the third one was Mastan's.

Two men lounging against its compound wall, conversing softly, who hadn't noticed their appearance. He could make out more shapes beyond them.

'Mastan's men?' Bear whispered.

'Could be. There's no one else out at this time of the night.'

Close to midnight. The city was still. Street lighting illuminating Park Road dimly.

'Three men at our end.' Meghan broke the radio silence. 'At a van. They've seen us.'

'Are they armed?'

'Can't tell from where we are.'

'Any other men?'

'No.'

'There are two on our side of the entrance.'

'Yeah, we can see their shapes. Vikram, anyone on your side of the sidewalk?'

'No.'

'We can take them out,' Meera said. 'They won't suspect us. We are women. They will be curious at our presence but won't be wary.'

'They'll see your vest,' Kohli pointed out.

'It will be too late by then. We'll be on them. If they are Mastan's men, they'll tell us where he is, how many more hostiles there are—'

'Go!' Zeb cut in.

CHAPTER 18

Meghan felt it inside her. A straightening, even though she knew nothing showed outwardly. It was her body's reaction, readying for a short, intense burst of action.

She could sense it in Beth, too. Her twin fingered her pony-tail, an unconscious gesture that she made every time they went hot.

Meera? She side-eyed the RAW agent. They knew Kohli well. They had been with him on missions but hadn't worked with his deputy before.

I'll bet she's as good as him if not better, she assessed, as she noted the operative's even strides and firm jaw.

The RAW officer's face relaxed as they got closer to the men, who stopped talking, stopped lounging and stared at them.

Our HKs are strapped to our backs. They'll see the slings but can't spot the rifles.

'Machis hai?'

Do you have a match?

Meera smiled as she brought out a cigarette.

The man in the middle reached for his pocket. His shirt flattened against his waist as he did so and outlined something hard and angular.

Gun!

Meghan lunged at him, trapped his wrist with her left hand and elbow-punched him in the throat. His breath left him in a choking sob. He staggered back, flailing. She followed him to reach underneath his shirt and brought out his gun, a Sig Sauer, and crashed its barrel in his temple. She pivoted to the thug on her right, but Beth had taken him out with a knee to the groin and finger jab to his eyes.

Meera had the third gangster in a chokehold and was squeezing hard.

'We need to question him,' Meghan told her. 'The other two can't talk.'

The RAW agent relaxed her hold, at which the thug attempted a backward headbutt, trying to catch her chin. She evaded the strike, spun around, and slammed him against the compound wall. Her hand streaked to her back pocket and came out with a wad of paper towels which she jammed into his mouth, muffling his shriek.

She bent down and drew a knife from her boot and ripped a piece of his shirt, which also went into his mouth.

The thug tried to attack, but he was dazed, slow and she shoved him back against the wall.

'What are you—' Beth began.

'This,' Meera hissed and plunged the blade high into the gangster's right shoulder.

The makeshift gag in his mouth choked his scream. Her slap rocked his head and split his lip.

She withdrew the knife and pricked his neck with its bloodied tip.

'This goes into your neck,' she snarled in Hindi, 'if you lie to us. Where is Mastan?'

. . .

'INCOMING,' ZEB WARNED MEGHAN.

She looked to her left.

The two men who were on his side of the gate were running towards them.

'We can take them out,' he said softly.

'Let them come,' she replied. 'We'll deal with them.'

She cast a look at Meera, who was interrogating the prisoner. *She doesn't need any help.*

She went around the RAW operative, her hands loose and ready, Beth joining her.

The men drew closer.

One of them shouted and drew his phone. The other's hand darted to his waist.

Meghan dove at the first man, body slamming into him and elbowed him in the nose. It broke. His yell turned into a choking grunt when she jabbed his chin with the base of her palm. She knocked him out with another elbow strike to the temple. She plasti-cuffed and gagged him and rolled his body underneath the van. Stumbled when the second heavy crashed into her. Caught him by the shoulder to find he was bleeding, eyes rolling. She smashed his head against the van and with Beth's help, shoved him beneath the vehicle too.

'Mastan is on the second floor.'

She turned at Meera's voice.

The gangster she was interrogating was on the ground, unconscious, blood spreading from the knife wound.

'Is he—'

'He's alive. These thugs are tough only when they have numbers on their side and guns in their hands.'

'Four-story building.' The RAW deputy briefed them swiftly as they cuffed the unconscious goon and hid him beneath the van.

She straightened and beckoned the rest of the RAW and Agency operatives.

'This is a blind spot from the building.' She gestured to where they were standing. 'The compound wall and those trees block the apartment views. On top of that, their windows are tinted, which reduces their night visibility.'

'Mastan is inside?' Zeb asked, checking out the building.

A pharmacy and a takeout joint, both shuttered, on the ground floor. Grills on the apartment windows, from many of which air conditioners jutted out. Their hum could be heard from where they were.

He scanned the neighboring buildings.

The banyans block their views as well.

'Yes, second floor. Four guards with him. More in the other stories. Twenty shooters in total. Heavily armed.'

'He bombed Crawford Market?' Kohli asked sharply.

'My thug didn't know. He was on sentry duty for several days. All he knows is Mastan came to this building yesterday.' She glanced at her watch to confirm the new day hadn't started. 'Gave instructions to several men and didn't step out. That restaurant on the ground floor serves them all day. Its owner and the chemist's don't know who they are.'

'Don't many such buildings have a watchman?' Broker asked.

'They do. There they are.' She grinned, pointing at the bodies beneath the van. 'Mastan appointed his men as guards when he took over all the apartments. These buildings—'

'Are housing societies. The developer transfers landownership to them. Apartment buyers own their properties outright and become members of the society with equal voting rights,' Chloe completed.

'Correct.' Meera smiled. 'You have done your homework. Since Mastan rented all the apartments, he effectively runs the society. Those shop owners didn't have a say. They might have suspected who Mastan is, but must be scared for their lives.'

'You got all this from him?' Kohli bobbed his head at the unconscious goons.

'I was very persuasive.'

His phone buzzed before he could reply. He broke away, spoke briefly, and raised his head.

'The backup teams are here.'

A shot slammed into the van and ricocheted into the night.

CHAPTER 19

Zeb ducked beneath the wall as more rounds crashed into the vehicle, searching for them.

'Someone must have seen us,' he spoke in his mic. 'Perhaps from the roof. Beth?'

'I've been working while you've been shooting the breeze,' she drawled. 'Meera's goon was right. Twenty bodies inside. Vikram, hook me up with your comms guy. I'll sync frequencies and you folks can take over.'

'Copy that,' Kohli confirmed.

The shooting had increased in volume as bullets sprayed the front of the building, none reaching them due to the compound wall's cover. Lights turned on in the neighboring buildings, heads appeared in windows and ducked out of sight quickly.

'This will turn into a clusterf—'

'We have to breach the building,' Kohli interrupted his deputy. 'We don't have a choice. I'll liaise with the cops and get them to mount a perimeter.'

'We'll cover the rear,' Zeb told him. 'Mastan's likely to have an escape route ... could be at the back.'

'Go!'

. . .

'AGAIN?' BWANA COMPLAINED WHEN ZEB RACED DOWN THE dead end and leapt over a building's wall.

'No other way to get behind Mastan's hideaway,' he grunted.

'POLICE!' he yelled in Hindi when a bleary-eyed resident stumbled onto the parking lot. 'GET BACK AND STAY INSIDE.'

'I can see movement on the second floor,' Beth said. 'Men rushing down the stairs. If you don't get there quickly, Mastan might escape from the back.'

'He might take hostages,' Chloe said grimly.

'What about Kohli?' Zeb asked.

'Can't you hear the shooting?' Beth snorted. 'His teams are fully engaged with the gangsters in the building. They can't go into the yard without exposing themselves.'

Or using heavy explosives, which might kill Mastan and we need him alive.

He increased his pace, ducking between cars in parking lots, dodging trash cans and waste bags as he led them into other buildings, guided by the younger twin until they circled to head towards the back of Mastan's.

'SHOOTERS!' she yelled in his earpiece.

Zeb was in mid-vault over the rear compound wall. He saw the two men emerge from the building.

They spotted him at the same time. Their AK-74s chattered in the night. A round slammed into his vest. His leap faltered and then he was pushed forward by a hand and fell to the ground, gasping from the impact, finding his HK in his hand as if by magic. It bucked as he triggered a short burst, which was drowned out in the roar of his team's guns, and the killers went down.

Zeb raced to the building, leapt sideways as another shooter emerged. He shot him point-blank in the chest.

'Duck!' Bwana said, as if enjoying himself.

He ducked and pulled goggles over his head. The flash-bang his friend tossed into the entrance turned the night into day temporarily. A teargas grenade, followed by two more stun grenades.

'Enter,' Beth announced laconically.

Zeb entered the building's lobby along with Bear and Bwana. A rectangular space, concrete floor, a security desk which was unmanned, two elevator cars with open doors.

Thick smoke. Three bodies on the ground; one was still, the other two were groaning.

None of them was Mastan.

Zeb knocked them out with his barrel while Bwana and Bear damaged their AK-74s. Meghan and Chloe went to the elevators and jammed them from working.

'ISMAIL?' a rough voice called from above.

He won't be coming.

Zeb took the stairs cautiously, Beth in his earpiece, relaying the RAW teams' status, the positions of the survivors in the building.

He went up, relying on her feed, his senses and his inner radar.

A head appeared. An AK-74 spat at him, but the shooter was hasty; his shots went wide and before he could trigger again, Meghan took out his head from behind him.

Six down.

First floor landing.

'Four men inside the first apartment,' Beth said. 'Two on either side of the door. They're waiting for you to cross it. DUCK!'

Zeb threw himself to the floor, shooting at the shadows that darted across the door.

A flash-bang arced over his head and landed inside the apartment. Someone screamed. He crawled to the wall, inched forward, ducked inside quickly and emptied his magazine at the bodies staggering in the apartment.

Second residence was empty.

The building shook from an explosion.

That must be Kohli's team.

A scream. Several groans.

Zeb didn't pause. He kept climbing the stairs.

Something clattered onto the steps.

Grenade!

He dove forward, caught it and threw it between the stairwells.

It exploded before it reached the ground floor. Windows rattled. A head poked around the concrete bannister to see if the explosive had worked.

Zeb shot the killer.

'That's how they take out grenades in movies,' Roger whispered.

He didn't reply. He slapped in a fresh magazine and raked the top of the ground floor bannister as he crawled up.

The building walls were old. They absorbed the rounds without causing them to ricochet.

The second flight of steps. No shooter.

'Door to your right,' Beth whispered.

His elbows hurt from grinding them on the steps. He ignored the ache. The universe was restricted to his HK's muzzle and what was in front of him.

Two more explosions sounded. The sounds of firing inside the building seemed to fade, but he couldn't be sure.

'Flash-bang.' He held a hand out behind him.

Someone slapped one in his palm.

Got to neutralize them before they toss grenades. We won't be lucky a second time.

He was arcing his hand to lob it when a voice yelled from inside.

'SURRENDER!'

CHAPTER 20

'It's him, Mastan.' Kohli's voice broke into their comms. 'He's left with only four men in that apartment. We fired grenades into the other apartments and took out the rest of his men.'

'COME OUT,' Zeb ordered. 'ONE BY ONE. HANDS IN THE AIR. THEY HAD BETTER BE EMPTY.'

A thug appeared in the doorway.

'UNDRESS.'

The gangster looked at him in astonishment.

'REMOVE YOUR CLOTHES, DOWN TO YOUR UNDERWEAR.'

Have to be sure he's not wearing explosives. He didn't know if Mastan had suicide bombers in his gang, but he wasn't taking chances.

He fired above the man's head to incentivize him. The killer removed his shirt hurriedly and dropped his trousers.

'Lie on the floor.'

The man obeyed, cursing softly.

The rest of the gangsters emerged and the last one was Mastan.

'I AM NOT UNDRESSING,' he roared.

Zeb shot him in the shoulder.

The mobster howled and swore but complied and stood shivering with shock and fury.

'Mastan Qureshi.' Kohli came up the steps and slapped the gangster. 'Why did you bomb Mumbai?'

'I DIDN'T!'

CHAPTER 21

Mastan stuck to his answer despite RAW's aggressive interrogation.

Kohli took a break from the questioning and joined Zeb and his team on the landing outside the apartment.

'What do you think?' He wiped sweat from his forehead. 'He says he has nothing to do with the bombing. Salil Ibrahim, who is like his second-in-command, was in Crawford Market when the explosion went off. He and a few other hitters. They were some distance away and weren't injured.'

'They saw us,' Zeb guessed. 'Worked out we were the ones attacked near CST, found out where we were staying—which wouldn't have been difficult—and attempted to snatch me.'

'Yes,' Meera confirmed. 'Most of these gangs have their informants in big hotels. That's how they identify targets for extortion or kidnapping. They put a watcher outside your hotel and when you went running, followed you.'

'Why?' Bwana growled.

'Mastan guessed you were of value to someone. He was going to put feelers out into the underworld once he had Zeb and—'

'Trade him,' Bear said, tight-lipped. He made a move to burst into the apartment, but Chloe held him back.

'Yes.'

Zeb looked at the ceiling. 'Who else was in the building?'

'Only his shooters, many of whom are dead,' Kohli replied. 'Why?'

'No women?'

'No.'

'Is that strange?'

'No. This isn't his usual base. He holed up here to carry out the snatch on you and sell you to the highest bidder.'

'He cleared out the building so quickly?'

'Nope, that was done a long time ago. His killers stay here occasionally. It's one of their many hideouts.'

Zeb peered inside the room and took in the mobster. Mastan's face was bloodied. He was bare-chested with visible cuts. He bared his teeth at the Agency operatives' glances.

'The other dude in the chair is Ibrahim?' Zeb asked.

'Yes; he too claims they had nothing to do with the bombing. What do you think?'

'I believe him. Mastan is vicious, ruthless, fast-rising in the Mumbai criminal world ... but he isn't that smart. The terrorists behind those explosions are pros. We have nothing on them. The bombs have no signature, do they?'

'No.'

'Nope.' Zeb nodded in confirmation. 'I am confident Mastan was telling the truth. But that doesn't mean...'

He trailed off and strode into the room. He caught hold of one of the cuffed thugs and shoved him towards a shattered window. The man resisted. He cursed and swore. Zeb ignored him, placed one hand on his belt and the other on his shirt and with a grunt, threw him out of the window.

Meera gasped. She and another RAW operative rushed to the opening and looked out. She turned back to Zeb in amazement.

'You killed him!'

'Yeah.'

CHAPTER 22

Zeb grabbed Ibrahim and dragged him to the window. Bwana chuckled and came to help.

'WHAT ARE YOU DOING?' The gangster shouted and dug his heels on the floor. Bear came from behind, kicked his legs out from beneath him and helped the African-American agent to lift him.

'STOP THEM!' Mastan shrieked at the RAW operatives. 'THEY WILL KILL SALIL.'

'That's the idea,' Zeb snarled as his friends thrust Ibrahim's head outside the window. 'Unless you start talking.'

'I TOLD YOU EVERYTHING. I DIDN'T ARRANGE THOSE BOMBS.'

'Your man saw the shooter.'

'YES. HE TOO TOLD EVERYTHING.'

'No, he didn't.' Zeb nodded at Bwana and Bear, who swung Ibrahim back like a pendulum, making to propel him out of the window. 'He followed the shooter and saw where he went.'

'YES, YES!' Ibrahim sobbed. 'I DID. HE WENT TO DHARAVI.'

'Where in Dharavi?'

'I DON'T KNOW. I DIDN'T FOLLOW HIM INSIDE.'

'Why should we believe him?' Bwana argued. 'He didn't spill that when RAW was interrogating him. He's lying to save himself.'

'Yeah.' Bear's biceps flexed as he tightened his hold on Ibrahim. 'Let's throw him out. We have to think of the planet. One less human on it means less CO_2 emissions.'

'THEY ARE CRAZY,' Mastan screamed. 'STOP THEM.'

Ibrahim thrashed in Bwana and Bear's arms and tried to rear back, but he was held tight.

'I AM TELLING THE TRUTH.'

'Why didn't you lead with that when we were questioning you?' Kohli growled.

'I AM SORRY. DON'T LET THEM KILL ME.'

Zeb looked at him speculatively for a moment and then nodded at his friends, who brought back the killer and thrust him in his chair.

Bwana smacked him on the face, a blow that made his teeth click together audibly, and gagged his mouth.

'How did you know he followed the shooter?' Meera asked him curiously.

'Lucky guess.'

'Really?'

'Yeah.'

If I were a gangster, Zeb thought to himself, *I too would have followed the shooter.*

Meera spun on her heel and slapped Ibrahim. 'Is this him?' She produced the digital sketch.

'YES. WHY DO YOU KEEP HITTING—'

'Because unfortunately I can't kill you. Not just yet.' She brought her knife and played with it. 'Did that man have anyone else with him? Who did he speak to? How did he go to Dharavi?'

'No.' he shrank when she thrust the blade at his neck. He exhaled in relief when it stopped short of his throat. 'He was alone. He took a taxi.'

'Do you remember its number?'

Salil Ibrahim licked his lips and looked at Mastan, who looked on balefully.

'He can't help you.' Meera caught Salil's chin and turned his head towards herself. 'If you wish, he can watch me cut your belly and pull your guts—'

'On my phone! I took a picture of the taxi.'

She went to a pile of phones in a corner and sifted through them until she held up one which had been tagged by the RAW agents. She returned to him, held it in front of his face to unlock it, and scrolled through the gallery until she came to the cab.

'We'll find him.' Kohli examined it. 'And bring him to our office before sunrise.'

CHAPTER 23

Zeb went out into the building's front yard and inhaled deeply.

'Drones are still up in the air?'

'Yeah,' Beth replied in his earpiece. 'Broker's at the dead-end. No sign of any hostiles.'

'Are you expecting trouble?' Chloe wiped perspiration from her forehead.

'Nope.' He shook his head. 'But there are so many questions.'

'I think they have far more than us.' Meghan nodded at Kohli and Meera, who emerged from the building deep in conversation.

The Special Agent smiled humorlessly when he came to them.

'We got Mastan, but nothing else. We are no closer to knowing.'

'Won't his capture help with the media?'

'It might.' He made a face. 'For a short while. But he's a small fish right now.'

He raised his hands apologetically when he realized how his words could be construed. 'Don't get me wrong. He was after you—'

'Relax,' Zeb told him.

Terrorist bombers are far more important to the Indians right now. Rightly so. We too would have placed them at the top of the priorities.

MUMBAI WAS STILL ON HIGH ALERT WHEN THEY MET THE NEXT morning. Traffic had picked up with the state government relaxing some restrictions, but the police and military presence was undiminished.

Bose was with Kohli and Meera when Zeb and his team entered RAW's Nariman Point office.

'I wish we could have met under better circumstances.' The agency executive shook their hands.

'Any progress?' Zeb took his chair in the meeting room and glanced at the muted TV on the wall, which was playing the day's news.

'A little. C4 was used in the bombs. Most of the previous terrorist attacks have used RDX, which means these killers are more sophisticated and better funded.'

C4 costs more in the black market, Zeb thought bleakly.

'We are shaking down the usual suspects.' Kohli continued. 'ISI-backed groups, insurgents, any malcontents who would have a reason to—'

'Who is that discontented to go make bombs and set them off in a crowded market?' Meera spat.

Zeb wasn't paying attention anymore. He was focused on the TV screen, on a wailing woman who was sobbing into another woman's shoulder.

ANOTHER VICTIM DIES. NISHA GAIKWAD, EIGHT YEARS OLD, YOUNGEST VICTIM IN YESTERDAY'S BLAST, the rolling banner read beneath the coverage. A file shot of a young girl came on screen.

Zeb wasn't aware he was gripping his water glass tightly until Meghan forced him to loosen his grip.

'Was that her? Nisha. The girl you saw in the market?'

She had to repeat herself twice before the words got to him.

'Yes.' He heard his voice come out distantly. He swung towards Bose. 'There are no rules.'

'We are RAW,' the agency head said expressionlessly. 'There never are.'

Kohli waited for several moments for Zeb to gather himself. 'We have some videos of three men leaving Crawford Market early in the morning, before it opened. They are not cleaners or maintenance people. No one seems to know who they are.'

Kohli hooked up his laptop to the TV and brought up the images. Three men, indistinct faces, fuzzy backgrounds.

'Taken from a camera outside the market that didn't have the best angle,' Bose explained. 'We cleaned up the images.'

Another click and clearer photographs appeared.

'Yes.' Kohli read the Americans' expressions. 'They could be anyone. Average-looking. Nothing memorable about them. In a city of over twenty million people, they could be anywhere. Or, they could have fled Mumbai, as well. We have distributed their photographs to the police, airport security, train stations ... so far, no luck.'

'For all we know, they might be some random men who were in the market for legitimate reasons,' Meera added.

'Can you share those with us?' Meghan asked.

'Yes.' Bose bent down to his screen and straightened moments later. 'The shooter ... no trace of him at the airport or any transit points.' He shrugged. 'Like I said, some progress, but not a lot.'

'We have better news with the taxi driver,' Meera said. She left the room and returned with a middle-aged man who was clearly frightened. He wore a khaki shirt and slacks, and his hands trembled when he took a seat at her nod.

'Anant Jagrale,' she introduced him. 'The taxi driver who took the shooter to Dharavi.'

'Inko batao woh kya bola,' she ordered.

Tell these people what he said.

'Maine bataya aapko, memsaab. Woh kuch nahin bola. Kidhar jaana hai, bas utna hi.'

I told you, ma'am. He told me where to go, nothing else.

'Did he give you an address in Dharavi?' Bwana growled.

The cab driver looked at him in astonishment, his surprise at the African-American's Hindi momentarily overcoming his fear.

'Nahin. Dharavi chalo, utna hi bola.'

No. Go to Dharavi. That's all he said.

'Did he speak English?'

'No, Hindi. But he was speaking like you.'

Zeb frowned and then his brow cleared.

'You mean like an accent?' He leaned forward interestedly.

'Yes.'

'What kind of accent?' Beth asked.

Jagrale shook his head. 'He sounded like a foreigner. I have had many such tourists in my taxi, but I couldn't say where he was from, from those two words.'

Beth whispered to Meghan and brought out her phone.

'Dharavi chalo,' she recorded in Hindi. She played with an app and placed the phone on the table.

'Come closer.' She beckoned to Jagrale, who rolled his chair to the table. The RAW officers and the Agency operatives bunched up.

'This app will play those same words in several languages. Listen carefully and tell us which comes closest.'

The taxi driver nodded. His eyes gleamed. His fear receded.

Beth pressed play.

A man's voice recited *Dharavi chalo* in Urdu several times.

Jagrale shook his head.

Arabic followed.

No luck.

Chinese.

'No.' The taxi driver shook his head emphatically. 'He wasn't Chinese or Japanese or Korean. I am sure of that.'

They moved on to European languages and at two of them Jagrale paused for a long while.

'Both of those,' he said after listening to the recordings several times.

Zeb didn't need to look over Beth's shoulder to see the languages she had scribbled on her notepad.

He had seen Jagrale's expression at the two utterings.

'Russian or Chechen.'

CHAPTER 24

Bose waited for Kohli to lead Jagrale out and on his return, brought up the shooter's digital sketch.

'What do you think?'

'He could be from either of those countries,' Zeb agreed.

'He's an SVR shooter?' Chloe wondered.

'I thought of that agency. We have history.'

'We heard.' Bose's smile disappeared as fast as it came.

'SVR has a new chief, Sergei Tuzov, who has retained the previous head's security team. Dusan Smirnov is their head, who we have had dealings with.'

Bear snorted at Zeb's description but made no other comment.

'Russia is isolated after it invaded Ukraine. SVR is busy dealing with oligarchs in the West who might turn on its president. No. I don't think the shooter was from that agency.'

'It's not their style, either.' Broker crossed his hands behind his head. 'A killer in a Mumbai market? Nope. They would go for a sniper or something more impactful.'

'Like plutonium poisoning?' Meera smirked.

'Yeah. But that doesn't rule out his being Russian. We have enough enemies.'

'Meera and I will take teams to Dharavi and question its residents. Someone might have seen the shooter. He might still be there for all we know.' Kohli got to his feet.

'Hold off on that,' Zeb said.

'Why?'

'Let me talk to Sule first.'

The RAW officers froze.

'Arjun Sule?' Bose asked cautiously.

'Yeah.'

'How do you know one of Mumbai's most feared gangsters?'

'He owes me.'

CHAPTER 25

'We haven't heard that story either.' Beth rounded on Zeb.

'It was on one of my lone missions. I was tracking a terrorist cell who were rumored to have linked up with Daesh. Sule had retired from criminal activities by then.'

'Philanthropy,' Meera said bitterly. 'He's big into that, now. He donates to charities, schools, sponsors events ... as if he's trying to whitewash his image.'

'He doesn't need to in Dharavi,' Kohli interjected. 'He's like a godfather to its residents. Sure, he headed Mumbai's largest gang at one time, but he did a lot for its residents.'

'Businessman,' Zeb said. 'That's how he referred to himself then and even now. Mumbai Police questioned him several times but never had enough to arrest him. He claims he was harassed—'

'How do you know him?' Meghan cut in impatiently.

'I saved his life a few times, from Irfan Shaikh's killers.'

'Shaikh. Isn't he the one whose gang replaced Sule's as Mumbai's largest criminal enterprise?' Broker snapped his fingers.

'Yes,' Kohli confirmed. 'Zeb, don't tell us you know him, too?

Mumbai Police, NIA, even we would love to arrest him. He has links to LET. His gang has been supporting that terrorist group, supplying them with weapons, vehicles and safe houses. He's one of the most wanted men in India.'

'I would like to see him in my Glock's sights, too,' Zeb said grimly. 'He tortured and killed one of my informers.'

'Get to it.' Beth ground her teeth.

'There isn't much to the story. A rainy night in Mumbai several years ago. I was walking to my apartment in Lower Parel, not far from where we took down Mastan, and a car races past. Its window rolls down, a hand comes out and fires at a man in a stationary vehicle. That was Sule. He was alone, returning to his place in Mahalaxmi after visiting his Padma, his daughter. No one else on the street. I got to him, found he was alive and took him to a hospital.'

Bose scratched his cheek. 'This isn't in the file we have for Sule.'

'No one knows of it. He was barely conscious when I reached him. Two rounds in the chest, one in his shoulder. He directed me to a doctor's residence in Mahalaxmi, someone he trusted. He was there for two weeks under heavy security. I was there the day he was discharged. The same day that Shaikh sent more shooters.'

'That I remember,' Kohli exclaimed. 'Four gunmen dead in an upscale building. Mumbai Police thought it was a gang killing.'

'I shot them. Sule didn't have any protection with him. They would have been noticed in the building. It turned out the doctor had been bribed and Sule's men killed him for his help.'

'Why were you there?'

'To turn Sule into a CI. My dealing with those killers gained his trust.'

'He didn't retaliate against Shaikh? I didn't hear of more killings after that.'

'No. He had retired. He had no interest in returning to the

underworld. He negotiated with Shaikh. Transferred several properties and warehouses to the gangster.'

'Shaikh didn't see that as a sign of weakness? He didn't demand more?' Chloe asked.

'Arjun Sule might have retired,' Meera said dryly, 'but he is still extremely powerful and if he snaps his fingers, killers will come out of the woodwork to defend him.'

'And then he helped you?' Meghan asked Zeb.

'Yeah.' He didn't elaborate.

'This cell you were hunting.' Bose regarded him keenly. 'Would it have been an ISI-backed one, operating in Assam?' He referred to a northeastern state in the country.

'It might have been.'

'We got an anonymous tip about it ... by the time we reached the gang's hideout, we found bodies.'

That was me, but I can't admit it. At that time, I suspected RAW had a leak and didn't take them into confidence.

'Sule knows who you are?' Bose asked him.

'He thinks I'm CIA.'

'We'll come with you.' Bwana stood up.

'I'll go alone.'

Bwana sat down.

Zeb got into a Range Rover and adjusted his rear-view mirror.

No second vehicle visible.

They'll be there, he smiled to himself. *Beth, Meg, Bwana and maybe the others too, even though I asked them to stay behind. They'll tail me and back me up if things go south.*

CHAPTER 26

Dharavi. Two square kilometers in which a million people resided. One of the most densely populated areas in the world and one of the largest slums on the planet.

Narrow lanes, ramshackle buildings and shanties, to which workers came from all over the country to work in Mumbai's factories, eateries, hospitality establishments and various other businesses. They came there because of Dharavi's low rents compared to the rest of the city.

The neighborhood had its own small-scale industries. Leather goods, pottery, garments and plastic manufacturing, along with fishing.

Zeb parked near Mahim Station, walked across the street, and entered the slum.

It was dirty. It stank. He had to duck overhead power lines and aluminum roofing. There was little privacy as residences jostled against each other. He stepped over human waste and walked past an open doorway in which a mother was feeding her child.

He could feel the neighborhood's energy, however. It throbbed beneath his feet and thrummed in the air.

That vibrancy feels like New York.

He ducked beneath a washing line, went past several leather manufacturers which were full of workers and entered a clearing.

Arjun Sule stood at a makeshift podium, addressing a small crowd. He was talking of representations he had made to the local government for better health and childcare. Hard-faced men stood nearby.

He's got protection ever since that shooting.

Zeb stood with folded hands as the speech wound down. The audience applauded. Sule bowed, greeted well-wishers and retreated to a kholi.

Zeb followed the retired gangster and found his way barred by one of Sule's men.

'Milne ka time khatam hua. Saab rest kar rahe hain.'

Meeting time is over. Boss is resting.

'He knows me,' Zeb said mildly.

'He doesn't want to be disturbed.' The CPO got close to him, eyes narrowing. Another bodyguard came to the door. Both of them wiry, lean, guns outlined beneath their shirts.

'Tell him it's—'

The first guard shoved him back. 'Don't you understand?' He hissed and raised a hand to punch. 'He's not meeting anyone.'

Zeb saw the blow coming.

Two more guards inside. Four in total.

He didn't want to go hot, but he didn't have time to waste either.

He trapped the incoming fist, pivoted and body-shoved the sentry, who crashed into the second guard and the two men staggered back into the kholi.

The two guards inside drew and cocked their guns and trained them on the intruder.

Movement from behind. A rush of air.

Bwana's voice, amused.

'Not so fast, boys.'

Zeb turned to see him and Bear on either side of the door, weapons out, presenting the narrowest profiles.

Sule got up from the bed he was resting on. He brushed away Padma, who was massaging his shoulder. He squinted at the Americans. His face relaxed and he waved at his men to stand down.

'You could have asked to meet me.'

'I tried,' Zeb replied and went deeper into the room.

Sule sat on his bed with his guards ranged behind him. A man at his right shoulder who seemed to be his aide. Padma, wide-eyed, on his left.

The room became small when the rest of the Agency operatives crowded behind Zeb.

'Are you here to arrest me? Do you have that authority? Why would you take me, though? I am a retired businessman—'

Zeb raised his palm to stop him.

'You heard about the bombings?'

'I am not deaf or blind.' Sule snorted. 'There is nothing else on TV. I—'

He stood up quickly. He sized up the Americans.

'You were the ones who were attacked! I heard of that, but I wasn't paying much attention. Why are you here?'

'A suspect came to Dharavi yesterday in a taxi after the explosions. He could be a Russian or a Chechen. This is him.'

Zeb unfolded a sheet of paper and showed him the sketch.

Sule inspected it and handed it to his aide, who glanced at it and shook his head.

'Dharavi,' Sule said bitterly. 'The rich people in their Malabar Hill mansions think it's an eyesore. Builders want to demolish this place and erect fancy apartments that they will sell to the rich. The government doesn't care about us. Do you know we have one of the lowest death rates in the world? We have become a role model in containing the virus. Dharavi *is* Mumbai. And now Mumbai Police think we are sheltering terrorists. Are they behind you?'

'Are you finished?' Zeb asked when Sule paused to draw a breath. 'The police will come, but if you can find out where this man went, who he spoke to, whether he is staying here, that might help.'

'Why should I help the police?'

'You said it yourself. Dharavi is Mumbai. Anything that impacts the city will affect your people, too.'

'Why are you here instead of the police?'

'We are working with them. We are part of the Joint Task Force.' Zeb showed him his identity card.

The gangster glowered at him for several moments. He made to speak when Padma tugged his sleeve. 'Isn't this the same man who saved you?'

'Yes, the American.'

'Do what he wants.'

Sule glared at her. She raised her chin and met his eyes defiantly. His face relaxed. He nodded at his aide, who scurried out.

Another man rushed in and whispered in his ear.

'Kal kyon nahin bola?' Sule roared and caught the man's shirt. *Why didn't you tell me yesterday?*

He was stopped by his daughter.

'What is it, Papa?'

The gangster had a haunted look in his eyes when he turned to Zeb.

'Something will go down today.'

'When and where?' Zeb rapped out.

The aide ran back. He presented his phone to Sule, who listened for a moment and licked his lips.

'It has happened. Bombs went off near Haji Ali.'

CHAPTER 27

'The Dargah!' Chloe exclaimed, referring to the mosque and tomb of one of Mumbai's most iconic attractions.

Sule picked up a remote and turned on a TV in the corner. 'It is intact! It is the approach to it that was bombed.'

BOMBS GO OFF AT HAJI ALI. SEVERAL PEOPLE DEAD AND INJURED, the rolling banner screamed.

The video scenes were chaotic as the reporter breathlessly announced the developments. Ambulances and police vehicles crowded on the road that ran along Worli's sea face, from which the causeway shot off to the site in the sea.

The concrete strip, which was normally above water during the day, was partly submerged. Khaki and blue-uniformed police officers and soldiers mixed with EMT staff in the knee-deep sea as they rescued the wounded, retrieved bodies and sealed off the site. A couple of police choppers circled the air, snipers bristling in their open doors.

'Haji Ali is one of Mumbai's most iconic shrines,' the TV journalist commented. 'Built nearly six hundred years ago to commemorate Haji Ali Bukhari, a Sufi saint, the site draws close to fifteen thousand visitors of all faiths each day. It now stands enveloped in smoke, with the cries of the wounded echoing through it and bodies carried away from it.'

The site was built in Worli Bay in the Arabian Sea, attached to Mumbai by a five-hundred-meter pedestrian causeway. The walkway was submerged during high tides, cutting it off from the city. The attraction opened to visitors when the water receded.

The journalist followed up the emotional opening with a factual account.

Eleven-thirty am. The causeway was crowded with visitors wishing to get into the attraction before the day's heat peaked. Three bombs went off in quick succession, instantly killing twelve people.

'Twenty-eight have been injured according to early reports. The numbers of both the dead and the wounded are sure to go up. Crawford Market witnessed a savage attack yesterday and now this. Surely the two bombings cannot be unrelated or coincidental, but Mumbai Police aren't speculating.'

Zeb tried Kohli's number. Busy. Meera and Bose's as well.

Call me asap, he messaged them and turned to Sule.

'What did your man tell you?' He gestured at the man who had rushed in, who was still in the room, a scared look on his face as he watched the TV.

'Mumbai is being attacked,' Zeb growled when the gangster hesitated. 'This isn't the time to protect your sources.'

'Nilu.' The former underworld don nodded. 'Got a call from a former foot soldier.'

The hitter had been smoking weed on the rocks on the sea face of Mahim, a suburb close to Worli.

'There isn't anything there,' the gangster continued. 'A road that parallels the coast, a concrete embankment to separate it from the rocks, and there's the sea beyond it. Nothing else. No one goes there in the night except couples who get away from the city to get some privacy there. It is ideal for gangs to conduct their business late in the night when Mumbai sleeps. Drugs and money change hands there. Suparis are given there.'

Supari. A kill contract to execute specific targets, given to gangsters.

'This soldier—I call him that, but he's not in the crime business anymore—was by himself. He works on a construction site during the day and at night goes there to smoke. He was there at ten pm, deep in the shadows, when he heard two men speak in Hindi. One of them said everything was set for the next day—'

'Next day?' Roger interrupted.

'Yes. This was the night before the Crawford Market explosions. Day before yesterday. The second man said Mumbai would begin to fear again. My man didn't think much of it until the blasts happened. He returned to the rocks yesterday night and waited in the same spot. The same men returned late. "The police are looking in the wrong areas," one of them said. "They will never suspect Haji Ali," the other man laughed. "Mumbai thinks Crawford Market was a one-off. The people will never think another explosion can happen tomorrow."'

'My man followed them to a car on the road. He got lucky. There was a passing taxi that was empty. He got into it and told the driver to follow the men to Goregaon. It's a—'

'A suburb on the Western line, to the north of the city. We know. Continue,' Beth said impatiently.

'He followed them to Polaris Tower, an upscale complex. He hid in the lobby and noted which floor they got to. Seventh. He returned to the building today and checked out their flat. It was locked. It was then that he called Nilu. This was around nine am.'

'WHY DIDN'T YOU TELL ME EARLIER?' Sule turned away from the Agency operatives and exploded at his man.

'Saheb.' *Sir.* Nilu put his hands together. 'I was getting those toilets and bathrooms installed. It slipped my mind. I rushed to you when I remembered.'

'CAN YOU SEE HOW MANY PEOPLE HAVE DIED—'

'STOP!' Zeb growled. 'Yelling at him will achieve nothing.'

He checked his phone again. No calls.

Kohli, Meera, Bose, they'll be swamped. I can't contact Mumbai Police. It will take me too long to get through to someone with authority.

'Where's your soldier? What's his name?'

'Bandya. I've been trying his phone. I can't reach him. It's taking a long time for calls to go through.'

'Networks are overloaded,' Zeb said. 'Did he describe these men?'

'No beards. He noticed that immediately. Average height. Jeans and T-shirts. They didn't look to be armed.'

'Did they look Indian?'

'He didn't see them from the front at all. He wasn't sure. But he said they spoke Hindi in a strange accent.'

'What did he mean by that?'

'It wasn't any Indian accent. He was sure of that. He thought they were foreigners.'

Russian? Chechen?

Zeb didn't speculate for long. 'Message him. Contact the JTF number.' He looked at Sule. 'Keep trying even if it is busy.'

'Where are you going?'

'Polaris Tower.'

CHAPTER 28

Zeb didn't ask his friends how they had found him in Dharavi. It wasn't important.

He didn't need to tell them to gear up. They strapped on their HKs when they reached the Range Rovers and drove away in a squeal of tires.

Meghan punched the address into the vehicle's mapping system and tuned the radio to a news station. She lowered the volume as Zeb stomped on the gas and sped through the city's near-empty streets.

They cut through Bandra-Kurla Complex and got onto the Western Express Highway. Several cruisers raced in the opposite direction, lights flashing, sirens wailing.

A police roadblock.

Zeb slowed and lowered the window to show his badge.

'JTF,' he announced crisply.

'JTF?' the officer asked, puzzled. He took in Meghan, Beth and Broker, went to the second vehicle and returned to Zeb.

'You are not Indian.'

'We're Americans, part of the Joint Task Force, working with Mumbai Police and RAW. Don't waste time. We're investigating a lead. Every second matters. Take down our plates and follow it up, but let us go. NOW!'

The officer's radio squawked. He took the call. Zeb used the opportunity to punch the gas and blow past him. He heard the man yell, saw the police officers raise their weapons in his rear-view mirror. He kept going.

They won't fire.

They didn't.

'Single tower,' Beth briefed them as they drove on the near-deserted highway. 'Twenty-six floors, each one having four apartments. Our targets' residence is on the seventh. We got floor plans from a real-estate broker's site. Their place overlooks Malad Creek that joins the Arabian Sea. Upscale place. CCTV cameras. Security desk. Gym. Gated compound with key code entry and a sentry to deal with visitors.'

'Not the kind of place gangsters would hang out,' Bear growled.

'It's exactly where I would hide if I were a terrorist,' Chloe corrected him.

Meghan dialed Sule and put the call on speaker. 'Bandya? Have you spoken to him?'

'His phone is unreachable. I haven't got through the JTF yet.'

'Keep trying.'

Zeb took the flyover exit from the highway. A suburban train passed beneath them, empty, its carriages rattling on the tracks.

That's normally packed with commuters. His lips thinned.

They came onto SV Road, a major arterial road that passed through the western suburbs. A pharmacy was open. A tea stall. A restaurant. Every other establishment was shuttered.

They entered Goregaon West. Highrises everywhere. Meghan pointed to a spire in the distance.

Polaris Tower.

She and Beth extracted the drones as they got closer.

Zeb got out of his ride when they rolled to a stop at the gate. He approached the entry and presented his badge.

'Police investigation. Don't tell anyone that we're here,' he commanded.

The guard, a middle-aged man in a dusty-blue uniform with the logo of a security company on his shoulders, shifted uneasily on his feet.

'Let us through,' Zeb snapped at him. 'This is related to the bombings.'

The guard eyed his credentials and nodded. He pressed a button and the gate rolled back.

'Don't tell anyone who we are and why we're here. Don't let anyone enter the complex. Not even residents. Give them whatever excuse you can think of,' Zeb warned him as they drove inside the large parking lot around the tower and eased into two vacant slots near the gate.

'Their apartment can't see us. No sight line,' Meghan said as she and Beth launched the UAVs. The elder twin reached down to her feet and came up with several rectangular pads. She scribbled *JTF, Mumbai Police,* with a marker and handed two to each of them.

Zeb Velcroed one of them to his chest and turned around for Beth to fasten the second one to his back.

'Ready?' he asked when they had finished attaching the pads.

'Yeah.' Bwana gripped his HK. 'Same formation as before?'

'Yeah. Beth and Broker at the vehicles to warn us if any hostiles turn up.'

'How will we recognize them?' Broker asked.

'If they come through the gate, they aren't friendly. Meg, Chloe and I will take the stairs. Bwana, Roger and Bear—'

'We'll disarm the elevators and cover you.'

'Occupants!' Beth snapped her fingers, her eyes on her drone's screen.

'Three men,' she added. 'It's definitely them. I can see through a window. They have guns. They look like AK-74s.'

These apartments have a single entry, Zeb thought rapidly. *No fire escape. Those stairs could be a problem.*

He didn't like shootouts on concrete steps. There wasn't any cover. There would be ricochets.

We can't repeat the grenade trick we did at Mastan's hideout. That building had no one else but the gangsters. This tower is fully occupied.

We have no choice.

'Let's go.'

CHAPTER 29

Zeb raced inside the polished-floor lobby. His footsteps echoed in the high-ceilinged space. Five elevators on a wall. A guard who was rising from behind his desk which was to one side, giving him full view of the comings and goings of people.

'Stay down,' he barked at the security man. 'We are with Mumbai Police.' He pointed to his chest pad. 'Don't let anyone enter the lobby. Where are the stairs?'

'WHERE ARE THE STAIRS?' he repeated while Bwana and Roger disabled the elevators.

The guard snapped his jaws shut and pointed to a door near a rolled-up firehose.

Zeb opened it cautiously. Concrete steps. Concrete banister. No cameras.

He wedged a spare magazine beneath the door to jam it open and took to the stairs. Meghan and Chloe behind him, Bear, Roger and Bwana well behind.

They went up swiftly, their rubber-soled shoes barely making any noise. The concrete stairwells blocked out any external sounds.

'Two of the men are packing their bags,' Beth warned in their earpieces.

'You have eyes on them?' Zeb asked.

'No, but I have their thermals.'

'Where's the third man?'

'In the living room, watching TV. I can see him.'

Fifth floor and then sixth floor landing.

'Those two dudes are out of the apartment.' Beth, her voice taut. 'I have lost their thermals. They'll be in the landing.'

They'll try the elevators, which won't respond. What will they do next? Will they go back inside or take the stairs?

Zeb got his answer when he heard voices as he climbed cautiously. One man swore in Hindi. The other one laughed.

And then they appeared on the stairs.

CHAPTER 30

The men had backpacks. Their AKs were clearly outlined beneath their shirts. They gaped at the operatives.

'Raise your hands. Slowly,' Zeb ordered.

He was prone on the stairs, his HK to his shoulder. He knew the rest of his friends weren't in sight.

They are on the lower flight, behind the banister.

The hostiles sprang apart. They reached beneath their shirts.

'POLICE!' one of them shouted.

'DROP YOUR GUNS,' Zeb roared, his finger taut on the trigger.

The shooters didn't obey. Their AKs came out. They fired, the rounds burning the air above his head. He shot into one man's thigh, felt a round nick his vest when Beth burst into his earpiece.

'THIRD MAN IS GOING FOR THE WINDOW!'

Zeb made the calculations automatically, without conscious thought, even as he fired at the men in an attempt to wound them.

Beth and Broker can stop that third dude, but what if more shooters come into the complex?

He was exposed. The rest of his team would back him up, but then the shooters were as good as dead since his friends would shoot to kill.

All this in nano-seconds as bullets edged closer to his body.

Zeb shot the first killer in the chest and crawled up at a loud burst from behind him as his friends opened up on the surviving man.

Both hostiles fell to the floor.

He lunged up and kicked away their AKs. He didn't waste time to check if they were alive.

Meg and Bwana will do that.

He sprang towards the apartment door, sensed rather than saw a neighboring door open a crack. His HK came up reflexively, and only his years of training and experience prevented him from shooting into it.

'BAHAR MAT AAO. HUM POLICE HAIN,' he yelled at the resident.

Don't come out. We are the police.

'Go! We'll deal with them,' Meghan hissed at him.

He went through the door and dove to the floor immediately when the man in the window turned at his entrance and sprayed in his direction.

'STOP!'

The hostile dropped out of sight in reply.

Zeb crouch-ran towards the living room window and snatched a glance. The shooter was scrambling down a nearby drainpipe.

'We have him in our sights,' Beth drawled. 'Should we take him out?'

'No. Don't show yourself. Watch out for other hostiles.'

'You'll go after him yourself? How?'

Zeb Velcroed his HK to his vest, climbed onto the windowsill, balanced for a moment and threw himself at the drainpipe, which was three meters away to his left.

His outstretched fingers felt the cylindrical surface, scrabbled desperately, found purchase and then gravity did its work and slammed his body against the wall.

'That had better hold,' Meghan said sardonically.

You and me, both!

He slid down rapidly, saw the shooter glance up his way, curse and reach for his AK clumsily. He gave up when Meghan and Bwana fired from the window, deliberately aiming around him.

Zeb swore when his combat pants snagged on the pipe's holding clip. He kicked out savagely to free it and ignored the burn in his palms as he resumed sliding down.

The shooter was several seconds ahead of him and even as he watched, the man landed on the ground, raised his AK and lowered it when his friends fired more rounds.

The hostile ran towards the gate.

Zeb let go of the pipe when he was four meters from the ground, landed, took a running step to balance himself and shot after the killer, who looked behind him desperately and changed track abruptly to lunge towards a nearby car.

He yanked its passenger door open and dragged out a young girl, turned towards Zeb and pointed his AK at her temple.

Zeb skidded to a stop.

A woman screamed. The child's mother, who came out of the second door, rushed around the car and halted when the shooter straightened his gun arm.

'DON'T. PLEASE!' she wailed.

The father climbed out from behind the wheel but stayed where he was.

'PLEASE LET HER GO,' he shrieked.

The girl trembled. Her eyes were wide, her mouth open, but no words came out.

'We can't risk a shot,' Bwana said bitterly.

'Neither can we,' Beth added.

Zeb nodded instinctively.

He knew his friends could take out the killer, but there was no guarantee the man's trigger finger wouldn't tighten even as he died, sending a burst through the girl's head.

He raised his hands slowly.

'Let her go,' he said softly.

'STAY WHERE YOU ARE!' the hostile shouted, spittle flying out of his mouth. He took several steps backward, dragging the girl with him.

'NO!' the mother cried.

'DON'T MOVE OR I WILL KILL HER RIGHT NOW.'

'Release her. Take me, instead.' Meghan, from behind Zeb.

He heard her approach slowly and then she came next to him, brushing his shoulder, her hands raised high in the air.

She must have found some cover to come up undetected.

'I am an American,' she continued, and took a step forward. 'You will have more negotiating power if you take me as a hostage. Think of it. Two countries will be impacted if you have me as a captive. You can make bigger demands—'

'STAY BACK. STOP TALKING.'

She ignored the killer and took another step forward.

Whoa!

Zeb took in the holstered Glock strapped to her back. It was loose in the sheath and trembled when she moved.

That's for me to draw it out easily.

He pictured it in his mind, going through the sequence as she took another half-step forward, giving him just enough room to make his move.

'The US government will provide you a plane to escape—'

The shooter swung his gun at her.

Zeb pounced forward and grabbed the gun with his right hand, shoving her sideways with his left, crouching down in the same move to rest one knee on the hard concrete of the parking lot while the Glock came up, his arm straight for him to sight down it and shoot into the killer's shoulder once and then a second time again to be sure.

He powered himself up with a palm and pounced forward

just as Beth and Meghan lunged towards the killer, the elder twin slapping his AK away and pinning him down with a knee to the chest while her sister searched him expertly.

The girl and her parents stood frozen, in shock and disbelief at the lightning turn of events. Broker reached the child and placed a hand on her shoulder to guide her to the mother, and their spell broke.

'Smart move,' Zeb told Meghan. He wiped sweat from his face. 'Risky.'

'It worked.' She grinned. 'I got Bwana to tape that gun to my back and took the stairs the moment you were halfway down the pipe. The shooter was at the car when I came onto the parking lot. He didn't see me hide behind another car.'

They watched the parents hug their daughter and sob loudly.

Zeb looked up when Bwana and Roger joined them.

'Those two men—'

'Dead,' Roger replied. 'Bear is with the bodies, to make sure the other residents remain inside.'

Zeb's phone buzzed. He brought it out, recognized the number, and took the call.

'I got several missed calls from you,' Kohli began. 'You heard about the—'

'Yeah. We have got one.'

'Got one of what?'

'A terrorist. Alive.'

CHAPTER 31

An hour later, Polaris Tower was flooded with JTF, Force One and Mumbai Police officers. The complex was sealed off to outside visitors, and media vans and reporters were pinned behind temporary barriers outside the building.

Kohli, Meera and Bose, fully up to speed, were in the shadow of a command van, along with Zeb and his team.

'Sule.' The RAW Special Agent mopped his face and drank from a bottle of water. 'We need to question him and his man, Nilu.'

'He will cooperate,' Zeb replied. 'These shooters spoke fluent Hindi but their accents ... Bandya, Sule's man, was right. They are not Indian.'

'Pakistani?'

'I don't think so. The survivor isn't talking?'

'No.' Meera ground her teeth angrily. 'He has clammed up. The only time he has opened his mouth is to drink water.'

'You found any identity on him? Beth searched him but it was a quick pat down.'

'Nothing. Indian rupees, spare change, a cell phone, but

nothing else. Not even a driver's license. That's what we found on the dead men, too.'

'You have an idea who they are? I can sense it in you.' Bose narrowed his eyes at Zeb.

He hesitated.

I have an idea, but it makes no sense.

'They sounded Iranian,' he admitted finally.

CHAPTER 32

The six men watched the TV in silence in the leader's room in the upscale hotel in downtown Mumbai.

The leader was in his early forties. Close-cropped hair with a hint of silver. Stubble on his face. Dark, hawk-like eyes. He was dressed casually in a half-sleeve shirt over jeans. He looked like a business executive, which was his cover.

The five other men were in their late thirties, a mix of looks, some clean-shaven, some sporting trimmed beards. All of them had similar builds. Lean, wiry, and fit. None of them sported any tattoos or visible scars.

'They had one job,' the leader said, 'and that was to lie low.'

He didn't raise his voice or pound the table in anger, but the rest of the men sensed his fury.

'They did.' Khalid defended the shooters as the camera cut to the two bodies that were being rolled into an ambulance. The surviving terrorist was out of sight. 'No one knew of them until today.'

'And now, we have lost them,' the leader countered sharply. 'They were our bombers. We don't have a second team. I can get one, but it will take time and we don't have much of it.'

'We have these four.' Khalid nodded at the four men, who were silent, observing everything.

'No. Their mission is different. We cannot risk them on this one.'

'I'll carry out the rest of the explosions, in that case.'

The leader regarded him through hooded eyes and nodded. He turned his attention to the TV.

'How did JTF find them?'

'Those Americans did.'

'They are part of JTF. Have you noticed how they are in the background? Their faces are never turned to any TV camera. No media outlet knows who they are. Mumbai Police have managed to delete every recording of their faces. Even today, there might have been several residents who recorded the shootout, but have you seen any footage on TV or the internet?'

He shook his head in reluctant admiration. 'We shouldn't underestimate RAW.'

'NIA is leading the JTF.'

The leader's eyes flashed. 'That's what India wants the world to think. I know how RAW works. They are leading this investigation. I know from our sources that Bose, Kohli and their upcoming star, Meera Ranganathan, are in Mumbai, leading the investigation.'

'Should we take them out?'

The leader whirled on him. 'Our mission is bigger than RAW's officers. Don't ever forget that.'

He rubbed his jaw thoughtfully. 'Asadi is alive. He will talk.'

'He won't.' Khalid shook his head. 'We recruited those three because of their discretion.'

'RAW will make him talk. Everyone breaks. You know that. The Indians will find out he and his team were Iranians. That might send them off the wrong trail for a while, but not for long. But, leave him to me. I will take care of him and even if he talks, he doesn't know much. He doesn't know where else we will be bombing. He won't recognize you. All he will say is he and his team were paid to set off those bombs. There is a loose end that we need to tie up, though.'

'The real estate agent?'

'Yes.'

'I'll take him out.'

'Do it right away.'

Khalid got to his feet. He was reaching for the door when the leader spoke again.

'Who is this other party who's interested in the Americans?'

'You mean that shooter in Crawford Market and that attack near CST?'

'Yes.'

'We can find out. Mastan might know.'

'Mastan is in police custody.'

'He is, but many of his gang members are out and about.'

'Find out.'

The leader brought out his phone, which indicated the meeting was over. Khalid left the room. The four silent men went out as well, to their rooms in the same hotel.

The leader channel surfed until he came to the news channel he was looking for. It had the same coverage, but that didn't matter. It was the media outlet he preferred.

He dialed a number, confident that the call would be bounced around the world, routed through several exchanges, proxy servers and internet connections, making it look like the call originated in Africa. The smart software in his phone automatically disguised his voice.

'You have seen the news?' he asked when the call was answered.

'Yes. Do we have a problem?'

'Nothing that can't be handled. The mission is still on track.'

'It had better be. Fifteenth and sixteenth are not far off.'

'The bots are ready?'

'Yes.'

The leader hung up.

He and the speaker had spoken in a language that wasn't Hindi.

Nor was it Farsi.

CHAPTER 33

'Some good news,' Kohli said. 'That man we captured and the dead men ... they seem to be the men in Crawford Market.'

'Those who were on camera?' Zeb asked.

'Yes. Their faces were fuzzy, if you remember, but our facial recognition program matched their cleaned-up photographs. They are our bombers.'

'We found C4 and detonators in the apartment,' Meera said.

'What was in their backpacks?'

'More explosives, spare magazines, rupees, several burner phones. We will check out their call logs, but if I were to guess, we won't get anywhere with those.'

'They were planning more attacks,' Meghan said bleakly.

'Yes. But we don't know where or when.'

'And whether there are more teams.' Bear looked at the young girl and her parents, who were being attended to by EMT staff.

'And now for some bad news.' Meera's teeth flashed in a humorless smile. 'We found your shooters. The ones who attacked you near Crawford Market. Six of them in a Byculla warehouse, not far from where we found their Toyota.'

'They aren't talking?' Zeb guessed.

'They can't. They are dead. Killed by single rounds in their foreheads.'

'An execution. Someone who knew them, tidying up loose ends.'

'Yes. We will run their prints and put out their details but with the luck we've had so far, we might not get anything.'

'They too are pros.'

'Yes.'

Zeb looked up at the building, at the residents who were peering out of their apartments.

'I've got my teams to warn them no one should take photographs and spread them on social media.'

'That wasn't what I was thinking of. This building ... it's an upscale one, right?'

'Correct,' Kohli said curiously.

'Who owns that apartment?'

'A businessman who lives in Dubai. He rents it out. Neighbors say our killers occupied it about a month ago. We'll check with the building society's records for exact dates.'

'How did they know of the apartment?'

'Through a broker, a real-estate agent—'

He broke off abruptly. His eyes lit up.

'He could be in danger!' Meera pivoted on her heel. 'RAHUL! KISHORE! Get two more members and come with us.'

'Where are you going?' Kohli called out as Zeb headed to his Range Rover.

'To talk to someone who knows a few Russians.'

CHAPTER 34

Sahil Gupta was balancing a phone on each shoulder as he alternated speaking in their mouthpieces.

'Madam, it is the only apartment with a sea view. Air conditioning, marble tiles, modular kitchen, it has everything you are looking for. Just a moment, madam.'

'Sir.' He switched to the other phone. 'I need a decision by today. There are many parties interested in this. Yes, sir, it is ideal for a four-person family. Yes, sir, it is close to that school. Hold please, sir.'

His cell phone buzzed. He ignored it. Such times gave him a rush. He was the go-to man for prime Goregaon properties. The number of calls he got was proof of that.

He was speaking to the woman when his door burst open.

'Who are you? No, ma'am, sir, that wasn't for you. Wait a moment please.'

He hunched his shoulders to secure the phones firmly against either side of his neck and glowered at the intruder. The man wore a hoodie, gloves on his hands and shades over his eyes.

Who wore those in Mumbai's heat, and indoors?

'Who are you?' he repeated. 'I am busy. Make an appointment with my secretary. She's outside. MAYA,' he bellowed. 'WHY DID YOU LET THIS MAN THROUGH?'

'WHAT ARE YOU DOING—'

His body slammed back into the leather chair as the round entered his forehead. It jerked when a second round tore into his chest. The phones clattered to the floor.

KHALID STOOD MOTIONLESS, LISTENING TO THE SOUNDS FROM outside. Gupta's office was in a commercial complex on New Link Road. Hair salons, restaurants, toy stores, pharmacies, and several other establishments in the area. It was set back from the road with a small parking lot in the front with paved steps to the shops.

He heard the sounds of traffic, an ambulance wailing in the distance, but no sounds of alarm, no rushed feet.

The phones squawked, reminding him the callers were still online. He ripped their cords out, checked that there were no cameras inside the office, and went around the desk. He hip-shoved Gupta's chair, which rolled away sluggishly with its weight.

The broker's computer was turned on. He went through several folders, grimacing when he found no rental records. A police cruiser's siren wailed close by.

He straightened, went to the body and started searching it when the siren drew closer. He hurried to the door without a glance at Maya, who was slumped back in her chair, and went out of the office.

He turned away casually and bent his head when a police cruiser flashed past. He hurried down the steps after it disappeared into the traffic and called the leader.

'The broker is dead. But I didn't have time to change his computer records or search him.'

'Asadi and his team gave false documents. The police will find nothing in them. He spent some time with them though, when he was showing them the property. He could have overheard or seen something about them that he would have told the cops, which is why he had to die. The rental payments came from a company bank account in Mauritius.'

'Won't the Indians find out who's behind that company?'

'I'll manipulate the bank's records so that they *do* find something.'

CHAPTER 35

'MOVE!' Meera yelled at the shoppers who were idling on the steps as she and Kohli went up with their men behind them. She scanned the shoppers' faces and shook her head. None of them looked like killers.

She pushed open the glass door with her left hand, her right close to the concealed holster on her waist.

'We're too late,' she spat at the sight of the receptionist. She checked the woman's body and nodded at Kohli, who drew his gun and covered her.

She burst through the second door, her gun raised. She lowered it instantly and rushed to Gupta.

'He's dead too. Body is still warm.'

'Rahul, Kishore,' Kohli rapped out. 'Take the rest of the men and interview everyone in neighboring shops. The customers, too. Ask them if they heard anything. Check for cameras.'

'Yes sir.'

Meera looked at the phones on the floor and traced their cords back to the sockets. They were old style but had a screen with a small caller log. She dialed the last number and winced when an angry voice came on.

'SAHIL GUPTA! HOW DARE YOU CUT ME OFF? DO YOU KNOW—'

'Ma'am, I am not Gupta. I am Meera Ranganathan with the Joint Task Force investigating the bombings. Gupta is dead. Did you hear anything—'

'DEAD? HOW? I WAS TALKING TO HIM JUST MINUTES AGO. WHAT ABOUT MY FLAT? WHO WILL I DEAL WITH NOW?'

Meera's lips thinned. 'Ma'am, there are more than thirty people dead in Mumbai and several injured. Now, what did you hear?'

'Nothing.' The woman's voice lowered. 'He asked me to hold and seemed to be speaking to someone.'

'Did you hear any name?'

'No. *Who are you?* That's what he said and then he yelled at some Maya, asking her why she had let the man through.'

That must be the receptionist.

'I heard a sharp sound. Like a book had fallen.'

'That was a shot, ma'am, from a silenced gun.'

The customer gasped. 'I don't remember anything else,' she quavered.

Meera took her details and hung up. She dialed the second number, got another irate customer who confirmed what the woman had said.

'No cameras here,' Kohli said when she hung up. 'His computer is still working, his cell phone is on him.'

'The killer was confident nothing would lead back to him or the terrorists.'

'Or, he didn't have time to do anything more.'

CHAPTER 36

Zeb got behind the wheel of his ride and fired it up to start the aircon. His friends crowded inside, the vehicle settling heavily on its shocks.

Roger sighed in relief at the cool air blowing inside and made to speak when Zeb raised a finger.

Zeb dialed a number and connected the call to the Range Rover's speakers.

'I was wondering if you would call.' Grigor Andropov, the head of a covert Russian agency, replied.

No *hi, hello,* or *how are you.* The spymaster, a close friend, knew there was a time for pleasantries. The day of the second bombings in Mumbai wasn't one of them.

'You know we're in Mumbai?'

'I guessed. I heard that a covert American agency was on a training exercise with RAW ... how many could there be! How can I help?'

'Are you aware of any Russian or Chechen killers interested in me?'

'Da.' Andropov chuckled. 'Many of them are dead. The few who are alive know better than to go after you. Why do you ask?'

Zeb told him about the Crawford Market shooter.

'Mumbai Police haven't any leads?'

'JTF and they are still investigating. We have contacts in Dharavi, but that place has over a million people. Are you aware of any shooters who are in India?'

'Nyet. But there is someone who might know.'

'Who?'

'Sergei Petrov. He is clued into the subcontinent's underworld.'

'Our contacts are, too. They haven't found anything.'

'Your contacts aren't Petrov.'

'What's special about him?' Beth cut in impatiently.

'Petrov is an old Afghan hand. He was in that country when Russia invaded Afghanistan. He trained its army to fight the mujahideen. He's seen it all, the Taliban, the American-led war. He deployed several Russian and Chechen killers to train the Taliban and, later on, to support Pakistani dissidents.'

Those folks were fighting the Pakistan government's support for the Afghan mujahideen, Zeb recalled.

'Da, it's a mess.' Andropov sighed heavily, reading his thoughts. 'Many of the problems in the world are caused by my country or your country or Britain's interference in other nations. But'—his voice sharpened—'if anyone will know of a Russian or Chechen killer in Mumbai, it will be Petrov.'

'Where is he?'

'In Mumbai. India is home for him, now.'

'What does he do here? Run gangs?' Broker asked sarcastically.

'No,' Andropov laughed. 'He's a changed man. He's running a charity for homeless children in ... let me look it up.'

They heard him punch keys and then his voice returned.

'Wadala. That's on the eastern side of the city. He's out of the spy business, but he's still plugged into his network.'

'Can you send us his address and number?' Meghan asked.

'Da. But don't call him. He won't respond to such requests on the phone. It's best you meet him in person. And, be careful.'

'Why?'

'He doesn't trust anyone from any government. Like I said, he has seen what went on in Afghanistan and Pakistan, how various countries interfered. He's out of the game, but he's still sharp and he hasn't lost his skills. He's also got guards with him.'

'We'll be careful,' Zeb assured him. 'Is there any way this Russian or Chechen killer might know of him?'

'Petrov is a legend—'

'How come we haven't heard of him?' Chloe asked curiously. 'He's not in our system. I checked while you were speaking.'

'Petrov knows where Russia's skeletons are buried. In Afghanistan. FSB and SVR feared he would spill our secrets from those days and sent out killer teams to take him out. He dealt with them ruthlessly. More killers were sent. They died. They negotiated a truce with him. They would leave him alone. He would stay silent and in return his records would be erased from our systems. That's why you don't know of him. But in the Russian and Eastern European contract killer world, which is active in the subcontinent, he's well known.'

'What of you?' Zeb asked softly. 'How are you doing?'

'Surviving.' Andropov laughed mirthlessly. 'My country is isolated from the world. But my president continues with this Ukrainian invasion. He has full control of the media that pumps out propaganda. Older Russians buy into it. They believe him when he says Ukraine is a threat to my country, that it is filled with Nazis.'

'Ach!' He made a dismissive sound. 'Don't worry about me. I have been in my business for a long time. There is no threat to my position. If anything,' he said, the smile in his voice perceptible, 'my agency has become more powerful after what you pulled off in Moscow.'

'That's good to hear. We were worried you would experience some blowback.'

'I can take care of myself. You know that.'

Zeb nodded. Few had heard of Grigor Andropov, but those

who knew of him had the highest regard for him even if they were adversaries.

'Has RAW or any other Indian agency reached out to you?' Beth asked.

'Not to us, but I know they have made contact with FSB. Standard stuff, whether we suspect anyone who could be behind these blasts. We haven't a clue.'

He took a deep breath. 'Help them, Zeb, if you can. An unstable India is dangerous for the world.'

CHAPTER 37

'What do we have?' Kohli asked his team in the evening.

Nariman Point. The setting sun in the Arabian Sea painted the glass-fronted towers in orange and gold hues. Nature's splendor, but no one was watching it.

'Zilch! Zero.' Meera bit her lip. 'That's what we have. Gupta's office didn't have cameras. The shopping center has a few, but conveniently, none at the front were working.'

'Sabotaged?'

'No,' Rahul replied. 'They were down for more than a week. The management company was in no hurry to fix them. It wasn't a priority.'

'Witnesses?'

'A few but none of them are reliable. All of them said they saw a man in a hoodie, shades and gloves.'

'Here.' Meera brought up a digital sketch on the screen. 'This is who they described.'

Kohli's lips curled in disgust at the image. The man, with his sunshades and head covering, had no distinguishing features.

'His diary? Computer records?'

'That's where it gets interesting.' Meera leaned forward. 'I take back what I said earlier. We have something, but it could go nowhere. Our prisoner is Hadi Asadi. A Persian carpet trader in Tehran. He has his own store. Karim Qaderi and Amir Hussain are the dead men, according to Gupta's notes.'

'Why were they in Mumbai?'

'To source Indian carpets. They were on a scouting trip to visit manufacturers all over the country.'

'Who referred them to Gupta?'

'No idea. We got all this from his diary and emails. He posts his properties on several real-estate sites. It's possible Asadi reached out to him through one of those sites. Our tech team is looking into that.'

'Passport copies?'

'There they are.' Meera brought up more photographs.

'Fake?'

'Yes. The Iranian Embassy in New Delhi says no such passports were issued by their country. In fact, we have nothing to say they are Iranian other than Zeb.'

'He could be wrong,' Kishore offered.

'He could be.' Kohli dismissed his suggestion. 'But I wouldn't count on it. He and his team know several world languages. If he says Asadi sounded Iranian, I'll believe it.'

'Why would Iranians bomb Mumbai? That too, in those two locations which have a high density of Muslim population?'

'They could be mercenaries,' Meera said.

'That's my thinking as well.' Kohli nodded. 'Look into Tehran, that store that they have. Airport cameras—'

'We are on it. You are not asking the key question, though.'

'What's that?'

Her smile lit up her face. 'Who was paying the rent?'

'All right, I'll bite. Who was it?'

'Hafeez Traders, an Iranian company, through its Mauritius bank account.'

'Banks carry out deeper due diligence on their clients,' Kohli said excitedly. 'We can find out who the company's officers are, who operates the account.'

'That's where we got road-blocked. The bank isn't cooperating.'

'They will. India is one of Mauritius's biggest trading partners. I will ask Bose to make a call. Good work.'

'Aren't you forgetting something?'

'What?'

'There might be more killer teams out there.'

CHAPTER 38

Zeb went to Wadala with Beth and Meghan.

It was a deliberate, psychological move that worked in their favor.

The twins were attractive. Just shy of six feet in height, their looks and inner confidence turned heads wherever they went. Their presence loosened up their suspects, who were invariably men, made them talkative.

'Let's face it.' Chloe had smirked when they had discussed the approach in the past. 'No one will feel like talking in Bwana or Bear's presence. Their size makes them intimidating.'

He parked their ride behind a container truck on a service road and checked out the surroundings. They were on P.D. Mello Road. Residential buildings on either side with a few stores interspersed.

Beth shoulder-nudged him to a squat, yellow-colored building.

'He hires that primary school in the evenings,' she said. 'He conducts lessons with volunteers. Numeracy and literacy skills.'

'How old are these kids?'

'Five to ten. His charity has over eighty children. Abandoned kids, those who have run away from broken homes. He takes them in, feeds them here, in the school and houses them with volunteer families and hostels in Wadala. He works with the city's adoption agencies to place them with families.'

'How's he funded?'

'Charitable donations.'

'How many staff does he have?'

'Two full time. Him and an administrative person. The rest are volunteers.'

'Petrov is a local celebrity,' Meghan interjected. 'There aren't many non-Indian folks who run charities in Mumbai. He's one of the few.'

'What's his backstory?' Zeb asked. 'What does Mumbai know of him?'

'He's created a believable cover that even the Indian agencies have bought into. He poses as a Russian businessman who used to visit India for trade, fell in love with the country and settled here. He sold his business, is well-off enough to not take any salary. That admin person is the only one who is paid.'

'Married? Kids?'

'He claims he had an Indian wife, but we couldn't dig up anything on her. No children of his own as far as we know.'

'Where does he live?'

'A fancy apartment in Worli. Just because he does charity stuff doesn't mean he has to give up his luxuries.'

'The guards that Grigor mentioned?'

'Nothing on them. This is India, in case you've forgotten.' Meghan grinned. 'Not everything is on the internet.'

He raised an apologetic hand, acknowledging her mild rebuke, and followed the sisters to the school's gates.

A chorus of voices reciting the English alphabet came out through barred windows. The school had a small playground, a main building and what looked like an administrative office to one side. It was overlooked by residential towers on three sides with the road at the front.

The twins followed the voices to an open door. They peered through it and entered. Zeb followed them inside a classroom.

Wooden benches attached to long desks, heavily scratched and scribbled on. Scattered about, bright-eyed children chorusing enthusiastically to the salwar-kameez clad middle-aged teacher who stopped at their entrance.

'Haan ji,' she started, took them in and resumed in English. 'Yes, can I help you?'

'We are looking for Petrov.' Beth smiled.

'Sergei is in his office,' a girl yelled.

'Yes.' The teacher chuckled and pointed at the admin building. 'You'll find him there.'

The children resumed their alphabet when they exited the building.

'You don't know what privilege is until you visit such places,' Meghan murmured.

'Stop,' her sister mock-reprimanded her. 'Zeb will go emotional and teary-eyed.'

He hid a grin. He was their verbal punching bag, and enjoyed it though he wouldn't admit it to them.

Petrov was easy to find. There was only one lighted room in the admin building. Its door was open and when they approached it, Zeb saw the sign on it. *Head Teacher,* with a woman's name on it.

The Russian was at a desk, poring over a file with two other men across from him. All of them seemed to be in their late fifties, sparse graying hair, stubble and with wiry builds.

Zeb saw ink on one of the men's forearms and recognized the Spetsnaz tattoo.

'Yes?' Petrov looked up when they entered. He spoke in English.

'Media interviews have to be scheduled,' one of the men spoke before they could reply. 'Call our office number tomorrow.'

'We aren't the media,' Meghan answered.

'You have children to enroll?'

'Nyet. We need to speak to Petrov. Alone.'

The three men's eyes narrowed at her fluent Russian. No other reaction. They remained expressionless.

'You know us?' Petrov asked mildly, in English.

'We have heard of you.'

'What's your business?' the third man asked. A shade away from being hostile or aggressive.

'It's with Petrov only.'

'You can speak freely in front of my friends.' The retired spy smiled faintly.

Zeb noted the way he sat. Alert. Ready. *Prepared to overturn the desk and hide behind it. He might have a gun taped beneath it.*

'We have a mutual friend,' he spoke. 'Grigor Andropov.'

The children's chorus filled the silence. A car honked distantly. Water dripped from a tap somewhere.

And then the first man spoke.

'We don't know that name. You have the wrong address. We are busy. We need to arrange dinner for the children.'

He stopped short of asking them to leave.

'Grigor said if anyone can help Mumbai, it is you,' Zeb said in Russian, his eyes on Petrov.

What was a white lie between friends?

'My friend is right,' the charity boss said. 'You have the wrong people. We run this facility for homeless children. I am sure you saw them as you entered the school. Helping Mumbai? Sure, what I do does help the city, but I am not the only one. There are thousands of—'

'Cut it,' Beth snapped. 'We know who you are. There are terrorists out there bombing Mumbai and if you really care so much for the city, you'll drop the act and help us.'

The third man went to the door, looked outside and closed it. He turned to them and leaned against it.

'Is this where you go strong-men on us?' Meghan drawled.

'Perhaps you should introduce yourself,' Petrov said smoothly.

'Meghan Peterson. Beth Peterson. Zeb Carter.'

'You are dvoynyashki?'

'Twins, yes.'

Petrov closed his file and leaned back. Man-at-Door didn't move. Third Man half-turned in his chair, ready to spring up and hurl it as a missile.

'If we were hunting you, you would be dead,' Beth said sardonically. 'We are here for your help.'

'You are CIA?'

'Something like that.'

'You were the ones who were attacked near CST.' Man-at-door snapped his fingers and returned to the table.

'Da.'

'How do you know Andropov?' Petrov questioned.

'It's his story to tell. Ask him.'

'What help do you need?'

'There is a Russian or Chechen fighter in the city. He tried to shoot me in Crawford Market the day of the bombing. Who is he?' Zeb asked.

The Russians didn't move.

'I don't know who that would be.'

He's dropped the businessman act at least.

'This might help.' Beth showed him the sketch on her phone.

Petrov looked long and hard at it and passed it to his men, who shook their heads after glancing at it.

'No one we know.'

'Can you find out? He went to Dharavi after the bombing. We know that much.'

'Dharavi,' Petrov repeated with no inflection.

'Yeah. You have a school there too, don't you?' Meghan challenged him.

'Is he connected to the bombing?'

'It's possible. JTF is interested in him as well.'

'Who else knows about me?'

He's asking if we told the police.

'Just us,' Zeb told him.

Petrov smiled faintly when the children began singing lustily. His men rolled their eyes at their out of pitch voices.

'All these years I have been here, and no one suspected who I was. I left that world behind and now you want me to go back to it?'

'We want you to tap into your network for that shooter. We know you still have active contacts.'

'And if I refuse, you'll expose me?'

'No. We'll continue our investigation. But if another bomb explodes in Mumbai or any other part of the city, you'll have to live with that. If something happens in Dharavi—'

'I get it. How can I contact you?'

Meghan scribbled her number on a sheet of paper and gave it to him.

Man-at-Door straightened his forearm to reveal more of his ink. He felt Zeb's eyes on it and his eyes glinted.

'You should have brought back-up ... if the meeting hadn't turned out this way you would have needed it.'

'No, we wouldn't have,' Beth said flatly.

CHAPTER 39

It wasn't hard for Khalid to find Mastan's gang. He drove around the refuse, gangster's territory, which was well known in the underworld, and threatened bar-owners and attacked street dealers until one of them confessed to being a soldier. That man pointed him to a lieutenant in a chawl, whom he tortured to get the names and locations of the commanders, the senior-most cadre who reported to the now-imprisoned Mastan.

Feroze Iqbal, one of the leaders who wasn't arrested, was in his apartment in a Dadar chawl enjoying the company of two women when Khalid approached the building close to midnight.

He was alone, but he knew what he was capable of and the caliber of the hitters he was facing.

There were three guards on the street level, lounging, smoking, leaning against a Honda.

'Is Iqbal inside?' Khalid asked them.

The men stared at him. Their looks were sufficient for Khalid, who drew his Sig-Sauer and shot them in the head. He shoved their bodies to the ground where they wouldn't be seen easily and took the steps.

Sounds of snoring and a child crying reached him. A man on

the passageway, bearded, scratching his belly to reveal the gun in his waist. His eyes widened at the stranger's arrival but before he could react, the gun spat.

Khalid stepped over his body and dealt ruthlessly with two more guards before shooting through the door and kicking it open.

The women screamed. Iqbal roared in rage, his anger turning to a howl when Khalid slashed at his mouth, breaking his teeth.

'What do you want?' the commander choked out.

'Information. Who was the shooter in Crawford Market? He was a foreigner.'

'Shooter? Foreigner? How would I know?'

'Find out and call me on this number.'

He slipped his number into the man's pocket.

'Do you know who you are—'

Khalid broke his nose with his gun barrel.

'I know who you are. You don't know me, however, and what I am capable of. That should scare you. If I don't hear from you in twenty-four hours, you are dead. If you want to send your shooters to hunt me, go ahead. See how many of them will be left alive. And then you'll have to deal with Mastan when he learns of it.'

Iqbal glared at him and shifted his eyes to the door.

'Your men are dead.'

The commander cursed and spat blood. 'What do I get in return?'

'You'll live.'

Khalid went out into the night satisfied with his work.

He was confident Iqbal wouldn't get back to him. That didn't matter, however. The gangster would be curious and would seek information on the shooter.

That foreigner will come to know of that if he is smart, and he will find a way to reach me.

Khalid waved down a passing cab and in its back seat, brought up a map of Mahim.

CHAPTER 40

The Russian met the Chechen at Leopold Café in Colaba. The bar was a city landmark. It had been shot up by terrorists in the 2008 attack on Mumbai and since then had become even more popular with tourists.

No one gave the men a second glance. No one could overhear their conversation amidst the loud Australian, German, and other accents. The Chechen's face had been on TV, but after the second bombing, he wasn't mentioned and the vast majority of Mumbai's residents had already forgotten him.

It was safe for him to be out and about in the city.

'You had him,' the Russian said. 'The market was busy. You could have easily gotten away afterwards.'

'He had seen me. There was no way I could have escaped, and then it was too late. I was lucky I survived the blast.'

The Russian sized him up. His companion had a faint bruise on his face from when the explosion had thrown him to the ground, but showed no other injury.

'I had to get the backup team to attack Carter.'

'They didn't do a good job.'

'No. I had to clean up afterwards.'

The Chechen looked at him. 'I didn't see that on TV!'

'Either the police haven't found the bodies or they haven't declared it. But they are dead.'

'We can take him out at his hotel. A sniper shot.'

'You don't know him as well as I do,' the Russian hissed. 'Carter or his friends never present a target long enough for a shot when they are in the open. They are continually on the move. When in hotels, they take random exits. They don't follow any routine. He goes for a run usually and we could take him then, but there's no predictability to his routine. He has so many enemies ... you think they wouldn't have tried the long shot?'

He sipped his drink and looked around casually to confirm no one was paying attention to them. 'Don't return to Dharavi. Carter was there. He has got Sule to search for you.'

'Sule? How does he know him?'

'I don't know. It doesn't matter. You are still sleeping in cars and buses?'

'Yes, ever since I fled from Dharavi.'

The Russian slid a key across the table. An address was scribbled on its tag.

'This is a flat in Mahim. It's clean. Hole up there until we work out our next steps.'

'Carter will be hunting us.'

'Da.' A feral smile split the Russian's face. 'We'll make sure he comes to us.'

Zeb and his team were in Dharavi, along with Sule's men. They had split up. Zeb and the sisters along with Nilu, with the rest of his team in smaller groups as they went through the slum showing the shooter's photograph to its residents.

They met three hours later in Sule's office, where an aide served them iced lemonade.

Bwana swallowed his drink in one gulp, snatched Chloe's from her hand and drank it too.

'I am bigger than you.' He wiped his lips. 'I need more cooling.'

She rolled her eyes, took another glass from the tray and turned to Zeb.

'Nada?'

'Yeah,' he replied. 'Someone is lying or—'

'There are a million people here.' Arjun Sule scowled. 'Sure, they live very close to one another, but it is highly possible for strangers to come here and stay for several nights without being remembered.'

'He would have to rent a kholi to stay here, wouldn't he?'

'Not necessarily. We have many people who sleep in the alleys at night.'

Would a killer do that? Zeb wondered.

Yeah. I would, if I were the shooter. Dharavi is the perfect place in Mumbai to get lost in. Sleeping outdoors makes it even more anonymous.

'I hoped someone would remember his accent,' Broker complained.

'There are hundreds of tourists who visit Dharavi each day.' Sule shrugged. 'Americans, French, Japanese, Russian, we get them all. Your man wouldn't stand out if he was staying here for a while.'

'Can you put the word out in your network? That this man is wanted.'

The retired gangster's eyes flashed. 'That life is behind me.'

'I am sure you or your men still have contacts, though.'

'The JTF published his photograph.'

'And Mumbai has already forgotten about him,' Bear growled. 'Everyone is talking of the bombings. Heck, he's a lower priority to Kohli too. We have taken the lead on finding him.'

'Put out the word,' Zeb urged, seeing Sule's indecision. 'What do you have to lose?'

'We are out of the gang business,' he snarled. 'All of my men ... we have changed our lives with great difficulty. None of us want to go back to it.'

'They should make a Bollywood movie on you,' Meghan said sarcastically. 'You say all that, but I bet you still have a finger on the underworld pulse. There is nothing that happens there you aren't aware of. Heck, Bandya, your man, still frequents the same haunts. Where is he? Did you find him?'

Sule's face darkened. 'Yes. He's dead.'

'How?' Zeb asked, shocked.

'We found his body in Goregaon, in a trash bin. His throat had been slashed.'

'When was this?'

'After he called Nilu. He must have gone back to Polaris Tower—'

'Those men must have seen him,' Bwana completed, 'and dealt with him. They must have tortured him to see who he worked for. That's why those men were packing up and leaving when we hit them.'

'Ask your network.' Zeb placed his empty glass on the tray and wiped his hands on his jeans. 'We need to find these terrorists and that shooter before another bomb explodes.'

He was silent as he drove back to their hotel.

We have nothing other than that shooter's sketch. That's of no help.

'Sule and Petrov.' Beth seemed to be thinking on the same lines. 'We have to hope they come up with something.'

CHAPTER 41

Hadi Asadi was chained to his bed in an ICU room in Kapadia Hospital in Goregaon.

The terrorist had been brought there to be treated after his capture.

He stared at the ceiling blankly. The police had interrogated him despite the hospital's objections, but he hadn't cracked. His room was guarded. The attendants who brought his food were vetted and his tray was checked thoroughly. His entire floor was filled with police officers. His room didn't have a window either.

There was no escape for him.

And yet he was determined to hold out. He wouldn't spill to the police.

He shifted on the bed and looked around when a male nurse entered his room carrying a food tray. An armed officer was behind him.

The nurse placed the food on a side table, sat on a nearby chair and spoon-fed him.

Asadi fell back when he was finished and closed his eyes.

He didn't open them again.

. . .

Kohli and Meera were the first JTF responders to the hospital.

The consulting doctor briefed them that Hadi Asadi had died of food poisoning.

'Not just him,' the tired-looking woman explained. 'We lost an entire floor of patients. The pantry is locked down. We are investigating what went wrong.'

This can't be an accident, Kohli thought as he ordered the entire hospital to close down and ordered their teams to investigate every employee, patient and visitor to the hospital. Delivery vans and their workers were stopped from going out.

It was a mammoth task, but by noon they knew what had happened.

'It was a ginger sauce.' Meera briefed Bose and several JTF and Mumbai Police officers in a consulting room that had been emptied for them. 'The hospital orders it from a specialist supplier in Kurla. An entire batch was poisoned. However, it was only that floor's trays that were affected since the ingredient was used only in their curries. No one else ordered that item.'

'What was in the poison?' the RAW chief asked, granite-faced.

'Botulinum. A high concentration of it. More than a gram of it in each tray. Even a few micrograms can be fatal.'

'This wasn't an accident.' Kohli looked up when Zeb and his team entered the room. 'Those sachets were deliberately infected with botulinum.'

'Asadi was the target?'

'Yes. All the other patients who died were innocent civilians.'

'The terrorists knew Asadi would talk eventually,' Meera said angrily. 'They were prepared to take out the entire hospital to kill one man.'

'The sauce supplier—' a senior police officer began.

'Its officers have been arrested. However, I am sure they weren't involved. It's a family-run business that has been around for years. We are likely to find someone infiltrated their staff with a fake identity and infected an entire batch. Mumbai Police are tracking down all the shipments from that supplier. We have made announcements on TV and radio, too.'

'Did he say anything before he died?' Zeb raised his hand to get her attention.

'No.'

THE LEADER AND KHALID WATCHED THE NEWS IN THE former's hotel room. They didn't fist-bump or have a celebratory drink.

'You took care of that man?'

'Yes,' Khalid replied. 'He's dead. Mumbai police will find his body in a day or two and work out that he was in the factory yesterday. He infected that sauce. But he was single. The trail won't lead to us.'

'What about the shooter? Have you made contact?'

'I have got people working on that,' the killer said, straight-faced.

FEROZE IQBAL'S MEN SPREAD THE WORD IN THE UNDERGROUND that they were interested in talking to the shooter in Crawford market. It wouldn't be a hostile meeting.

Mastan's gang had a presence in the darknet. They offered their services and got contracts via specialist websites and forums that civilians didn't know of. Feroze's men broadcast discreetly on those mediums too.

THE RUSSIAN WAS ACTIVE ON ONE OF THE DARK WEB SITES. HE saw the message and even though it was obliquely worded, knew it referred to him.

He contacted the sender and asked why the gang wanted to

meet. The website was designed such that person-to-person messages were automatically erased after a few seconds.

A matter of mutual interest, was the reply.

How do I know you aren't police?

How do I know that of you?

The Russian drummed his fingers on his thigh. It was a fair question.

Who are you?

Someone in a similar business as you.

Who do you represent?

Mastan.

The Russian raised his eyebrows. *Why is that gang interested in me,* he thought to himself.

Meet and find out, was the answer when he posed the question.

How will I know who I am meeting?

The gangster turned on his webcam to show a swarthy man in a dimly lit room. He held up a newspaper to show an article and a photograph.

The Russian squinted as he read about Feroze Iqbal, a wanted lieutenant in Mastan's gang. The image matched the man's.

Now, you.

No, the Russian replied. *You want to meet, you'll have to take the risk that I am the shooter. I will decide where the meeting happens and when. Take it or leave it.*

Iqbal took it.

THE RUSSIAN ARRANGED THE MEETING FOR THAT NIGHT. Horniman Circle Gardens would be the venue.

It was in downtown Mumbai, a landmark location that was overlooked by the Asiatic Society of Mumbai, a colonial-style building that had been featured in several movies.

He conveyed the location to Iqbal and ignored the gangster's protests that it was a high-risk place for such a meeting.

That's why I chose it, he smiled to himself and briefed the Chechen.

IQBAL'S MEN REACHED OUT TO KHALID WITH THE information, who listened silently and gave a single command.

'I will meet Iqbal at Horniman Circle.'

CHAPTER 42

Nariman Point. The conference room in the JTF's office.

Bose was tight-lipped after the video call with India's Home Minister ended. It hadn't been a pleasant discussion. The elected official had criticized the JTF for its slow investigation.

'What have you got to show?' The minister had challenged the assembled representatives from NIA, RAW, Mumbai Police and various other investigative agencies. 'Sixty people have died in total and that number might only go up, considering the injured. The only progress you have made is finding out about some estate agent, who is dead, and in capturing Asadi, who too has been killed right beneath your noses. You don't know who is bombing our country. You don't know if more explosions are being planned. What do you know, ladies and gentlemen?'

Bose looked over the JTF team in the conference room. His eyes flicked over Zeb Carter and the Agency personnel at the back of the room. He didn't blast the gathering. He didn't indulge in petty theatrics. He knew everyone in the room was working flat-out. No one had gone home ever since the first bombing. They all showed signs of exhaustion. Bags beneath their eyes, the faint smell of perspiration that deodorants hadn't killed. Lines around their mouths.

'Kohli, Meera, where are we?'

'We have identified the man who carried out the poisoning,' the deputy got to her feet and replied. 'Kewal Patel, a worker in a pharmacy shop in Kurla. He got into the factory's premises using a false pass yesterday. We have CCTV images of him at the assembly line, inspecting the ginger sauce packages.'

'Where is he?'

'Missing. His apartment in Dombivli is empty. His friends don't know where he is. His cell phone is turned off. They say he had several gambling debts. Our theory is he was coerced into injecting that poison.'

'We will find his body somewhere,' a NIA officer said flatly.

'Yes, that's our assumption too. We are investigating the dead attackers in Byculla, interviewing every resident in Polaris Tower again, going through camera footage of all—'

'You don't have much. We don't have much,' Bose corrected himself instantly, but he knew his words had hit hard by the way she reacted, a hurt expression that she swiftly masked.

He sighed. 'I am sorry. That didn't come out the way it should have. I am aware of the effort you all are putting in. I know how these investigations work. I know you are aware of the criticism we are getting on TV, social media, newspapers ... everyone with an opinion is blaming us for not showing results.'

He raised a hand. 'That's noise. Ignore it as best as you can. Continue chasing down every lead, however slim. Leave the criticism to me. That's for me and my peers at the other agencies to handle. That's what we are paid for.'

His thin-lipped smile drew a few chuckles. The mood in the room lightened. Meera nodded imperceptibly at him and took her seat.

Kohli got up. 'We will be raiding every known terrorist or insurgent's location, sir. Nationwide, in coordinated attacks with local police. We will arrest them if we find them, and question them. It might feel like clutching at straws, but we are chasing down every possibility.'

'What about Irfan Shaikh? Why haven't we acted on him? We know his Lashkar-e-Taiba connections. He is our prime suspect. What are we—'

'We have raided many of his hideouts and cells, sir. His soldiers haven't given us anything. He himself is—'

'In either Dubai or Karachi, sir,' Meera intervened. 'We have taken it up with those governments, but both have said he isn't there. Pakistan has firmly denied ISI is backing LET.'

'That's what they always say. No one knows where Mumbai's most-wanted criminal is?'

'If they are, they aren't telling, sir. The Home Ministry—'

'I'll get them to apply diplomatic pressure. But, yes, Zeb?'

He looked down the room when the American raised his hand.

'Someone might know where he is.'

'Who?'

'Arjun Sule.'

CHAPTER 43

'You are here again?' Sule asked angrily when Zeb and his team entered the man's Dharavi office.

The retired gangster's face darkened when Kohli, Meera and a couple of RAW officers joined them. 'You have heard of cell phones? Whatever you want, couldn't be asked on a call?'

'Being in front of you, in person, gives weight.' Bwana smiled at him.

Zeb cut off Sule before he made to respond.

'Where is Irfan Shaikh?'

The room fell silent. The former gangster clenched his fists.

'I told you,' he said softly. 'I am a businessman, a philanthropist. I spend my time with charities these days. Gangsters, killers, drug-dealers, weapons-smugglers ... I have nothing to do with them.'

'We never said you had,' Meera said disarmingly. 'But you know him better than any other person in this city. Your gang and his were engaged in street war at one time.'

'Let me guess,' Sule barked. 'You want me to tap into my network and find out where he is.'

'Yeah,' Zeb acknowledged.

'You.' The man flared at him. 'You know what happened to me. You know I worked out a deal with Shaikh.'

He's no longer hiding what he was involved in or what went down, Zeb thought. He saw the same understanding reflected in Kohli's and Meera's eyes as well, but the RAW agents didn't speak.

'You worked out a deal with a man who is suspected of helping LET, the same terrorist organization that carried out the 2008 attacks. You are lucky Mumbai Police didn't brand you as a terrorist supporter as well, otherwise you wouldn't be here, a free man. Don't pull the pity act on us.'

Sule swallowed, but he didn't budge.

'Padma, my people ... he will hit them hard if I break my word. They are civilians. They don't deserve to be targeted by killers.'

'So, you can find out where Shaikh is?' Beth inferred.

'I ran Mumbai like I owned it, at one point.' Sule allowed a note of pride to creep into his voice. 'There was little that went on in the city that I didn't know of, even if the perps weren't in the city. I got my network to inform the Mumbai Police during the 2008 attack. We shared whatever information we had on those terrorists, anonymously. I am sure I can find his location if I want to. But I won't.'

'What if we take him off the board?'

The Dharavi man stared at Kohli.

'You can do that? He has never been arrested. He hasn't even been questioned. Every agency in the country is hunting him and yet he has evaded them all. You don't even know where he is. Even if you did, you have to follow the laws.'

'No.'

Sule closed his mouth with an audible click of his jaws. He glanced at his daughter, who nodded.

'Help them. It is *our* Mumbai.'

. . .

A LATE EVENING BRIEFING IN THE JTF OFFICE. TIRED VOICES updating Kohli on various threads of the investigation.

Zeb felt his phone vibrate and brought it out.

Pingleshwar. Until tomorrow night. The bird will fly early morning, the day after.

He got to his feet.

'We know where Irfan Shaikh is.'

Meera took his phone, read the message and sprang to her feet. She hooked her computer to the screen and brought up a map of Gujarat, a western state.

'Pingleshwar is a remote beach in that state,' she said excitedly as she zoomed in a satellite feed. 'It isn't far from Sir Creek, a marshland area which is the water border between India and Pakistan. It is disputed territory. Both countries argue about where exactly the border lies in those waters. It has become the new entry point for smugglers. Pakistani gangsters move meth, guns, cocaine there.'

'Great location for a criminal to hide out.' Kohli rubbed his jaw. 'Shaikh can escape to Sir Creek and onto the Pakistani side of the marshlands if he suspects we are coming.'

'Is he backed by ISI?' a RAW officer asked.

'We suspect he is,' Meera replied. 'We have got enough circumstantial evidence, but the Pakistani outfit denies it.'

'He could have set off the bombs in that case.'

'He could. He hasn't hidden his hatred for our country. There is no particular reason for it ... he's grown up surrounded by propaganda on how Muslims are marginalized, have no voice, and are treated like inferior citizens. He believes Kashmir should be part of Pakistan.'

Not all of it is propaganda, Zeb thought. *Several Indian governments have used the Muslim population as a vote bank and have ignored their development.*

Meera bobbed her head when she caught his eyes, as if she knew what he was thinking.

She said firmly, 'Not all of it is propaganda. Governments

have failed the Muslim population either deliberately or by accident.' Her voice strengthened and she turned back to the map. 'But, we aren't here to discuss politics. Pingleshwar. It will be difficult to capture Shaikh there. It's a small town. The presence of strangers is noticed immediately. This is his villa.'

She pointed her laser at the house on the screen. 'It looks to be two stories. Concrete compound wall. There will be guards, cameras, there could be dogs. There will be boats to escape into the sea.'

'Is it a tourist beach?' Meghan asked.

'It's not like Goa. It's off the beaten track. But it does get a lot of visitors, both Indian and international.'

Zeb hid a smile when Meera regarded the twin thoughtfully. Kohli nodded to himself.

They've cottoned on to why Meg asked that question.

'You capture him,' Meera stated, looking at the Agency operatives.

CHAPTER 44

The RAW agents stirred. Several of them scowled at the Americans.

'Are they better than us?' one of them challenged.

'No,' Zeb began and stopped when Meghan leaned forward and smiled disarmingly.

'Of course not,' she scoffed.

It drew a few laughs.

'But we are foreigners. We will look like tourists. You all, on the other hand ... super-fit men and women ... the local people will notice you. Word might get back to Shaikh.'

'She is correct.' Bose added his weight. 'In case anyone is forgetting, they are JTF too. We have one objective; to capture Mumbai's terrorists and everyone associated with them. Park your egos at the door. Besides, I know the Americans. They keep a very low profile. It's one reason we rarely take their names even in our offices. They will not want credit.'

Zeb nodded and his gesture along with the RAW chief's words, seemed to reassure the Indian agents.

'There are only eight of them.' The speaker didn't give up. 'That compound might have thirty or forty men.'

Zeb looked at Bwana. *Don't make your flippant remarks,* he telegraphed with his eyes.

The Black agent grinned, lightening the mood. 'How many would you take in your attack team?'

The RAW agent scratched his cheek, clearly not expecting to be put on the spot. 'About the same, eight or ten people. But we would have backup.'

'And so will they,' Meera said crisply and signaled for RAW agents to leave the room.

Bose gripped Zeb's forearm tightly for a moment and followed the Indian operatives out.

'Let's plan,' Meera said as she was joined at the screen by the twins.

'Heli. Drones. Stealth-painted SUVs.'

Zeb leaned back in his chair, crossed his hands behind his head as their voices washed over him. He was focused on Pingleshwar's beach and the villa on it.

Drone to confirm Shaikh is in the house. One team to cut off the sea route. Snipers to take out the guards. We'll have to go hot and loud but that won't matter if we choke off Shaikh's getaway routes.

'Are you paying attention?' Beth asked, irritatedly.

'I am,' he replied.

'Here's what we've come up with.'

He was unsurprised when it matched what he had figured out.

'We go tomorrow?' Broker stifled a yawn and stretched.

'Tomorrow,' Zeb confirmed.

CHAPTER 45

The Russian and the Chechen scaled the Asiatic Society's building at night and found a vantage point on its roof.

It was an imposing building with a flight of long concrete steps that led up to several columns and a grand entrance. The roof was pitched, but there were enough flat surfaces for maintenance.

The two men had arrived at five pm, dressed in coveralls with the logo of a well-known roof cleaning company. They had presented their work order to the guard and rappelled up the side of the building. They mounted their equipment on one of the flat surfaces overlooking Horniman Circle. The roof's elevation gave them ample cover and as the sun set, the Russian opened a flask, poured coffee in two mugs and they sipped as they waited.

'I DON'T THINK YOU SHOULD BE THERE,' KHALID SAID AS HE drove his rental Toyota from the downtown hotel.

'I want to see who this shooter is.'

'He may not show himself. He may not be alone.'

'Doesn't matter.'

'Iqbal will be there.'

'He will have to be! How else will the shooter know who he is meeting? But don't worry. I will be masked. I won't show my face.'

'This could be a trap. Horniman Circle could be flooded with police.'

'It won't be. My contacts in Mumbai Police have said there is nothing unusual going on down there.'

The rendezvous was busy that time of the evening as offices emptied and staff began their long commutes home. The gardens were enclosed circularly by an array of Victorian-style buildings with columned walkways, on which street vendors sold food and trinkets. Several restaurants faced the walkway, all of which were crowded. A busker sang lustily but few passers-by gave him any attention.

Khalid circled the garden once and pointed out the Mumbai Police cruiser parked in front of a building.

'See how alert they are.' The leader smirked as the police officer within yawned boredly. 'They aren't here for us.'

Khalid went down towards Flora Fountain and turned back. He cruised several alleys until he found a parking spot in Homji Street from where they could observe the garden.

They waited.

THE RUSSIAN CRACKED A KNUCKLE AND ZIPPED UP HIS coverall when night set in. He and the Chechen had NVGS with which they scanned the circle. No signs of Iqbal.

'He'll come,' he told the Chechen reassuringly.

'What does a petty gang want with us?'

'They are the second largest outfit in the city.'

'With their leader locked up in prison.'

'That doesn't make them any less dangerous.'

'We'll see.'

Lights turned off in office buildings. Restaurants emptied and shops shuttered down. The street vendors disappeared in the dark and the busker had long departed.

The police cruiser rolled away silently.

By ten pm, Horniman Circle was deserted except for a few passing cabs. The restrictions on traffic had lightened, but the city's residents hadn't taken to the roads fully. There were a few vehicles which seemed to be abandoned, judging by their condition.

The black SUV entered the circle when it was past eleven pm. It drove leisurely around the garden, went inside several alleys, returned and parked in front of the Asiatic Society.

A man got out, walked around and went back to the vehicle where he leaned against it with his arms crossed on his chest.

'That's not Iqbal,' the Russian whispered. 'But it could be one of his shooters. There are more people inside that vehicle.'

'Traffic?'

'None.'

'Police?'

'No.'

'Call the number.'

'THERE'S A PHONE RINGING.' THE SHOOTER STRAIGHTENED from the SUV and looked around.

'Find out where it is,' Iqbal said impatiently from inside.

The man hurried away searching for the source. He darted towards a parked car, leaned inside its open window and came out with a phone. He ran back to Iqbal who squinted at the screen. Number withheld.

He thumbed it on cautiously.

'Hello?'

. . .

'IT'S ME,' THE RUSSIAN REPLIED. 'DO YOU RECOGNIZE MY voice?'

'Yes, but where are you?'

The gangster climbed out of the vehicle and looked around. He peered up at the buildings and shook his head at himself.

'I am nearby. What do you want to talk about?'

'There is someone who wants to meet you.'

The Russian stiffened. He felt the Chechen grow alert beside him. They scanned the circle again and searched the alleys but didn't detect any cops.

'Who's that?'

'I don't know. He killed many of my men yesterday and came to me. He said I had to find out who you were.'

'That's why you made contact on the darkweb.'

'Yes. He wants to meet.'

'Where is he then? Who is he?'

'Wait, I'll call him. He knows I have set it up here—'

'Is it him?' the Russian asked sharply when the Chechen nudged him. He trained his NVGs on two figures who emerged from Homji Street. Both walked casually as they approached the SUV.

Both were masked, their hands raised non-threateningly.

They saw Iqbal turn to them and one of them pulled up his mask briefly as they got closer.

'Did you see him?' the Russian hissed.

'No,' the Chechen said disgustedly. 'It happened too fast.'

'Yes, that's him,' Iqbal confirmed on the phone. 'But I don't know who the other man is. He's masked too.'

'I can see that.'

The Russian watched them walk up. They seemed to exchange words with the gangster and then with one smooth, deceptive motion, the first man, the one who had briefly exposed himself, drew a gun, shot Iqbal and the shooter, leaned inside the SUV and killed the rest of the men.

He bent over the lieutenant's fallen body, picked up the phone and gave it to the second man.

'I wanted to meet you.'

'Who are you?'

'An interested party. Let's leave it at that.'

The Russian listened carefully for any accents but didn't identify any. The stranger spoke English neutrally.

'There are many such parties in the world. I have nothing to do with them. Identify yourself. State your business. Don't waste my time.'

The men at the vehicle stood confidently, unafraid, not worried that a police cruiser might approach.

'They are pros,' the Chechen murmured.

The Russian nodded.

'Hadi Asadi was my man.'

The Russian stared down at the gardens, wondering if he had heard correctly.

'That's all you need to know.'

'Why are you—'

'None of your business. You are the shooter in Crawford Market?'

'Yes.'

He wasn't, but there was no need for Masked Man to know that.

'We might have similar objectives.'

'We don't. I am after a different target.'

'What's that?'

The Russian weighed the question. *I am not interested in what he's doing, but if his bombings can help me ...*

'I am after the Americans.'

'Americans? That special team who's working with the JTF?'

'They are part of the task force now. Yes. Them.'

'Who are they?'

'Don't you know?'

'I am aware of them, but I haven't been able to get their identities.'

'They are a covert American agency. Very few people have heard of them. Their leader is Zeb Carter. He has seven other operatives with him.'

'You want him?'

'I have unfinished business with him.'

'He will be at Pingleshwar tomorrow, at a villa on the beach.'

The Russian jerked in surprise and almost dropped his NVGs. He fumbled with it and trained it on the masked men again.

'How do you know that? Are you sure of that?'

'No, but I know a JTF team will be there tomorrow to capture Irfan Shaikh who's in that villa. Shaikh—'

'I am aware of him.'

'If I was the JTF, I would send the Americans instead of an Indian team. They would look like tourists.'

The Russian nodded in the dark. *That's what I would do, too.*

'Why are you telling me this?'

'If you can take out Carter and his team, that's fewer people hunting me.'

'How do you know Shaikh will be there?'

'Because I arranged for that information to be leaked.'

CHAPTER 46

The heli took the Agency operatives to a strip of tarmac in a deserted farm on the Vanku-Pingleshwar Road, forty minutes away from the small town.

'Some rich dude,' Meghan yelled over the whirling blades, 'decided to set up an organic farm. Gave up when he found it was too much hard work.'

There were two SUVs waiting for them at the residence. Mitsubishi Pajeros, black, dull paint to remove any shine and with darkened windows.

Bwana and Roger nodded appreciatively as they inspected the vehicles.

'Rental vehicle,' the Texan observed, pointing to the yellow-on-black number plates. 'That will confirm our cover as tourists.'

'Privately owned vehicles, commercial ones, hire-cars ...' Chloe grinned. 'India must be the only country where we can identify what kind of vehicle it is from the number plate.'

'Yeah,' Zeb agreed. He knelt and checked out the tires.

Kohli said they would be run-flat ones.

They were. The brand etching on them stated that. He joined his team and helped transfer their gear from their heli to the vehicles, waved at the pilot and got behind the wheel of the first Pajero.

'They're our exfil ride?' Beth watched the chopper in the mirror.

'Yeah. There will be a couple more helis and back-up teams and rides in the night. Kohli and Meera along with them.'

He donned his shades and set off on the road to the town.

The state of Gujarat, in which the town was, had lifted its travel restrictions during the day, as a result of which there was a fair amount of traffic on the road. Most of it seemed to be tourists heading towards the beach, but as they drew closer to the town, trucks and buses crowded the road.

Pingleshwar was a riot of color, sound and smells. A temple's bells chimed in the distance. Street vendors crowded their ride when the twins lowered their windows and presented trinkets to them.

'Not now.' Meghan laughed at a young boy who waved a flower garland at her.

'It'll look good on you, ma'am,' he said in broken English.

'Later,' she said and rolled up her window.

Zeb didn't stop in the town. They carried on down the road, which turned into the beach road and arrived at a makeshift parking lot, where an attendant took money from them and directed them towards the far end.

'We don't want our cars to be damaged,' Zeb told him.

'I'll watch over them myself, sir,' the man promised with a toothy grin when Beth tipped him generously. 'No one will come near it.'

They unloaded picnic hampers and went to the beach, which at ten am was getting busy. A line of palm trees and vegetation, that offered cover from the sun, from which the sandy beach started and stretched towards the waves.

'There.' Chloe pointed towards the shade, away from the rest of the visitors.

Zeb and Broker spread blankets on the ground, on which

they placed their hampers. The elder operative breathed deeply and stretched.

'Finally, a proper vacation.'

'We aren't on one.' Beth corrected him.

'Spoilsport. We are on a beach. Ergo, we are on holiday. That's our cover, in any case.'

Zeb uncapped a bottle of water and drank deeply as he checked them out. They were in standard beachwear for tourists. Colorful tees and shorts, sneakers and shades. Their only weapons were their Glocks, which were hidden beneath the food and drink in the baskets. A larger hamper had their drones and their control screens.

He grimaced when the breeze flattened Bear and Bwana's tees against their torsos, outlining their biceps.

Nothing we can do to hide their builds. Wearing combat pants would have drawn attention.

'Go,' he told them. 'You'll only get in the way here and people might wonder why we aren't in the water.'

Bwana let out a whoop and raced to the sea with Bear, Roger, Chloe and Broker.

'I heard some American accents.' Beth nodded at a group of men and women several meters away. 'And those, beyond them, are speaking German.'

There were several families as well, a school group and many couples who split away from the main groups and drifted up the beach.

'Make a guess.' Meghan looked at him. 'Who do you think is behind these attacks?'

'LET, other Islamic terrorists who want Kashmir to be part of Pakistan, insurgents, Maoist extremists who are active in the country, people unhappy with the government ...' He shrugged. 'Take your pick. This is a big country. There's always some explosion and killing somewhere.'

'All of those would work in such a planned, coordinated manner? This feels like an LET attack.'

'They haven't claimed responsibility. Kohli and Meera are pressing hard on their cells and informers. Bose would have said they are a prime suspect if he thought—'

'He has.'

'They are one of the suspects.'

'The media—'

'Indian media is no different to what we have back home. They are speculating.'

'Come on. Why don't you speculate and tell us!'

Zeb looked towards the sea, at his friends splashing and swimming. The sounds of enjoyment, the smells of food wafting their way, momentarily dispelled the thought that the country was under attack.

'Not yet,' he said.

'You know something,' Beth growled, punching him hard in the bicep.

'I don't.' He made a face, rubbing his arm. 'I have a feeling, but I don't have any proof.'

He ducked when she drew her fist back, then his phone rang.

'Meera,' he said unnecessarily. Her number on his screen was visible to them.

'Yeah.' He took the call.

'Kewal Patel,' she said in a tight, clipped voice. 'We found his body by the train tracks near Kurla station. His throat had been cut. His friends say there was no need for him to be there. He didn't commute by locals.'

Locals, Zeb figured out what she meant instantly. *That's what Mumbai's residents call the suburban trains.*

'We are interviewing everyone but—'

'You don't have anything.'

'Correct. Have you seen the news?'

'No. Another bomb?' Beth asked urgently.

'Thankfully not, but this could be just as bad. Our Home Minister has accused ISI of being behind the attacks. Pakistan has responded strongly. It has rejected the accusation. In turn, its officials have said India is war-mongering and they are ready for it. That we should not forget they too have nuclear weapons.'

'They said that?' Meghan said in disbelief.

'Yes. You should understand—'

'Pakistan's government is in crisis. Their previous prime minister was ousted in a no-confidence motion. The current PM was elected by parliamentarians. He's new. The country has been in an economic crisis for years. Couple that with political instability and you get social unrest. Politicians resort to populist measures in such times.'

'You read geo-politics well,' Meera said after a short pause.

'We have to,' Beth said with a laugh. 'Many of our missions are in such regions. How much of this is saber-rattling?'

'Some of it. But overnight, Pakistan moved several battalions closer to the Kashmir border. That has put us on higher alert.'

'But why?'

'Our analysts say their prime minister wants to distract his people from their domestic problems. Unfortunately, we had to respond too and moved our army closer to the border. There has been firing from both sides overnight. The situation is tense.'

'But can be scaled back diplomatically.'

'Yes, but right now, neither party is interested in that. Perhaps in a day or two ... you can imagine though, the media headlines.'

'Yeah.' Zeb nodded.

Talk show hosts will go to town on this.

'You're in position?'

'Yeah. We'll start our surveillance shortly.'

'We'll roll in the moment you go hot.'

THE TWINS LAUNCHED THE DRONES AT LUNCH TIME. THE SUN was beating down by then and while there were several people in the water, their numbers had reduced.

Their UAVs rose under the shade of the palm trees and went

out of the cover, unnoticed. Zeb followed them casually until their automatic camo-paint blended with the blue sky and they were unspottable.

He turned at a shoulder tap and took the topped coconut from Bwana. He sipped at its fresh water and went out on the sand.

'It's to your eight o'clock,' Beth spoke in his earpiece. 'Shaikh's villa. A hundred and thirty meters from here. That thick line of palm trees on our left is hiding it from our view. They have planted several trees in their compound as well, making it difficult to be seen from the sides or the back. There's an unrestricted view from the sea, but if you look to your left, there's no one on the beach on that side.'

Zeb turned his head casually to confirm her observation. 'There must be guards who clear the strip of sand in front of the villa.'

'Correct. Four of them. Armed. They must be licensed.'

'They have to be. Guns are heavily regulated in India.'

'The villa has a ten-foot-tall iron gate and a concrete wall that goes around it. You can see the villa above it from the beach or the sea, a balcony, but not much else.'

'What's inside?' Bear slurped loudly.

'I'm getting to that, hotshot. Large lawn. It must take some effort and bag loads of money to maintain it, here. Pool. Three women bathing in it.'

'Welcome to OG life.' Chloe sniggered.

'Tinted glass rolling doors to the inside of the house, which is two stories.'

'Six rooms downstairs,' Meghan commented. 'One large living room, kitchen, dining room, a bathroom and two bedrooms. There is a backyard and three dorms.'

'How can you see the layout?'

Zeb grinned. He could sense Beth rolling her eyes.

'We have two drones in the air, dumbass. Both of them with zoom lenses that professional photographers would sell their kidneys for. They can see through windows. Werner collates the feed from both the UAVs and builds the inside of the house. Any more questions?'

'I need food.'

'Three dormitory kinda buildings in the back yard. That must be for the guards. Nothing in them other than bedrooms and bathrooms. They probably come to the main house for food. There are garages, big enough to house SUVs and trucks at the back as well.'

'Six more rooms upstairs,' she continued. 'One is the living room that has the beach-facing balcony, the rest are bedrooms.'

'How many guards?' Zeb asked.

The twins fell silent as they counted.

'Thirty men. One of them could be Shaikh. He isn't outdoors. Five women,' Beth announced. 'Two of those are in the kitchen.'

'Guns?'

'Eight guards in the front and backyard, four each. All of them have AK74s. The ones at the front gate have the same weapons.'

'What do Pingleshwar's residents think of this villa? Who do they think owns it?'

'An industrialist, which explains the security.'

That cover won't be hard for Shaikh to fabricate. He's got legitimate interests.

'What's around and behind the house?'

'Trees, lots of them, except for two openings on the side away from us and to the back. Undergrowth. A bed of rocks going around like a moat.'

That's smart. Those stones will make it harder for an approach from the sides and the back.

'Lots of cameras,' Beth commented. 'Mounted on the wall. We should expect motion sensors, infra-red movement detectors, the works.'

'Are there any other exits to the house?' Zeb visualized the villa's location mentally. 'Doesn't the Nayaro River flow on its other side?'

'Yeah, that's some hundreds of meters away, but there's a creek closer to the side wall.'

Beth navigated the drone, humming to herself. 'Gotcha. A side door that looks like it's part of the wall. Big enough to accommodate a truck.'

'Any boats?'

'Nope. You think the creek could be a getaway route? It is deep enough.'

'Yeah.'

'No boat. No dock or moorings either.'

'If I were Shaikh,' Chloe drawled after finishing her coconut water, 'I would have a dinghy with outboard motor in the house. That way, it's safer and I'll need fewer guards.'

'The garages are big enough for it,' Meghan agreed.

'No rear exit?'

'There is one!' Beth exclaimed. 'The gates are painted so well, we nearly missed it. There's a path that goes from the house, between the garages and to it.'

'Where do they get deliveries?'

'Side or rear exit or even the front. There's the rock moat around the sides and the back, but men could carry crates over them.'

Zeb took a food plate that Broker served and dug in with a plastic fork. He ran through the layout, working through the attack vectors.

'Here's how we'll do it,' he told them between mouthfuls.

Shaikh came out after six pm when the sun had set, but there was enough light to make him. He was short with thick facial hair, his shirt unbuttoned all the way to his waist to reveal his graying chest hair.

The gangster sat on a deck chair by the pool, watching the

women splash in it. He was continually on his phone while his men served him food and drink.

He's here. We have eyes on him. Zeb messaged Kohli and Meera.

Take him!

Zeb chuckled, showing the others Meera's response.

'You can sense her anger.'

'Who wouldn't be?' Bear slipped into a light jacket and zipped it up. 'He's enjoying the tourist life while the country is hunting him.'

The lights in the villa and around the walls came on at seven pm and an hour later, when the darkness had fallen, the beach started emptying.

They went to their rides and geared up in the shadows.

'Dinner,' Beth said briefly.

'I'll pass,' Bwana patted his belly, his HK looking like a toy slung around his chest.

'Not you, dumbass. Shaikh. He's being fed a multiple course meal by his girlfriends.'

'It'll be his last such meal.'

CHAPTER 47

Bwana and Roger went out to the beach at eleven pm. It was just them and the sounds of the sea. A thin moon high up in the sky which failed to illuminate the sand.

The villa's bright lights made up for it, however; an oasis of white in the surrounding darkness.

'Here?' the Texan asked when they came onto wet sand.

Bwana felt it with his toes. The waves were lapping quietly behind them about ten meters away. The villa was around a hundred meters away, with the sand stretched down in a gentle slope towards them. The four guards at the metal gate were conferring as they looked in the operators' direction.

'Here,' he agreed. He laid down the Barrett he was carrying, mounted it on its tripod and adjusted it, slapped on a scope and put his eye to it.

'They aren't happy.' Roger snickered when an angry yell reached them. One of the guards gesticulated furiously. 'Doesn't look like they've seen we are armed.'

The sentries stood out brightly in Bwana's scope. Angry Guard continued to yell but didn't make a move towards them.

His finger curled lightly over the trigger.

He waited for the signal.

. . .

BEAR, CHLOE, ZEB AND MEGHAN HUSTLED THROUGH THE trees, dodging low branches and picking through the undergrowth.

'Don't get any closer to the compound wall,' Beth warned in their earpieces. 'They might have infrared cameras, in which case you'll be detected.'

'It won't matter in a few minutes,' her sister panted.

They had to cut a wide loop to go behind the villa, where Bear and Chloe split away to cover the rear entrance while Zeb and the elder sister continued to go around its side and come to the creek exit.

He took cover behind a tree trunk and checked out the sliding door, which was expertly fitted into the wall. The rock moat was a meter wide, jagged edges and uneven surfaces.

Definitely laid out to deter approach.

'Come on,' Meghan hissed impatiently.

He ghosted from tree to tree until he joined her at the corner from where they could view both the front and the side exit. He could hear guards shouting at Bwana and Roger to clear the beach.

'They haven't made us yet. We are close to the cameras. Whoever is monitoring them couldn't have missed us.'

'Everyone's attention is at the front probably,' he told the elder twin.

'Ten,' he whispered in his mic, removed it and his earpieces, and inserted them in a Faraday foil.

Meghan mimicked his moves and gave him a thumbs-up.

Ten seconds later, the lights went out.

Zeb waited a beat and then removed his comms gear and inserted them back in his collar and ear.

. . .

'EVERYTHING IS EMPED,' BETH SAID LACONICALLY. SHE AND Broker had moved closer to the villa and were at the edge of the tree line, from where they could look down the front as well as the side. They were both prone on the sand, the elder operative cradling his HK, watching intently.

The control screens of the drones were in front of her, her rifle and Glock at her side. She reached for her phone and sent a message to Meera.

We're going hot.

CHAPTER 48

Bwana didn't react to the sudden darkness, nor to the shouts that came to them. The guards were gesticulating furiously and replying angrily to those within the villa.

He aimed at the tallest man and sent death hurtling at eight hundred and fifty meters per second. The guard's head exploded. His body collapsed. The men with him stared in shock and then reacted, grabbing for their guns.

Bwana put them down ruthlessly. The front gate went silent.

'WAIT,' ZEB WHISPERED.

We need that gate to open.

'They know they are under attack,' Beth briefed them. 'They aren't panicking. Every man is armed. The guards from the dorms have come out too. Shaikh and the women are in the upper floor bedroom. I'm guessing it's him since the three women are there with a man. The two women in the kitchen are hiding in the pantry. WAIT! One man is kneeling in the front yard. He's got a gun ... grenade launcher! Bwana, Rog, the gate's opening. They'll fire at you.'

Zeb heard the rumbling and squeak of wheels as the gate was pushed back. He tensed, prepared to burst.

'NOW!'

Bwana and Roger dove away from each other at Beth's shout.

The beach behind them exploded, showering them with sand.

Dude didn't have time to aim. He fired in our general direction. Bwana rolled to a stop and brought his Barrett to his shoulder and nestled his cheek against its stock.

He got the man in his sight. The shooter was hastily reloading, nodding as other hitters shouted and screamed at him.

Bwana triggered, saw the man fall back, and rolled back to his original position, from where he and Roger had the best firing angle.

It will expose us to them too, but Beth will warn us of incoming fire.

'Pick your targets,' he told the Texan and started firing at the shooters in the front yard.

Zeb and Meghan burst through their cover, crouching low. They slowed when they came to the gate, both their left arms swinging high and over repeatedly to lob flash-bangs into the compound.

The explosions were muted by the headsets they wore and the intense light dimmed by the customized night-vision shades around their eyes.

'Some of them are helmeted or masked. They aren't suffering from the bangs. ON YOUR ELEVEN!'

Zeb dove to the ground as he burst through the gate. He sensed Meghan going low as well, to his right. He spotted the shooter Beth warned them about, who was adjusting his aim.

His HK chattered in a long burst, the rounds ripping through the man's chest and taking out another one behind him.

He felt a round whisper above him and rolled again until he was on the lawn, to its side. He felt a shadow move. A man raised his hand.

Too close for me to turn and shoot.

Zeb lunged at him, body slamming him, bringing him down and clubbing him furiously with his barrel until the man went still.

'We're coming closer to the gate.' Roger, emotionless. 'We'll have a wider field of fire. We can cover you better.'

Smoke filled the yard, within which shadows moved and screams and yells sounded. He and Meghan were outnumbered as they raced down either sidewall towards the house, but the deadly hail from Bwana and the Texan provided them with cover.

Someone lit flares, brightening the night.

'Not us,' Bwana said laconically.

Zeb threw a bang at a hostile who was shooting at him and fired from his hip as he kept running.

Staying still made them targets.

He zigged and zagged, shooting at shadows, knowing that the glow-patches on his and Meghan's arms and backs would identify them to Bwana and Roger.

Zeb staggered when a round glanced off his side. He threw himself to the ground when he felt the shooter move.

He's to my right. Can't turn my gun far enough. He rolled desperately, heard a gun boom and looked up to see the man fall.

That's Bwana. Or Roger.

The glass door shattered when one of his friends fired at it.

'Thirteen down,' Beth announced. 'Five men are making a break to the backyard. Probably to the rear exit. Eight are going into the house, likely to protect Shaikh. Four more are still in the front yard, behind statues and furniture.'

'Leave them to us,' Bwana said cheerfully. 'We're inside the gate. Zeb, Meg, we can back you up from here. All the glass at the front of the house is gone. We can see inside and fire.'

'We'll take care of the five at the back,' Chloe said.

MEGHAN LEAPT OVER A FALLEN CHAIR IN THE YARD. A HOSTILE reared up from the concrete bank of the swimming pool. He was uncoordinated from the bangs, tears streaming down his face, but the grip on his AK was steady as he shrieked at her in rage and turned the weapon on her.

Her rounds caught him in the chest and throat. She landed lightly and fired through the shattered front door at the shadows running across the floor.

With the sliding door destroyed, the front of the house was nothing but a big hole that ran the width of the house. She threw herself on the polished marble, wincing as glass shards cracked beneath her.

One of the shooters turned on the steps to aim at her. He went down before she could fire.

Zeb was inside the house too, at the other end, and threw a bang at the steps.

She lobbed one too, and sprayed wildly with her HK in the hostiles' direction. The flashes lit up the room. The bodies of men were illuminated and that provided a big enough target for her, Zeb, Bwana, and Roger to shoot.

The hostiles fell, rolling down the steps, their bodies jerking from more shots.

'Those three,' she panted at Zeb as the hostiles disappeared into the landing, 'will wait for us.'

'Yeah,' Zeb replied.

He took the lead up the stairs, crouching low and reaching down into a pocket to remove a grenade, unpin and throw it blindly up and over the steps.

A gangster yelled a warning. Someone screamed as it

exploded and then he and Meghan were onto the top floor, diving to either side, firing at the surviving killers.

One of them was alive. He lunged towards a door which opened. Zeb made out a shadow inside.

'That's Shaikh!' Beth called out.

Can't let Shooter Dude go inside. They'll barricade themselves, making it harder for us to grab the gangster.

'He's mine!'

He sensed Meghan nod. He raised his HK to fire and slipped on a shard of glass. His shots went wide into the night. He swore beneath his breath and turned his stumble into a lunging dive to crash into the hostile against the door, which flew open.

He fell on top of the killer, shot him point blank in the chest and rolled away desperately when he felt the air above him move.

Shaikh, looming over him, teeth bared in a snarl, his knife slicing through the night.

Zeb bunched his knees and slammed his feet into the man's chest, sending him staggering back. He hurled upwards and caught the gangster's wrist and snapped it, grimacing at the howl that echoed in his ears. He twisted the arm up and behind the man, kicked out his legs from beneath him and slammed his face to the floor.

The gang boss struggled. He kicked and jerked and swore as he tried to escape, but Zeb smothered him with his body weight and zip-tied his wrists and legs.

'Secure!' Meghan told him.

He looked up to see her secure the last woman and check the thug he had shot.

'Dead.'

'We have got a few prisoners,' Bwana announced from downstairs.

'What about the five that escaped to the back?' Zeb asked.

. . .

BEAR AND CHLOE CROUCHED AT EITHER SIDE OF THE REAR door. The petite operator raised three fingers in the air as its wheels squeaked.

She timed it perfectly. The gate rolled sideways when her last finger curled.

She swung her HK in a short, sharp arc at the ankles that emerged and nodded approvingly when Bear mimicked her move at the other end.

They didn't expect us to be that low to the ground.

She sprang up and crashed her rifle's butt into the heads of the falling men, reversed her weapon expertly and thrust its muzzle into a man's throat.

'We got Shaikh!' she said triumphantly.

'We too have him,' Meghan replied, puzzled.

'IS ... HE BETRAYED ME!' the man she had captured shouted.

CHAPTER 49

'It's him.' Zeb pointed at Chloe's captive when Megan and she stood the two prisoners side-by-side. 'The man we took is a body-double.'

'Smart.' Broker nodded approvingly. 'It's a move that would have worked if we weren't covering the rear.'

Zeb sized up the gang leader, who was tight-lipped, forehead bleeding from a gash, an angry scowl on his face.

They were in the front yard with eight other prisoners who stood sullen-faced, looking into the distance. None of them paid any attention to the bodies in the garden. A few of them had cursed softly when Bwana and Roger had come up to them, identifying them as those responsible for the brutal shooting.

'Who betrayed you?' Zeb asked Shaikh.

He ducked his head when the gangster spat at him.

'You are not Indians,' the criminal said after a string of curses. 'Who are you?'

'Do you remember Afzal Khan? He was my—'

'That traitor! He was ratting me out. It was to you! You should have heard him scream when I gutted him.'

The darkness rose in Zeb instantly. It flooded him, making

him curl his fists, and it was only his iron control that held him back from delivering a fatal throat-jab to the prisoner.

Shaikh seemed to sense the killing instinct in him and took a hasty step backwards to join the other prisoners.

Zeb swallowed his fury and made a circling motion in the air. It was time to leave.

'We can't take all of them,' Beth told him.

'We take Shaikh, his double, and any one of his men. It doesn't matter who. We'll leave the rest here. Meera will send her people to take them in.'

They hustled to their Pajeros with Shaikh in the first vehicle while the other gangsters went in Bear's ride.

Bird's captured. He messaged Meera. *We are on our way*.

CHAPTER 50

'Check in,' the Russian spoke into his radio as he peered through the window of the outbuilding.

There were three helis on the tarmac, several yards away, a dim row of portable lights surrounding them on the ground. Four shadows in the first one, one of which moved occasionally.

'All quiet,' his man replied from within the chopper. 'The pilots are still unconscious.'

The Russian trained his NVGs on the shadows behind the choppers, where seven of his men were holding guns on ten JTF operators. Three of them were women. All of them were gagged, sitting on the ground with their ankles and wrists tied.

Kohli and Meera. He knew their names from their badges had worked out they were the senior-most officers.

He had slapped one of the women and put a blade to her throat and she, at Meera's nod, had admitted that Carter was on his way with Shaikh as a prisoner.

'All quiet,' one of his sentries echoed from the approach road.

There were eight more men there, wearing JTF uniforms, ranged out along the entrance to the farm. The men whose uniforms they wore were dead, their bodies in a nearby ditch.

It hadn't been hard to capture the JTF operators.

The Russian, the Chechen and their fifteen men had burst upon the Indian agents as they had arrived in their two vehicles. They had shot the first team ruthlessly and had surrounded the second team. The pilots, who had climbed out of the helis to greet them, had been captured too.

They weren't expecting us. He smiled in the dark. *They thought there was only the chopper and its pilot, here. We didn't give them time to set a perimeter.*

'Let's go.' He tapped the Chechen on the shoulder and went to the door.

'Are you sure? Hiding far away in the field seems excessive.'

'I know how Carter works. He'll have drones in the air. They'll be equipped with night-vision, thermal imaging and technology I am not aware of. I don't want to risk being anywhere near them until they are captured. We'll observe from the field across the road, out of range of their UAVs, and come here only when we have them.'

'Remember,' he reminded his team. 'Don't shoot until they are on the tarmac. You on the road—don't hide. They don't know all the JTF operators. They will think you are Kohli's men. Go to their Pajeros when they arrive, make a show of confirming their identities and let them through. They will then be trapped between you and the guards at the heli. Whatever happens, don't kill Kohli and Meera. We might need them as hostages.'

'What about Shaikh?' one killer asked.

'I don't care about him. Shoot him if you have to. We'll join you as soon as Carter is captured.'

He went out into the night with the Chechen behind him, onto the tarmac and to the road, into the sugarcane field beyond. The tall stalks rustled as they pushed deep inside and when they were three hundred meters away, they stopped.

The Russian stood on his toes and applied the NVGs to his eyes. He grunted in satisfaction when he spotted the line of men at the farm's entrance and the heli, visible through the entrance.

He moved laterally until he could see within the cockpit as well as the prisoners behind it.

Carter won't see Meera and Kohli. The angle from the entrance is wrong for them.

He settled down to wait.

He was cautious. He was wily. He was smart. He had been hunting the American for a long while. He had studied the Agency man to such detail that he felt he could predict how the man would react.

He felt the satisfaction well inside him.

He'll be my prisoner soon.

CHAPTER 51

The Russian couldn't predict the round that flew in the air and burst through the head of one of the sentries on the road.

One down. Bwana turned his Barrett a centimeter, aimed at a second guard who fell before he could fire.

That's Roger's kill.

He aimed at the next guard and took him out.

The two men worked in near-silence, their shots muffled by the suppressors, as they put their shooting skills to use.

The sentries had no time to react as their bodies fell to the ground. Even if they did, they didn't have targets to fire at.

The night was quiet, the fields were still, and the shots seemed to come from nowhere.

'All down,' Roger said cheerfully.

Broker grunted in acknowledgment.

Part one, accomplished. It was vital that the first perimeter be taken out without any alarm being raised.

That was done.

He settled deeper into the loose soil of the field and focused his Leupold on the first heli. He could see four shadows inside. One man behind the others.

He waited for Beth, beside him, to confirm who the hostile was.

'The one at the back,' she replied a moment later, without raising her eyes from her screen. 'He's holding a gun on them.'

Only Broker's finger moved. It pressed gently on the trigger and sent his bullet speeding towards the hostile, who jerked back in his seat.

ZEB WAS RUNNING ACROSS THE TARMAC FROM THE SOUTH SIDE of the field when he heard Beth's confirmation that the heli's killer had been shot.

Meghan to his right, racing as silently as him, two shadows distinguishable from the ground only because they were moving.

Bear and Chloe closing in from the north, all four of them coming up from behind the hostiles who stood over the JTF prisoners, all of them facing the entrance.

One of the killers seemed to sense their presence.

He must have heard us, Zeb thought as the shooter started turning, and then his body fell down when a round blew his head apart.

'STAY DOWN!' he yelled when Meera and Kohli twisted around to see what had happened.

Zeb's second round tore into a hostile's shoulder and the third slammed into his chest.

By the time he was fifteen meters away, four of the seven killers were down and when he was three meters away, all were dead.

He and Meghan bent over the fallen men and confirmed they weren't a threat. They kicked away their AKs as a precautionary measure and then went to the JTF prisoners. He sliced Kohli's ties and helped him stand up.

'Clear.' Bwana and Bear came out of the outbuilding.

'There were two masked men in there,' Meera said savagely. 'They went onto the road and didn't return.'

'No one around.' Beth looked up from her screen. 'They must have escaped.'

Zeb helped pass around water bottles to the RAW agents, who uncapped them and drank deeply.

Kohli wiped his lips and turned to his team. 'Arjun, Dhir, Kishor, Rahul. Go to the road and put up roadblocks. Physical ones. No one should pass this field. The rest of you—'

'No need to cover the rear,' Zeb stopped him. 'Our drones are in the air. We'll know if someone's coming through the surrounding fields.'

Bwana, Bear and Roger joined the four Indian agents and went onto the road to set up the barriers.

'They killed an entire team of ours. Eight men.' Meera caught Zeb's eyes. 'There's a drainage ditch over there. They piled the bodies in it.'

His lips tightened. He looked towards the out building she was pointing to. *It must be far behind, otherwise Bwana and Bear would have seen it when they were checking it out.*

'We didn't stand a chance,' Kohli said bleakly. 'They opened fire as we were unloading our gear. By the time the rest of us had found cover, their second team was on us.'

'One of them was making to kill Neelam if she didn't tell them why we were here.'

Meera went to her and hugged her tight. The RAW agent returned her hug and wiped her eyes. She looked defiantly at the Agency operators.

'I would have resisted, but Meera and Kohli persuaded me to give in.'

'They were right,' Zeb told her. 'Your life is more important than what you knew. Intel that's aggressively extracted ... that has value, obviously, but not as much as any person.'

'You didn't have any drones in the air?' Beth asked Kohli.

'They aren't working,' Meera replied. They got damaged

when we were getting here. Those attackers were on us before we could fix them.'

'How?' Kohli swallowed his drink and wiped his hands on his combat pants. 'How did you guess we were captured? Where did you come from?'

The RAW team drew close to listen in.

'We were driving through Pingleshwar,' Meghan said, 'with our windows rolled down to let in the night air. It was empty, but a tobacco shop was open. We heard someone comment about fireworks at the beach. That was our shooting. Another man said someone was setting them off at the Vanku-Pingleshwar Road. That alerted us. We drove out of the village and waited for a while until we saw two men on bicycles. We hired them to drive our SUVs.'

'You could have hired a couple at the shop.' Meera frowned.

'We didn't know whether those fireworks were genuine or were sounds of shooting. Shaikh could have had a network of informers in the village. We didn't want to take any risk.'

'Makes sense.'

'We told the villagers to drive slowly.' Beth smiled briefly. 'Which gave us time to split up. Bwana and Roger on the field across the road, the rest of us coming up from the farms behind this one. I launched our drones when we came into sighting distance, and you know the rest.'

'Where's Shaikh?'

'In one of the Pajeros.'

'Isn't that a risk? He might convince the driver to release him or the villager might call—'

'We handcuffed both drivers to the wheel and took their phones.'

An involuntary chuckle escaped Meera before her face hardened again.

Neelam caught Beth's hand and squeezed it hard, a gesture that turned into a hug. The younger twin held the trembling operator until her shivering stopped.

'Your first mission?'

'No, but it's the first one where I could have died.'

'You held up better than me. I puked when I was threatened like that. I won't say it gets easier, but our minds get better at compartmentalizing.'

'Who did the talking? The masked men?' Zeb addressed Kohli and Meera.

'No. They didn't speak in our presence. That first man you shot, he seemed to be some kind of leader—' Kohli began.

'He wasn't,' Zeb interrupted him. He looked across the road, towards the field. 'One of those masked men was. They got this other dude to speak up.'

'Why go through all that?'

'Because,' Zeb answered slowly, working through his thoughts as some of the jigsaw pieces fell into place. 'He or both men knew you would know their accents. Russian or Chechen.'

Meera sucked in her breath sharply. 'Your shooter! He isn't working alone.'

'He never was, it looks like. I am sure you'll find these men were hired killers, like the ones who attacked us near CST Station.'

'Why did they go away?'

'They're smart. Both of them, or at least the leader. We could have rolled up and would have been captured. They weren't counting on it going as easily as that, however, which is why they left the airport.'

'They are out there?' Meera followed his gaze. 'Why didn't your drones spot them?'

'They could be. If I were them, I would have left the moment it went south. Our drones ... they must have been wearing thermal camouflaging. Our outfits'—he gestured at his vest and pants—'have those capabilities. And on top, they must have been hiding out of our range.'

Beth nodded in agreement. 'I zoomed in to look for immediate threats.'

Zeb stiffened suddenly. 'Shaikh, the real one—'

'The real one?'

'He had a body double in that villa. The gangster spoke just once when he was captured. He said he had been betrayed.'

He looked at his friends and the RAW agents, letting them digest the revelation. He wasn't surprised when Meghan was the first to make the connection.

'Shaikh was given to us. We were set up.'

Zeb searched the night, his eyes moving from shadow to shadow as if he could see through the darkness.

'Not just that,' he said softly. 'Our shooters have now hooked up with the terrorists.'

CHAPTER 52

The Russian cursed.

He and the Chechen alternated in driving their rental car from Pingleshwar, during which time he swore and pounded the wheel or the armrests bitterly.

They had escaped from the field after the last of their killers had been shot. They had retrieved their car from where it was hidden in another sugarcane field and had started the long drive back.

'We could have shot Carter from the field if we had long guns,' the Chechen said.

'FOOL! I thought you were smarter than that. Yes, we could have shot him and maybe we would have killed him. Do you know how our men reacted on the road? They stood there even as the shots came from the field. They were sitting ducks. Carter's team isn't like that. His friends will drop to the ground at the first round. They will escape. And then they will start hunting us. Those drones ... you really think we would have escaped them? LEAVE THE THINKING TO ME!'

He had calmed down by the time they reached the Gujarat Maharashtra border. He drove into a service station where they fueled up, freshened themselves and breakfasted.

'They'll know it was us.' The Chechen brooded over his coffee.

'Yes, but they still won't be able to identify us.'

'They could track down the men we spoke to in Horniman Circle.'

'Fool.' The Russian sneered. 'Those men are the terrorists. If the JTF find them, that bust will be so big they might not be interested in us at all. In any case, those bombers didn't see us.'

'Should we stop? Return to—'

The Russian caught the Chechen's wrist and squeezed it so hard that the man yelped.

'DON'T EVER SAY THAT AGAIN. WE WILL NOT STOP UNTIL CARTER IS DEAD.'

The killer breathed deeply until he controlled his fury.

'Carter will come to us. We'll have to make the invitation attractive enough.'

THE LEADER SMILED WHEN HE HEARD THE POUNDING ON HIS door. He opened it to let Khalid in.

'Did you hear it?'

'Yes,' the leader laughed. 'Join us.'

He pointed at the four silent men who were sprawled on the bed. 'They came before you. We have been following the news since it broke out.'

'Irfan Shaikh captured in Pingleshwar in a daring raid by Gujarat Police,' Khalid read the headline. He snorted. 'I bet it was the JTF who walked into our trap.'

'The Indian authorities won't admit that. I know from my sources that they lost eight men, but there's no news about them either. They have covered it up well. They are saying there was a second attack outside Pingleshwar, where Shaikh's men tried to rescue him. I know the JTF men were killed there, but not by the gang.'

'The shooter!'

'Yes, but I think he got away. If he had been captured, the Indian authorities would have made a song and dance about it.'

'They will wonder whether they were set up.'

'Let them. They won't be able to get to us.'

'What about Shaikh? Will he talk?'

'Of course he will. JTF will break him. He knows me only as a voice on the phone. He will say I asked him to stay in his villa because he'd be protected. Even if he recorded my calls, the JTF will get nowhere. My voice was disguised; the numbers were false ones.'

'He'll admit which agency you are from.'

'No. He'll never confess that. He knows he will not live if he does. We can take him out even in prison if he reveals the agency name. No, he'll throw the Indians a bone. He'll admit he has helped LET several times, which is true. That will be enough for the Indians. They may not even interrogate him further. They'll take that confession as a win. Have you taken care of the importer?'

Khalid nodded. 'He won't be talking to anyone, anymore.'

'What about Kurla? Are the bombs in place?'

'Yes.'

ZEB WENT FOR A MORNING RUN.

The return from Pingleshwar had been uneventful, and after they had reached their hotel late at night, they had crashed in their respective rooms.

He went down Marine Drive, past the spot where Mastan's men had attacked him and went all the way to Chowpatty, a small sandy beach on the promenade, before turning back.

Is he someone I know?

He went through his enemies as his feet pounded the sidewalk. The Russians, Chinese and Iranians were the most interested in him, but there were other intelligence agencies who wanted him dead, too. The North Koreans, some Turkish,

Brazilian and Filipino outfits. And then there were the organized crime gangs on every continent.

It could be anyone, he grimaced. *That those two men are Russian or Chechen does not mean much. They could be contract killers acting for someone else.*

Mossad, MI6, the Germans, and other allied agencies had come back negative. None of them had any information on any killer who was actively hunting him.

What will they do next?

They'll set a trap for me.

'WHERE ARE YOU GOING?' HE ASKED, WHEN HE AND HIS friends reached the JTF office later in the day to see Kohli and Meera leaving.

'Sule,' the deputy replied in a clipped tone.

He took in her face and understood instantly.

'We'll come with you.'

'We don't need your help.'

'We'll keep you from killing him.'

MEERA SPRANG FORWARD AS SOON AS THEY ENTERED SULE'S Dharavi office. She yanked him from behind his desk and slammed him against the wall.

She ignored Padma's scream and Nilu's yell.

'YOU SET US UP!' she spat at him. 'WE LOST EIGHT MEN IN THAT RAID BECAUSE OF YOU.'

'WHO? WHAT? I DON'T KNOW WHAT YOU ARE TALKING ABOUT!' Sule attempted to free himself.

She slapped him hard and stepped back.

'Irfan Shaikh. You must have heard about him. That was us. But we were ambushed and an entire team died. Because of you.'

The Dharavi man's face turned gray. He waved away his daughter, who was pulling out her phone. He jerked his head angrily at the door when several of his men crowded it. They melted away at his gesture.

'Tell me everything.' His voice shook as he reached for his chair and settled heavily on it.

Meera looked at Kohli, who nodded once. She gave Sule the abbreviated version.

'Why did you want to kill us?'

'No.' The retired gangster raised his hands defensively. 'You have it wrong. The CIA man'—he nodded at Zeb—'asked me if I could find out where Shaikh was. I got the information from a narcotics dealer, someone who was my informer in the old days. I passed it on to you. I don't know anything else.'

Meera observed him, weighed his words and took a further step back.

I believe him.

She sensed the same sentiment in Kohli, Zeb, and the Agency operators.

'Who's this informer? Where can we find him?'

'Karim Abbas,' Sule said promptly. 'He's got a shop on Wadi Bunder. He's a textile importer. That's his cover.'

'You'll find him. Dead.'

Meera nodded at Zeb's words. *We have to find him, nevertheless.*

She issued an order into her cell phone and turned to Sule.

'Shaikh said he was betrayed. Was he referring to you?'

Sule looked surprised. 'Me? He and I have had no contact for years. I didn't know he was in Pingleshwar until Abbas's information reached me. Haven't you interrogated him?'

Not yet. We want him to feel he is safe and then begin.

The Dharavi man didn't need to know that, however.

She put on her game face and moved towards the door. *Coming here was a waste of time. Sule does not know anything.*

She saw the quick glance Padma threw at her father. Heard him clear his throat and spun on her heel.

'Don't you want to know about that Russian or Chechen?'

CHAPTER 53

'You found him?' Zeb straightened from the wall he was leaning against.

'No.' Sule shook his head. 'But there is something that could help you. Usko leke aao.'

Bring him.

Nilu left the office and returned with a young adult. He was dressed in a tee and long shorts and sported a trim beard. His eyes were alert as they took in Sule's visitors. They lingered on the twins, Chloe and Meera.

Hormones, Zeb grinned inwardly.

'This is Manas, Manas Patel,' the retired gangster said. 'He's at university but also works in a leather factory here, at night. He doesn't have anyone. No parents or relatives. He sleeps in the passageways at night, wherever he finds space and, in the mornings, takes food from families. Dharavi is his home. We will support him.'

Patel nodded at them, smiling awkwardly.

'Manas, these people are from JTF. You don't need to know their names.'

The smile left the young adult's face. He turned serious.

'Tell them what you saw.'

'That man—'

'This one?' Meera asked sharply and showed him the sketch on her phone.

'Haan, madam.'

Yes, ma'am.

'He and I slept in the same passage three times. This was a week before the Crawford Market bombing. It was just him and me in the gully next to the nala behind the leather factories. No one else sleeps there because of the smell.'

Gully, lane. Nala, drainage ditch. Zeb automatically translated the words internally and looked at his team to confirm they had understood.

They had.

'He was wearing a hoodie all three times, but I could see his face clearly enough. We never spoke to each other. I greeted him the first night, but he only responded with a nod. The next two nights, I didn't even bother. I didn't know he was a foreigner, then. Yes, he was fair, but there are Kashmiris in Dharavi who look like they are from America.'

'Do you know where he came from or where he went in the morning?' Zeb asked.

'No. I wake up at six o'clock, but he was gone all three days before that. I find my place to sleep at nine pm. He used to come about half an hour later.'

'Food? Did he have any with him?'

If he brought takeouts, we can check if the shops remember him.

'No. He had a backpack from which he removed his bedding and an inflatable pillow.'

'Did you see anything else in his bag?'

'No.'

Zeb swallowed his disappointment. *Patel saw him but that doesn't help us in any way.*

The youngster seemed to read his expression.

'The way we sleep,' he continued, 'is single file. We lie down, one behind the other, our feet close to the other person's head.

We never sleep side to side. That way we don't block the passage. This foreigner was behind me. We slept in the same formation, but head-to-head instead of feet-to-head since there were only two of us.'

Beth stirred.

Let him speak, Zeb telegraphed with his eyes.

She nodded.

'I was on my phone. I was recording myself.'

Zeb straightened. He realized instantly what was coming.

'The next morning, I found out my video had captured him when he was on his phone as well.'

'Show us!'

Patel nodded at Zeb's command and pulled out his phone. 'I showed it to Nilu and Sule, sir, but they couldn't make out what was being sent.'

The Agency operators and Meera and Kohli crowded around him as he turned on his video, forwarded it to the time stamp and paused it.

The shooter's head was a dark blob on the edge of his pillow. They could see him hold his phone in his right hand, on which a messaging app was open.

Signal. Zeb recognized the application. It was a highly secure application that was growing in popularity because of its encryption standards. It was used by extremists and terrorists for that reason.

The chats were blurred because of the angle and light reflection, but a few lines of conversation were visible.

Where will you sleep?

In Dharavi.

Nazyr, have you lost your mind? There?

Yes. I'll sleep here, now onwards.

NO! It is not safe.

It is. No one pays any attention to me. There are so many people here. Relax.

Have you rented a room?

No. I am sleeping in the passage.

Won't it be crowded?

There's just another kid here. He doesn't talk. He's on his phone all the time.

'We have names!' Meghan clenched her fist.

'Names? You can read the conversation? It seems to be Cyrillic?' Meera asked.

'We couldn't read it either,' Sule admitted.

'It's Russian,' Zeb clarified. 'Nazyr is the shooter, the man who was sleeping. The second man's name is on the top of the chat window. Misha.'

'Nazyr?' Kohli frowned. 'Is he an Islamic terrorist?'

'N-A-Z-Y-R.' Zeb spelled it out for him. 'It's a Chechen name. The taxi driver guessed his accent correctly.'

'You know them?'

'No. We haven't come across those names.'

Zeb took the phone from Patel and turned it to catch different angles, but the previous conversations remained blurred.

'Can you—'

'Yeah,' Meghan replied. 'If Manas can forward that chat to us, we'll run it through Werner to see if we can read the previous lines.'

'And to us too,' Kohli told the youngster.

Patel nodded. His fingers danced on his phone as he punched in the numbers Meghan and Meera gave him and sent them the conversation.

'You did well.' Zeb smiled warmly at him. 'Let us know if you remember anything else.'

'I will.'

His smile disappeared when the young man left the room.

Misha. He seems to be the leader. Why are he and Nazyr after us?

CHAPTER 54

'Let me,' Meera told Kohli when they were at Arthur Road Jail later in the day.

'You want to interrogate Irfan Shaikh?'

'Yes. He will be arrogant, seeing that I am a woman. That will be his mistake.'

Kohli chuckled as they showed their badges at the entrance and were led by an armed officer to the interrogation room. The prison had been made famous in numerous Bollywood movies. It had housed stock market scammers and terrorists. Kasab, the terrorist from the 2008 Mumbai attacks, had been jailed there as well.

The corridor to the interrogation room was lined with guards. It had iron gates which were manned by a sentry who examined their badges, checked them on his computer and only then let the barrier roll open.

'No recording,' Meera warned Kohli when he went to the observation room. 'No other witnesses.'

'Agreed.'

She went inside the room where Irfan Shaikh was chained to a metal desk, his legs fastened to his chair.

'You?' the gangster exclaimed in Hindi. 'I was expecting a

bruiser to rough me up. They sent a woman? Are you going to seduce me into confessing?'

He laughed at his own joke.

Meera didn't reply. She removed her suit jacket and tossed it carelessly to the floor. She brought out a slim tube from her trouser pocket that was the length of her palm and pulled at its ends to unfold the two-foot-long cane.

She slashed at Shaikh's face without warning.

The interrogation had begun.

SHE STOPPED NINETY MINUTES LATER, LOOKING dispassionately at Shaikh, whose face was bloody but with no other marks on him. His breath came out tortuously, his eyes were half-closed. His defiance had vanished, and he looked like what he was.

A defeated man.

She went out to join Kohli, who gave her a towel. She wiped her palms and face, took the water bottle from him and drank deeply.

The guards in the passage avoided looking at them.

She wiped her lips and capped the bottle.

'He has nothing to do with the bombings.'

CHAPTER 55

Kohli watched the evening press conference with Meera in the JTF office.

Suman Shekhawat, the NIA head, briefed the journalists. She spoke about Shaikh's capture and said the gangster had confirmed his links with LET.

'He has confessed that he has supported them in various terrorist activities, in not just supplying them with safe houses or weapons, but in also giving them personnel to help in intelligence gathering and even shootings. With his capture, we have taken out one more enemy of the country.'

'She's smart,' Meera said dryly. 'She has deflected the narrative from the fact that we have made little progress in these attacks.'

'The Home Minister didn't mince his words,' Kohli said soberly. 'Bose told me he was savage.'

'He has a right to be. We are supposed to be India's best. All our results so far have been mostly because of Zeb.'

'He's part of the JTF.'

'Yes,' she snarled in frustration, 'but what have we achieved? What have we to show?'

Her phone rang before Kohli could reply.

His did too.

They took the calls simultaneously and their faces paled when they looked at each other.

Meera lunged for the door.

'ZEB!' she yelled at the American who was at Shahadat, the coffee bar, along with his team.

They looked at her. Heard her tone, read her expression and raced to the conference room.

'What?' Zeb demanded.

'Another bomb,' Meera said hollowly. 'In Kurla. Just as the press conference was going on. This is bigger. People are already talking of more than fifty bodies.'

CHAPTER 56

Zeb and his crew went to the scene.

A crowded vegetable market on Kurla Pipe Road. Several smoldering stalls. EMT workers and police clearing bodies. Media vans cordoned some distance away. All civilians cleared from the road. Uniformed and armed officers everywhere.

'It went off at ten to six,' Kohli yelled above the wail of a siren. 'The market was busy. People doing last-minute shopping before going home. Office workers, women, homemakers, kids.'

Zeb took it in.

They were in their Range Rovers, watching from a distance.

There's nothing we can do. We'll only get into the police's way if we go to the market.

Kohli and Meera were at his window with Bwana, Bear, Roger, and Chloe behind them.

'LET?' Meera thought aloud. 'Revenge bombing for Shaikh's capture?'

'No.' Zeb shook his head. 'Whoever's behind this has planned out their attacks. They are not acting on impulse. They would have selected these sites carefully, would have checked them out for security cameras ... all that takes preparation. Mumbai was still on very high alert before this blast. Everyone carrying bags or backpacks is being looked at carefully. Nope, they didn't wake up today and decide "let's bomb Kurla Pipe Road."'

'Tell us,' Beth prodded him. 'This theory you have.'

'You know something?' Kohli looked at him sharply. 'Share it with us! We need a break. Heck, have you seen the conspiracy theories floating on the internet? That it's Hindu extremists who are behind these attacks.'

'They *have* been in Muslim populated areas.'

'Yes,' Meera acknowledged. 'Everyone is aware of that. But making the leap to Hindus—'

She looked at the Americans and raised her hands. 'No, I am not saying this because I am a Hindu. I know very well there are Hindu extremists. India and Pakistan are shelling each other at the border because of these blasts. The two prime ministers are making veiled threats about using nuclear bombs. But Hindu extremists haven't gone to this extent before. I don't believe it's them.'

'You're right,' Zeb said. 'These blasts have nothing to do with them.'

'Who then? What do you know?'

'I know as much as you all do. I am just speculating here. There's a lot of organization required to carry out these attacks. Explosives that can't be traced, site surveys, people who won't be recognized ... these terrorists recruited Asadi and his team, but they were disposable. They haven't stopped bombing even after that team died.'

He jerked his head at the grim scene in front of them.

'What are you getting at?' Meera asked somberly.

'Organization. These aren't Hindu extremists or any other outfits who carry out bombings in India. LET is capable, but even they haven't carried out serial explosions.'

'There's always a first time.'

'No. They have always been on your radar. After Crawford

Market you went after them with a vengeance and arrested several people suspected of associating with them. That didn't stop the Haji Ali bombing or this one. It's not them.'

'Who then?'

'There are only two outfits who I think can carry out such explosions. ISI—'

Kohli slammed his palm against the Range Rover's roof. A passing medic looked at him curiously and hurried towards the scene.

'ISI! It is one of our prime suspects. The Home Minister wants us to go after that organization. We'll—'

'Back up,' Zeb said sharply. 'You need to work out what's in it for them as well.'

'Isn't it obvious?' Kohli flared. 'They want to create chaos in India. They want to weaken and destroy our country. That's been their mission all along. They supported the 2008 attacks! What more do you want?'

'I am aware of all that. But these attacks are putting pressure on them, too. Your government isn't sitting quietly. It has accused Pakistan of aiding these bombers. The current political and military tensions are because the two governments have been accusing each other.'

'That does not mean ISI isn't involved.'

'I'm not saying that. I don't think it's the main suspect, however.'

'Who, then?' Meera asked softly.

'ISIS.'

They stared at him. His friends looked at him as well in surprise.

'ISIS? India has never been a major target for them. It has focused on the West all along. Besides, its organization is in tatters.'

'It could be regrouping and finds India is a soft target. The destruction of India and Israel are the objectives of every Islamic terrorist group. Do you remember what Shaikh said when he was captured?'

'That he was betrayed by someone.'

'Yeah, but before that he said started off with *IS* and then broke off and said *he betrayed me*.'

They fell silent. Zeb watched the medics and police officers at work at the scene while his friends, Kohli and Meera digested his theory.

'It's possible,' Kohli admitted. 'RAW has long believed ISIS, Taliban and Al Qaeda will focus on India at some point.' His stubble rasped when he rubbed his jaw. 'We aren't aware of any active cells in the country, however.'

'I know someone who might.'

'Who?'

'Lieutenant General Nawaz Khan.'

Meera rocked back on her heels. 'That's the ISI chief!'

CHAPTER 57

'How do you know him?' Meera asked.

'We saved his daughter from a situation in Los Angeles,' Chloe said. She hesitated and at Zeb's nod, resumed. 'She lives in America now. This was when she was a student at UCLA. She and several students were kidnapped by an organized crime gang. They picked on wealthy families' kids.'

'Nawaz Khan is rich. Just about every senior politician, military officer and agency head in Pakistan has siphoned funds to their personal offshore accounts.'

She's right, Zeb thought. *Most of them money-launder.*

'The gang didn't know who she was. They were targeting some other students, but Khan's daughter was at the party they attacked. They took out her security team and those of the other students and moved them to Mexico to begin their extortion.'

'I didn't know you took on such missions.'

'We don't. We were in the country, however, and coincidentally, we were interested in that gang.'

Their outfit was selling weapons to terrorists.

'We took out the gang's leader and rescued those students.'

'I bet Khan wasn't very grateful,' Meera spat. 'I am sure he didn't stop ISI's meddling in other countries.'

The laugh escaped Chloe before she could control it. Her mirth died quickly as an ambulance rushed past them.

'You are right, but he owes us.'

'You'll call him?' Kohli shifted on his feet.

'No,' Zeb replied. 'I'll meet him.'

CHAPTER 58

Zeb took the Lear, which was still in Mumbai International Airport. He used a diplomatic passport, officially issued by the State Department, but in a false name, and slipped through the immigration line in Jinnah International Airport in Karachi at two am without any incident.

In, he messaged Beth and Meghan when he checked into a fancy hotel on Rashid Minhas Road.

He shook his head when they thumbs-upped in acknowledgment a few minutes later.

You aren't asleep? He messaged the younger twin.

I was. You woke me up!

Nope, he couldn't win against either of them. He showered, lay down on the bed and stared at the ceiling.

Misha and Nazyr. He thought about all their missions, the countries they had been in. Neither of the men registered with him.

And yet there was something in his memory, deeply buried. A feeling that one of those names was important, that he had some kind of relationship to the man. He lay still, motionless, waiting for that particular jigsaw piece to fall into place, but it didn't.

. . .

ZEB TURNED ON THE TV IN THE MORNING.

A press conference being conducted by the Pakistani prime minister, who was responding to a reporter's question.

'Yes, we want to be good neighbors, but if India attacks us, we will defend ourselves. With everything that we have.'

'What about India's stand that ISI is behind these bombings?' a journalist asked.

'Those are baseless accusations,' the leader said angrily. 'The Indians are making these claims to divert attention from their internal problems and the lack of progress in their investigations. The majority who died have been Muslim. How do we know it wasn't Hindu extremists behind these bombings?'

'What about the shelling on the border, sir?'

'India started those. We didn't. We moved more troops there because they did in the first place.'

'Will you comment on the rumors that you will authorize nuclear weapons, sir, if war breaks out?'

'We will do whatever it takes to defend our country.'

Zeb turned off the TV.

Unbelievable! These two governments aren't holding back their words.

They were ratcheting up the pressure instead.

President Morgan spoke to both leaders yesterday. That didn't seem to have any effect.

He pinched the bridge of his nose and went to the window to look out.

You have reacted like an ignorant Westerner, he berated himself. *You should know better. You have studied their history.*

The two countries had a deeply entangled and bitter history. Pakistan was created by partitioning the Indian subcontinent in 1947 to create independent countries, the Muslim-majority Pakistan and Hindu-majority India.

It was an act that was preceded by communal violence and succeeded by mass displacement and killing of people on a scale the region hadn't ever experienced.

About fifteen million fled their homes, Hindus from Pakistan to India and Muslims in the opposite direction. Up to two million were killed in the ensuing communal clashes.

How and why the two governments react the way they do … there's violent history behind it, he reminded himself.

He put the press conference out of his mind when he walked out of his room at eleven am and went onto National Stadium Road.

It was hot. His tee stuck to his back. His shades cut out the glare but did little to protect his eyes from the dust that swirled in the air from passing traffic.

I could have hired a vehicle, but this place is walking distance from my hotel.

This place was Karachi Golf Club, the oldest such establishment in the city. It was more than a century old, formed before the partition of the subcontinent, when the British ruled it.

Zeb spotted the dark SUV near the club's entrance immediately. A man in a white shirt tucked into dark pants leaned against it, watching him impassively.

Another such vehicle in the club building's patio, but this one had armed men in it.

He climbed up the stairs and went to the reception desk.

'I'm with the American Embassy.' He smiled and presented his diplomatic passport. 'I want to check out the club. I might become a member.'

'Mr. Travis.' The elegant woman inspected his credential and handed it back. She got to her feet, returning his smile. 'I'll be happy to show you around.'

'If you don't mind, I would like to wander about on my own. I don't need the hard sell.'

'Go ahead, sir. The club building and course are well-marked. You won't get lost. But if you do, here's my card. Call me. I'll find you.'

Zeb pocketed it and made a show of inspecting the club's

facilities. He went onto the green finally, breathing deeply the clean, crisp air.

The city's traffic and smog are just a few hundred meters away. Here, it's an oasis!

He went past the first hole, where two men were discussing the stock market. Near another hole, a couple of women were in an electric buggy, watching their partners swing with interest.

Broker will like this place.

The eldest operator among them made it a point to visit golf courses whenever they were in new cities.

It was at the ninth hole that he saw the two armed men. They made no pretense of looking friendly. They scowled at him and tightened their hands on their HKs when he got closer.

The man at the hole stopped his swing. He removed his shades and stared at Zeb.

'It's all right, Rahim,' he said in Urdu. 'I know this gentleman. Can you give us some privacy please? In fact, why don't you arrange a table and get some drinks.'

'Zeb Carter, well, well,' Lieutenant General Nawaz Khan, chief of Pakistan's Inter-Services Intelligence, ISI, greeted him in English with a cut-glass accent.

He studied in Britain and spent several years there before returning to Pakistan.

It was a route taken by many from privileged families in that country, before they entered politics or joined the military.

They then invest their illegal money in London, buy properties, in case they have to flee Pakistan, he added to himself.

'When I left my home to putt, the last person I expected to see was you.'

He broke away when Rahim and the other bodyguard returned with a folding table, a couple of chairs and an umbrella. They set everything up, went to the buggy and returned with ice-cold lemonade that they poured into two glasses and served.

'When I left Mumbai last night,' Zeb said as he raised his

glass in a silent toast to the ISI head, 'I knew I would find you here today.'

'You have done your homework on my routine.'

Khan radiated authority. He was in a golfing outfit, blue tee and khaki pants, but his thick hair with streaks of gray in it, neatly trimmed mustache and clean-cut jaw, told strangers to stay away.

The presence of armed guards helped as well.

'Mumbai.' Khan's eyes sharpened. 'You were there.'

'Yes. I was at Kurla Pipe Road less than an hour after the explosion.'

'Why is America interested in those bombings?'

'The only country that doesn't seem concerned about them seems to be Pakistan.'

A muscle twitched on Khan's cheek. His eyes veiled.

'Our prime minister has spoken to India's leader. He has expressed his shock and anger and offered every possible help.'

'What about ISI? Has it offered help to India's agencies?'

'There is nothing to offer,' Khan said stiffly. 'We don't know anything about those explosions. Why are you here? What are you accusing me of?'

'Is ISI involved? Is your agency supporting the killers the way it helped the LET terrorists in 2008?'

'We had nothing to do with that. ISI—'

'Save it,' Zeb said coldly. 'Everyone in the intelligence world knows ISI's role in those attacks. We have all seen the reports. That's in the past, however. I am interested in these explosions. ARE. YOU. INVOLVED?'

He enunciated slowly.

Khan got to his feet abruptly. He slipped on his shades. His men looked over at his sudden move.

'We are done,' the ISI head said tightly. 'This conversation is over. Go back to Mumbai or wherever you want to go, Carter, before you face any unpleasantness in Karachi.'

Zeb didn't move. He looked up at Khan, who was unfolding his shades.

'How is Zeba? I heard she is working in a big law firm in LA.'

Khan's face twisted in fury.

'You take her name? You use her to make me feel guilty? To blackmail me? Have you no shame?'

'The death toll in Mumbai was one hundred and seventy-eight when I checked in the morning. That's more than in 2008. Your country and India are on the edge of war. I will mention anyone if it helps me.'

'I TOLD YOU ISI IS NOT INVOLVED IN ANY WAY.'

Khan's guards shifted uneasily. There was no one else within hearing distance. The other golfers were out of sight.

The ISI chief breathed harshly as he glowered at his visitor, his shades clutched in one hand.

Zeb took him in. *He's telling the truth.*

'Are you following what's being posted on the internet? Hindu extremists—'

'Yes, I know of all that. I am confident it's not them.'

'Why not? It's Muslims being killed. My country is again suspected of supporting terrorism. It's exactly what the extremists would do.'

'Because they have nothing to gain by such large-scale killing.'

'You would say that. You would support the Indians. You would believe whatever they say.'

Zeb sighed inwardly. *This same discussion with Meera and Kohli, but from a different perspective.*

'My team looked into the Hindu extremist angle. We didn't find it credible. As for your issues with India ... that's between you and them.'

He doesn't need to know about our vacation or the shooters after us.

Khan snorted but made no other comment.

'Are there any ISIS cells in India?'

'How would I know?' Khan snapped.

Zeb kept looking at him.

'I am sure the Indian agencies will know.'

'I came here to ask you. Your agency has relationships with various outfits. Taliban, the Haqqani group ... no,' he cut off Khan before the man could speak. 'Don't deny it. You will know of ISIS in India possibly before they know of it.'

The ISI chief sat down. He mopped his forehead with a handkerchief, which he folded neatly and slipped back into his pocket.

'ISIS is looking to regroup,' he acknowledged. 'I haven't heard about it targeting India, but it makes sense.'

He looked away for a long while and seemed to come to a decision.

'You are sure about the Hindu—'

'Yeah.'

Khan unfolded a paper towel and scribbled an address on it. 'That's a cell in UP, Uttar Pradesh, that's an Indian state.'

'I know India well.'

'Right. That town is about an hour away from New Delhi. Four men in that group. They are British. Yes.' He smiled mirthlessly. 'They are British Muslims who joined ISIS in Syria. They fled when the terrorist group collapsed, but instead of going to their home country, they went to India.'

'They have Indian origins?'

'No, but they have fake passports and documentation that shows they have.'

'No one knows about them? The British, the Indian agencies, American outfits?'

'No. Only ISI.'

'And you kept this to yourself?'

'Yes,' Khan said unapologetically. 'It's how ISI works.'

Four men. Zeb fingered the address. *They would be more than enough to plant the Kurla bombs and set more off.*

He memorized the address, pocketed the paper, and got to his feet.

'Hadi Asadi and his outfit. They were Iranians.'

'They had Iranian passports,' Khan corrected him. 'They could have been ISIS, too. I don't know.'

Zeb turned when the ISI head looked beyond him and frowned.

That's the guard who was on National Stadium Road, he identified the approaching man who had his HK in his hands.

'What happened, Salim?' Khan asked him.

Salim raised his gun and shot the two bodyguards.

CHAPTER 59

Zeb reacted instantly.

He flung himself at Khan and toppled him to the ground. He fell on top, twisted around desperately and upturned the table to offer them some cover.

The HK chattered. Rounds spat into the ground. Mud and turf flew in the air.

We don't have time. That table is flimsy. It won't protect us for long. He's standing, we're on the ground.

Zeb looked around desperately. No one in sight. No other cover.

'When I move,' he whispered, 'dive to your left.'

Khan nodded and flinched when the table shuddered from bullets ripping into it.

Zeb didn't wait for their thin cover to splinter.

He jammed his feet against it and kicked out with all his strength.

The wooden table flew into the air towards Salim.

Zeb sprang out to his left, drawing his Glock, sensing Khan dive to his right.

The killer, five meters away, his HK held high, easily dodging the flying table.

Zeb felt a bullet slam into his chest and stumbled backwards. His own round went wide.

The shooter fired again.

Zeb felt it graze his side.

His feet slipped on the grass, sending another of his rounds harmlessly in the air.

Salim's lips twitched.

He turned his HK a centimeter down.

Zeb went with the slide. Felt the rounds burn the air above his head and then his Glock was bucking, his burst ripping into Salim's chest, throwing him backwards, his last bullet taking the killer's head away.

Zeb fell to the ground, gasping as he fast-changed his magazine.

'Stay down!' he wheezed at Khan, who was making to move.

His chest hurt as if a mule had kicked him. His side throbbed as well. He compartmentalized the aches and scanned the golf course.

It was still empty.

'I thought he was your guard.' He winced as he stood upright and helped Khan to his feet.

'I thought so, too.' The ISI chief was in shock. He was shivering.

Zeb bent over the fallen CPOs and checked them. Both were dead. He took one man's HK, searched his pockets for spare magazines and took those as well.

'He was after you.'

'I figured that.' Khan drew out his phone and started dialing.

'Don't call anyone. Not right now. Let's get you to a safe house.'

'My house.'

'You have people there?'

'It's my residence. My personal one. I have guards there, people who have known my family for years.'

'Get behind me. You'll need to show your badge if anyone stops us.'

'Leave that to me,' Khan growled.

Zeb led the way down the green, moving fast.

Were those golfers a cover? No one's around on the course.

He went inside the building, past the restaurant where guests were being served.

They didn't hear the shots.

Past a few staff who stepped back to let them pass and into the reception.

'Mr. Travis.' The woman who had welcomed him started rising. 'Oh ...' she trailed off when she saw the HK in his hand and Khan. 'Is there any problem, sir?'

'Three bodies on the green.'

She looked at him disbelievingly and then they were out into the portico.

'That's your vehicle.' Zeb spotted the SUV which had been in the patio and was parked in the driveway.

He tried to see through its darkened windows.

'They should have seen you come out. Stand behind this pillar. Call out if you see any gunmen coming from inside.'

He didn't wait for Khan's reply.

He ducked and raced towards the vehicle, looked through the window and straightened.

'They're dead.'

He went to the next vehicle in the driveway. No keys. The third one, a Ford sedan, had them in the ignition.

'Come!' he barked at Khan who was looking inside his SUV.

The ISI chief hesitated for a moment and joined him.

'Drive,' Zeb told him.

'Me?'

'Yes, so that I can use the gun if we're attacked.'

'I haven't driven in—'

'You are the ISI chief. The police won't stop you if you cause any accidents.'

Zeb adjusted the rear-view mirror when Khan drew jerkily out of the club. He saw the receptionist come out into the portico and stare at them, and then she vanished when they turned.

Zeb drew up the HK when they went out of the gate, but no one attacked them.

'That's Salim's vehicle.' He nodded at the SUV. 'Looks like he was alone.'

Khan grunted in reply. His eyes were tense, his shoulders hunched as he drove the unfamiliar car through the city.

Zeb checked their mirrors and got him to go through red lights and turn abruptly into streets and alleys.

'We're clean,' he announced finally. 'Get us to your home.'

He turned on the car's radio and switched to a news station. Weather, sports, discussion on the prime minister's press conference.

'There has not been any coup!' Khan exclaimed.

Zeb side-eyed him.

'That was on your mind?'

'Yes. I thought the army had taken over and bribed Salim to kill me.'

'And now?'

'This is Pakistan.' The ISI chief relaxed in his seat. He put on a burst of speed and honked loudly at a taxi. 'I have several enemies. One of them must have turned him. My schedule ... quite a few people know I play golf regularly. I'll rip apart Salim's life, find out who was behind him and those people will wish they had never been born.' He ended in cold fury.

They entered Clifton, an upscale neighborhood close to the seaside. Fancy villas behind high walls, private security, quiet roads and well-maintained gardens.

'My family is wealthy,' Khan said defensively.

How else would you have made it to your position?

'How far are we from your home?'

'There.' Khan pointed at a white-painted house on the intersection of two streets, half a kilometer away.

'Park here. Behind that blue van.'

'Why?'

Zeb didn't reply.

He was out of the Ford, hustling to the van. He broke its windows.

No alarm. Good.

He opened the door from inside and beckoned at Khan who came over.

'Sit inside. Take this.' He thrust the HK at him.

'Where are you going?'

'To check out your house. There might be more killers waiting there.'

'I told you—'

'You want to risk yourself, be my guest. Go home.'

Khan didn't move.

Zeb left him and went down the sidewalk with his arms swinging freely. He went to the residence. An armed, alert, HK-toting guard at the door eyed him expressionlessly.

He felt the man's gaze as he went past.

It feels quiet. Khan has a family. Wife, two kids. Are they home? There didn't seem to be CCTV cameras at the gate. I should have asked him about those.

He turned back and went to the gate, seeing the guard stiffen.

'Khan saab hain kya?' he asked the guard in Urdu.

Is Khan Sir there?

'Nahin. Niklo yahan se.'

No. Go away.

Zeb caught his HK and punched him in the throat. Drew him away from the gate and knocked him out with the rifle's barrel. He laid the man down and swung the door open carefully.

Tiled driveway. Water falling in a fountain somewhere. Trees and potted plants.

He went down the side of the house and risked a glance inside through its darkened windows.

A woman watching a TV.

Must be his wife.

No sign of hostiles.

A guard appeared, however. From behind the house.

'WHO ARE YOU?' he roared.

Zeb sprinted towards the gate.

I didn't come here to get shot.

He heard the guard yelling at him as he squeezed through the door and thought he heard a woman's voice, and then he was on the sidewalk and crossing the road and still heard the sentry shouting when Khan came out from the van and hustled across.

'ZAFAR! HE'S WITH ME. DON'T MAKE A RACKET.'

The guard stared at his boss and then at Zeb.

'He attacked Minaf, sir, and was inside the compound.'

'Yes, I know. I was watching him. I will explain. Let's go inside.'

'Not me,' Zeb told him. 'You'll be safe at home. I'm done here. I need to get back to Mumbai. I'm sure you've got a lot on your plate.'

'Yes,' Khan said with a clenched jaw.

'Have you thought of sending your family to somewhere safe?'

The ISI chief's head jerked up in shock. Light flared in his eyes. 'I didn't think of that. I'll get them away from Karachi.'

He called a number, spoke softly, gesticulating furiously as he looked at the house.

Zeb saw a shadow appear at an upper window and disappear when he waved at it impatiently.

'She's not happy,' he said when he hung up. 'She never wanted me to take this job. She's blaming me for the upheaval.'

His wife isn't wrong. This role paints a target on his back and on those of his family.

Zeb slipped his hand in his pocket and felt the slip of paper Khan had passed over.

'You should have told the Indian agencies of the ISIS cell.'

The ISI man didn't respond.

'Or the British.'

'Don't tell me how to run my agency.'

Zeb shook his head in disgust.

'I have to leave.'

'I'll get a guard to drive you to the airport.'

'I don't need your help.' He eyed the house. 'Be careful.'

'I will. Carter, this does not change anything. We aren't—'

'Aren't friends. I know.'

Zeb didn't shake his hand. He returned Khan's head nod and was crossing the road when the ISI man called out.

'Azhar Mirza.'

'Who?' He returned to the house.

'Lieutenant General Azhar Mirza. Be careful of him.'

'Who is he? What has he done?'

Khan didn't respond. He went inside the compound with his guard, who shut the gate.

Zeb was buckling in the Lear when he remembered.

Azhar Mirza! He was the Pakistan Army general who attempted a coup last year. He's dropped out of sight.

Why did Khan mention him?

CHAPTER 60

Zeb was back in his Mumbai hotel late at night. He crashed into bed and woke to sunlight streaming through his window. He stretched and hurried to the shower when he remembered Khan's intel.

His team was lounging in the hotel's lobby when he emerged from the elevator car.

'When did you arrive?' Beth sprang up. 'We called and messaged several times—'

'Let's get to the JTF office.'

He drove in silence, aware of Meghan, Beth, and Broker's curious looks.

'Saves me from explaining over and over again,' was all that he offered.

'Get Bose,' he told Kohli when they joined the RAW Special Agent and his deputy.

'Why? Did Khan tell you anything?'

'Please get him.'

'Don't look at us!' Beth shrugged. 'He's been Mystery Man ever since we met him.'

Kohli went out and returned with the RAW Director.

Zeb brought out the piece of paper and gave it to the RAW head.

'What's this?' Bose examined the address and passed it on to Meera, who read it and gave it to Kohli.

'A four-man ISIS cell. British Muslims who have fake documents that show they have Indian origins.'

No one reacted for a moment, and then Meera snatched the slip from Kohli's hands and read it again as if she could picture the men.

'Khan kept it from us?' Her cheeks reddened in anger.

'Yes, and from the British too.'

'How long have they been in India?'

Zeb cursed himself inwardly. *I knew I had forgotten something!*

'I don't know. I didn't ask.'

He raised his hands apologetically at the looks he got.

'I would have but things happened—'

'What things?' Meghan rapped out.

'Khan's bodyguard tried to kill him.'

'Vikram,' Bose said in the heavy silence that followed, 'can you arrange coffee? I think we'll need it.'

'YOU DIDN'T THINK OF TELLING US?' BWANA GROWLED WHEN Zeb had finished summing up the previous day's events.

'Things happened too fast.'

'You could have called us on the way to the airport. Or while in the Lear. It is equipped for secure calls. Or when you reached the hotel—'

'It was late.'

'It wouldn't have mattered.'

'I didn't want to disturb you.'

'It's not in the news,' Meera said quickly before his team argued further.

'It wouldn't be. Khan has hushed it up,' Bose said, his face revealing none of his thoughts. 'Does he have any suspects?'

'He said he had many enemies. He didn't say anything more,' Zeb replied, smiling gratefully at Meera for changing the topic.

He would willingly face down a bunch of terrorists rather than deal with his friends' anger.

'What?' His smile faded at Kohli and Meera's expressions. 'That's a red-hot lead, that ISIS cell. You don't seem to be happy about it.'

'Happy isn't the word for it,' the deputy said tonelessly. 'We'll arrest and interrogate them, but we too have had some developments.'

'Like what?'

'Hafeez Traders.'

Zeb searched his memory for the name. 'That's the company that paid Asadi's rent.'

'Correct. From an account in Mauritius. We got the bank to disclose its holder. It's Praveen Kumar.'

'Praveen Kumar?' Zeb shook his head, puzzled. 'That name's supposed to mean something?'

'He's a senior aide to the Home Minister.'

Bose added heavily. 'He's also a senior leader in Hindus For India.'

CHAPTER 61

'HFI. A country-wide organization that supports the current central government. It has chapters in every state.' Kohli briefed them rapidly. 'Kumar is in the media constantly. He's giving speeches, going to ribbon-cutting ceremonies. He's one of the most powerful people in the government.'

'He is a Hindu extremist?' Zeb asked, stunned.

'It looks like that.'

'Have you arrested him?'

'No,' Bose answered. 'Imagine the headlines if we did that. The conspiracy theorists on social media would go nuts. There would be riots in the country if it got out that the killings were masterminded by these extremists.'

'It's not a conspiracy anymore, is it, sir? We have proof,' Meera challenged him.

'What do you think?'

Zeb took his time replying to Bose's question.

'You have a team on him?' He asked a query of his own.

'Yes. Not one. Three. We have tapped his phones, those of his family, his friends, every associate of his.'

'And?'

'Nothing suspicious.'

'Social media?' He looked at the twins. 'I haven't looked at what's trending on Twitter.'

'It's going nuts. Hindus attacking Muslims. Indian and Pakistani government officials accusing each other. ISI being blamed. RAW being named. There was a knife-stabbing in Delhi last night. A Muslim youth was the victim. In Haryana, a Hindu woman was assaulted. It's happening.'

'It won't take much to spark a riot,' Zeb guessed.

'No. Praveen Kumar's name is not needed. Another day of hot debates on the internet and I fear the worst.'

'The military—'

'India and Pakistan have put their air forces on full alert. More battalions have been moved to the border. Both countries have rejected President Morgan's suggestion of a neutral intermediary to host a discussion.'

'Was there anyone else's name on the account?' Zeb looked at Kohli and Meera.

'No. Praveen Kumar, alone. His signature, his bio-metric identity, the bank has it all. It was opened several years ago, but regular transactions have started only recently, for Asadi's rent. We are looking into the rest of the payments, but they are for small amounts. Purchases at various airports, from the looks of it.'

'What do you think, Zeb?' Bose repeated.

'We're being set up.'

CHAPTER 62

'Kumar's name wasn't concealed. There was no shell company, no obscure trail.' Meghan sat up straight.

'Yeah,' Zeb agreed. 'It was as if the masterminds wanted you to find it.'

'You mean he's innocent?' Meera asked doubtfully.

'I don't know. Right now, we have two suspects. That ISIS cell and him. But if I had to put money on it, it wouldn't be on him.'

'ISIS is capable of that? Hacking into a bank account to plant his name and identity? Why would it do that?'

'Beats me,' Zeb said in frustration. 'That's not how it operates. It's not into such clandestine—'

'ISI!' Kohli snarled. 'It's got to be them. That's how Nawaz Khan works.'

'I was with him. I believe him.'

'You might. We don't.'

'Enough.' Bose snapped his fingers. 'We won't gain anything by arguing among ourselves. Keep tailing Kumar. Get that ISIS cell and sweat them—'

'And get ahead of the curve,' Roger broke in. 'Check out

Muslim-majority neighborhoods in Mumbai. Get search teams and explosive squads there.'

'We are doing that,' Meera replied. The RAW team got up, as did the Americans.

Zeb remained sitting, however.

'What?' Meghan asked him, exasperatedly.

'Go.' He motioned. 'I need to think.'

'Leave that to us,' the elder twin quipped, but it was half-hearted.

Zeb brought out his screen when he was alone and typed in a name for Werner to research.

Azhar Mirza.

CHAPTER 63

Mumbra was to the northeast of south Mumbai. It wasn't a part of the city but was within the Mumbai Metropolitan Area, which comprised several satellite cities and towns around the most populous city in the country.

The town was home to two hundred and thirty thousand residents, many of whom worked in Mumbai and commuted via locals.

The bomb was detected by a police sniffer dog who barked, pointing its snout towards an empty carriage on a track.

Within minutes, police had emptied the station. In half an hour, a JTF team had taken over and ninety minutes from detection, the explosive had been defused.

'C4,' Kohli briefed the JTF that afternoon. 'Same batch as that used in Kurla. There was some undetonated explosive there which has some faint wrapper markings, similar to what we found here.'

His words amped up the room.

'Congratulations to the Mumbra Police for detecting it and for our bomb-disposal teams for getting there in time. It had a timer that was set to go off in the evening, during rush hour. That particular carriage was a women-only one that would have been attached to peak-hour trains to make them longer. For those of you who are new to Mumbai, the local trains are operated by two divisions of Indian Railways, Western and Central. The latter is responsible for the locals to Mumbra.'

'The terrorists knew of that carriage and the Central Railways routine.'

'Yes.' Bose confirmed Meera's guess. 'It wasn't hard to find out. Anyone could have stood at Mumbra station for a few days and would have seen that carriage being hooked to an evening train. And that's also the problem we have. There aren't many security cameras there. It is a busy station. It's impossible to find out who was surveilling the station. There's more good news. I said the explosive batch is linked to the previous explosion. Same C4 was used in Crawford Market and Haji Ali.'

A ripple of excitement went through the room.

Zeb put his hand up.

'Are you sure you want to ask what's on your mind?' Beth sniggered softly.

'Yes?' Bose asked him.

'How did you find they are the same batch? I thought C4 is so popular with terrorists because it's untraceable.'

'It is. Your country came to our help, however. Your Department of Defense has been using some space technology, used for identifying Moon and Mars rocks ... do you want to know the details?'

'No, sir.'

'Thought not!' Beth crowed in a whisper.

Zeb knew it was coming when Bose paused to turn to the wall on which a projector was playing images. The RAW chief pressed the remote button and four photographs appeared.

'Karim Abdullah, Ijaz Ahmed, Salman Ghani and Wasif Khan. An ISIS cell that we captured in Ghaziabad about two hours ago.'

Murmurs swept through the room.

'They are British but masquerading as Indian in origin. They were fighting with the terrorist group in Syria but when it collapsed, fled to our country with false papers. We are working out how long they have been here. We found maps on their phones. Old Delhi. Lucknow. A few other cities.'

All of those have a significant Muslim population.

Zeb stirred. *Was it them all along? Are they the bombers?*

'You didn't involve us in the takedown, sir?' Rahul raised his hand.

'There wasn't any time. Our New Delhi team could move faster.'

'This isn't public news?'

'No, and it will remain like that until we complete our investigation. Clear?'

'Clear,' the assembled agents chorused.

Bose made a gesture at which the meeting broke up. Zeb and his crew joined him, Kohli and Meera.

'This is it!' The deputy's eyes shone. 'I think we have cracked it.'

'You don't believe that?' Bose read Zeb's expression.

'I have been wrong before. Let's see what their interrogation comes up with.'

'Have you heard from Nawaz Khan?'

'No. He must be busy tracking down his enemies.'

'Azhar Mirza is well-known to us. He's a bitter enemy. He's one of the few generals who blames India for everything. His family were in Punjab before India's Partition. Several of their members were killed in the riots that followed. Maybe that's the reason he hates us. I don't know. Did you work out why Khan mentioned him?'

'No, sir.'

'He's dropped out of sight. His own government is hunting him, to put him on trial for the coup. Anyway.' Bose shrugged.

'Good work, all of you. Get some rest. I have a good feeling about this ISIS cell's capture.'

'You don't think it's over?' Chloe asked Zeb when they were alone in the conference room. 'I mean the bombings.'

'No.'

CHAPTER 64

'This is a problem.' The leader mused over dinner.

'I didn't expect them to search Mumbra.' Khalid played with the food on his plate. 'I was thinking they would focus on central and south Mumbai. That's where we exploded the previous bombs.'

'Uh huh.'

'I've enough C4. I can plant some of it in Byculla or Mahim. I have got a list of locations.'

'Fifteenth and Sixteenth of August are less than a week away.' The leader sipped his drink and wiped his lips. 'Leave it with me. I will decide.'

'We need to have one more explosion before those two days—'

'I said I will decide.' Steel in his voice that Khalid didn't challenge.

The leader reached into his briefcase and brought out four passports. He handed them to the four silent men.

'Your identities.'

'As Indians? Hindus?'

'Yes.'

'You didn't tell us we had to change our religion.'

'You aren't. Those passports are fake. Do you have any objections? I thought you were professionals. Did I make a mistake in recruiting you? Aren't you already staying in this hotel under Hindu names?'

'We thought we wouldn't need those covers on the fifteenth and sixteenth.'

'You *will* need those new identities on those two days.'

The men looked at his hard, implacable face and nodded.

'Remember your mission,' he reminded them. 'You will set off bombs in Dharavi on the fifteenth, India's Independence Day. You will show your faces. That's why those passports are important. The Indians need to know who you are. Your false identities. After the detonation, you'll go to the airport where you'll buy tickets for—'

'Islamabad, where we'll set off bombs on the sixteenth. Got it.'

'I will hand over the C4 and the detonators to you on the fourteenth,' Khalid said.

'Go to your rooms,' the leader commanded.

'Will they create any problems?' Khalid asked when it was only the two of them.

'I hope not. Our sponsor sent them. He said they were the best kill team.'

'What about a bombing before Independence Day?'

The leader looked out of the window at Marine Drive for several moments.

'Mumbra was to be that blast. How easy will it be for you to plant explosives before then?'

Khalid made a face.

'With the security being what it is, it's anyone's guess. I can hide them, but they won't be discovered. Dharavi—'

'No. That's our finale in India. You have surveilled it several times. Our men can get in easily. The slums are not searched for bombs. We don't want to draw security there by exploding before the fifteenth.'

'There's a player on the board we have not accounted for.'

'Who's that?'

'The shooter.'

The leader shrugged. 'He has his own agenda. There's no overlap with ours.'

'There isn't, but I hope he doesn't complicate things for us.'

'How can he? Even if he reports our meeting to the police, what can he say? That he spoke to two masked men in Horniman Circle on the phone?' The leader slapped his thigh and laughed in disbelief. 'Even if they believe him and don't arrest him, how will they find us? No, he isn't a problem.'

'He's after Carter and the rest of the Americans.'

'Yes, I am aware. But stop worrying about him. Instead of his being a problem, he's an asset. He will be helping us indirectly by attacking them.'

PETROV HADN'T FORGOTTEN ABOUT THE AMERICANS' REQUEST.

He hadn't made it a priority either.

He put out a cursory word and didn't bother following up even when Kurla Pipe Road happened.

'Nyet.' He shrugged at Viktor and Dmitri. 'It's not our business.'

'You told the Americans you would help.' Viktor trimmed his nails with a file, blew on them and examined them in the light.

'That was because they were here. What I told them is true. We have nothing to do with that world anymore.'

'That was a big bomb on Kurla Pipe Road.'

'I have made up my mind.'

And then Mumbra happened.

He listened to the news on a radio app on his phone as he went through the charity's accounts and closed the books when the reporter announced the bomb had been defused. He leaned back in his chair and crossed his arms behind his neck. He contemplated the ceiling for a long time, making a mental note to get the cobwebs cleaned. He came to a decision and went to the door.

'I am going to the Russian Consulate,' he told his friends, who were at a small table in the front yard.

'What for?' Dmitri looked up from the playing cards he was holding in his hands. Viktor folded his and placed them face down.

'To see if they know of any killer.'

'I thought you weren't going to help the Americans.'

'These bombers need to be stopped.'

'I am sure the Indian authorities would have already contacted our government.'

'Da, and our people would have said they don't know of any such killer, otherwise the Americans wouldn't have come to us. I still know some old-timers, however, and my discussions will be different.'

He caught a taxi to the consulate in Malabar Hill and presented his identification to the security team.

'You can't walk in like this,' the guard said boredly and returned his passport. 'You need to take an appointment.'

Petrov hunched down to look the man in the eye.

'Tell Leonid Zerov that I want to meet him. If he finds out that you turned me away, you'll be posted back to Russia. You'll find yourself cleaning toilet bowls in Serbia.'

The guard flushed. He made to retort, but something in the visitor's eyes and demeanor made him pause. He muttered an oath, dialed a number and spoke softly.

'He'll see you.'

Petrov went through the barriers, through the security checks and into a waiting hall where a gray-suited, silvery-haired man was waiting for him.

'Come.' Zerov beckoned and led him to a meeting room.

'My Dharavi school has its third year anniversary next week.' Petrov presented the invitation to him. 'Please come to it.'

The old-timer opened the envelope, read it swiftly, and

nodded. 'I'll be there. I wouldn't miss it. What you are doing for Mumbai is getting noticed in Moscow.'

'I am not doing it for the politicians.'

'Da. Everyone knows that but still, you are making our country proud.'

They exchanged pleasantries for a while and then Zerov removed a cigarette case from his pocket.

'I haven't been able to quit the old habits,' he laughed. 'Let's go out.'

Petrov followed him to an enclosed garden.

'Here.' Zerov sat on a bench and tapped out a smoke. He lit it and exhaled in contentment. 'This is a blind spot. There are no cameras. We won't be heard.'

The former spy brought out the sketch the Americans had given him.

'Do you know him?'

Zerov looked at it for long and shook his head. 'Nyet. Should I know him?'

'He's the shooter in Crawford Market.'

'I heard about him, but this is the first time I'm seeing him. The Indians haven't released his sketch to the public.'

'That's because they want all international agencies to get back to them. I am sure they would have contacted you—'

'Not me. Andrei. He's the SVR representative here, passing as the legal attaché.'

'He's after my time.'

'He's young, ambitious, thinks people like you and me are dinosaurs. He hasn't ever been in the field. He hasn't pulled a trigger. What does he know of the real world? He thinks a computer can give him all the answers.' Zerov snorted in disgust. 'But why are you coming to me with this?'

'Because he's a Russian.'

The consulate officer paused in the midst of drawing a puff. He coughed, cleared his throat and looked at the sketch again.

'Why are you involved?'

'Some JTF agents came to me. They knew of my previous life. They asked me to ask about this man.'

There was no need for Zerov to know of the Americans.

'We have no active operation in India. This country is our ally—'

'I know. JTF know that too. But can you ask around?'

'Da. Is he involved in the bombings too?'

'I don't know.'

'If he is, he's made a big mistake. Our people will kill him for that.'

CHAPTER 65

Zeb squinted at his screen and tried for the umpteenth time to read the indistinct letters on it.

They remained illegible.

'I told you.' Beth looked over when he growled in frustration. 'We ran that screenshot through Werner. We tried everything. No luck. Vikram and Meera tried at their end too. The rest of the conversation on that phone is unreadable.'

Zeb glowered at the image from Manas Patel's phone as if his angry look could make the Signal conversation legible.

'There are hundreds of Mishas and a few Nazyrs as well in our database,' Meghan chimed in, 'but none of them are of any interest.'

He laced his fingers and stretched. Got to his feet, filled several mugs with coffee and served them to his team.

'We won't get anywhere in this manner. We've got to get ahead of their curve.'

'Explain,' Broker suggested.

'We have got to get the Russian and Chechen to come for us.'

'How will we do that?'

'We tell them where we will be.'

'Where is that?'

'Some place plausible and yet where we can capture them.'

They returned to their screens and researched likely locations in Mumbai.

Someplace crowded, Zeb thought, *which can offer anonymity to these killers. A place they would have chosen themselves.*

Slums were the obvious choice, and then high-rise buildings like the ones Hadi Asadi had hidden in.

'Somewhere close to local train stations, taxi stands and bus stations,' Chloe said aloud.

'And where they can easily hire cars,' Roger added.

'Why do they have to be apartment buildings?' Bear questioned. 'They can be hiding in under-construction ones in places where foreigners are quite common.'

They searched Mumbai and came up with three locations.

Malabar, Andheri West and Worli's seafront.

We have to decide where to suck them in, Zeb pondered as he blew up a map and projected it on a wall.

Beth lit it up with crosses and check marks, the former to denote under-construction buildings and the latter for tall, residential ones.

Zeb went to the wall, crossed his arms and studied the map.

'What's that?' Meera came up from behind, along with Kohli.

'That's where we get killed.'

CHAPTER 66

'Ma'am, you need to be a fluent liar.'

Bose rubbed his forehead at Zeb's comment. Meera fidgeted while Kohli pointedly looked out of the window.

Suman Shekhawat, head of India's National Intelligence Agency, didn't react immediately. She pretended to ignore Beth's sharp jab in Zeb's side.

Then she smiled. 'I'm a government official. Being creative with the truth is a job requirement.' She fingered the spectacles that were dangling around her neck from a bead necklace and studied her notes.

'Who started this rumor that the JTF is interested in under-construction buildings in Malabar? That it suspects the Crawford Market shooter is hiding in one of them?'

'It's not a rumor, ma'am. A couple of tweets are all there are on it.'

'Who posted those?'

'We wouldn't know, ma'am,' Meghan said blandly. 'We spotted them and showed them to Vikram.'

'We don't want the sites to become a tourist spot, ma'am,'

Kohli commented. 'Which is why we want you to deny the rumor.'

'You want me to say the JTF isn't interested in those places. That we have better things to do and are working on keeping Mumbai and the country safe.'

'Which isn't wrong, Suman.' Bose nodded his head.

'I am guessing you have signed off on whatever your team has come up with.'

'They are working on investigating whether that ISIS cell has planted any more bombs.'

'You want me to believe that?' Suman Shekhawat scoffed and then held up her hand to stop him from answering. 'I'll do it. My press conference is coming up shortly. I'll deal with those tweets then. What about Praveen Kumar?'

'He's not to be mentioned, Suman.'

'Anything suspicious from him?'

'No. He's either extremely smart or he's innocent.'

'We are taking a big risk by keeping his identity from the home minister and the prime minister.'

'Let's give it a few more days and see where we get to with the ISIS cell's interrogation.'

Suman Shekhawat put on her glasses, signaling the meeting was over.

'You think it will work?' Beth whispered when they filed out of her Mumbai office.

'We'll hit the buildings tonight and see.'

MISHA BECAME AWARE OF THE TWEETS ONLY WHEN SUMAN Shekhawat categorically denied that the JTF was investigating any under-construction buildings in Malabar.

He brought them up on a map and turned on satellite images. He was studying them when he felt a shadow over his shoulder.

'Are those the buildings the tweets mentioned?'

'You know of them?'

'No, but I looked them up when the press conference mentioned it,' Nazyr replied. 'Why would the JTF think we or the terrorists are hiding there?'

'We, not the bombers,' Misha corrected him. 'The Indians think the ISIS cell they captured in Ghaziabad are the terrorists. They are now looking for us. Those buildings are good cover, that's why they suspect we could be there. Civilians will not suspect we could be hiding in them.'

'Who will be looking for us? The entire task force or just the Americans?'

'Let's watch those buildings and then we'll know. But before that, let's fill them up.'

'Fill them up? With what?'

'Whom, not what. With several homeless people.'

'To fool the Americans' drones!' Nazyr caught on immediately.

'Da, and then we pick one building and wait for them.'

The Russian shut his laptop and looked around. Leopold Café was crowded, but no one was paying them any attention. They were another couple of foreigners in the crowded restaurant, with several languages and accents floating in the air.

'Have you heard of Sergei Petrov?' he asked his companion.

'Da. Hasn't he retired from the game and settled down here, in Mumbai?'

'Yes. He's one of the few who's still alive from those days. I never met him but know a few agents who worked with him. They all said he was one of the smartest and deadliest agents our country produced.'

Nazyr shook his head in confusion. 'What's he got to do with any of this?'

'I heard he's looking for us.'

'Petrov? He knows our names?'

'No, but he's got your sketch.'

The Chechen froze for a moment. 'How—'

'It's not surprising. There must be a few people from Crawford Market who remember seeing you. They must have described you to the police.'

'Why didn't they circulate the sketch?'

'Going public will be a last resort. They'll get thousands of crank calls if they do that. They want to find us before they do that. But none of that is important. Why's Petrov asking about us? That's crucial.'

'Let's ask him.'

'Da.' Misha patted his laptop. 'But first, let's check out Carter.'

CHAPTER 67

There were four buildings of interest. Two were on Walkeshwar Road and had sea views as the street went up the upscale, green neighborhood.

Suman's press conference was several hours ago. Enough time for Misha and Nazyr to pick one of the buildings and lay a trap for us.

If they watched it, Zeb told himself.

They will. If I were them, I would be following all official information and I would see the opportunity to sucker us in.

Zeb side-glanced to take in his team. They had split up and were drifting up the sidewalks on either side of the road, keeping pace with him.

'Nice place to live,' Beth whispered.

'If you have the money,' Bwana snarked. A Lamborghini was parked on the road to demonstrate his point.

The overhang from the tree line blocked many of the street lights, but there was enough ambient illumination for them to weave through the shadows.

Zeb waited behind one of the parked cars on the road while the sisters flew their drones high over the construction site of the first building. Several trees had been chopped down to clear the construction area, which hugged the slope to look over the Arabian Sea.

'Twelve floors, each one of them with two apartments. Basement parking, concierge service, biometrics-operated elevators, fancy security—'

'Are you reading the brochure?' Chloe asked.

'Nope, reciting from memory.' Beth tossed her head. 'But there are occupants!'

Zeb froze. He peered over the top of the car he was crouching behind and looked down the dusty track that led away from the road. A rope barrier with a sign on it warned civilians to keep away from the site. He could make out concrete-mixers, diggers and bags of sand on the ground, and beyond them was the dark shape of the tower.

No lights in it.

'Are you sure?'

'Yeah. About eight or nine people on each floor.'

'What are they doing?'

'Sleeping.'

'They could be the workers,' Bear offered. 'Several construction companies use contract companies for labor. Those firms employ folks from all over the country.'

Zeb nodded. The workers were a common sight in the city. They were impoverished, drifted from project to project, and often lived near the sites in crude tents.

'Mumbai. City of dreams built on the backs of the less fortunate,' Broker said grimly.

'That's the case in every country.'

'It's different, here. The inequality is in-your-face.'

'Let's debate the development of countries and their social systems later,' Meghan said impatiently. 'Zeb, the construction firm on this project is reputable. I don't think they would allow workers to sleep inside the site.'

'Homeless people?' he guessed.

'Yeah.'

'Let's check it out.'

'Take over my drone too,' the older twin told her sister, who responded with a thumbs-up.

Meghan jammed her screen in her backpack, tightened its straps and joined Zeb, Bwana and Roger.

They ghosted down the track, filtering through the equipment on the ground until they came to the steps.

'No snipers, no hostiles, none of those folks have moved,' Beth informed them.

Zeb went up the stairs carefully. Loose gravel crunched beneath his feet.

Can't do anything about those sounds. Beth will warn us if anyone moves.

The sounds of snoring on the first floor. Shapes huddled beneath thin blankets. A child cried briefly and then fell silent.

He picked his way carefully down the passageway and returned to his friends who were covering him from the stairs.

'Civilians.'

They checked out the remaining floors and returned to ground level forty minutes later.

'Clear,' he told Beth when they joined her and the rest of the crew.

'The next building is up the road.'

'The third one is deeper inside, right?'

'Yeah. Off Ridge Road, near a temple. Several other residential towers near it, all of them occupied.'

'Let's check that one out.'

'A more crowded neighborhood. Offers more protection,' Bwana agreed.

Twenty minutes to climb up Walkeshwar Road, cut through the parking lots of several buildings, scale their compound walls, circle the Malabar Hill Police Station to get to Ridge Road.

Zeb could see the temple's dome rising between the shapes of two buildings. Its flag fluttered and snapped in the light breeze. He looked down at the screen in Beth's hand when she came abreast.

'It's at the end of that lane that shoots off from Thakkar Marg. The temple is ahead of it.'

'That's where I would hide,' Zeb murmured. 'That temple ... it makes people instinctively think there won't be anything hostile near it. I would pretend to be one of the homeless people—'

'There are eight of us, only two of them,' Chloe objected.

'We know only two names. There could be more. But our numbers don't matter. They can't take us out all at once. They can cut us down, however.'

'And escape in the night,' Meghan agreed. 'We have our drones, but once they are out of the construction site, there are a lot of other buildings they can run through or hide in. Our birds can track them for sure, but they could take hostages or merge with a crowd, like climbing into a night bus.'

'That's assuming they aren't thermo-camouflaged,' Beth countered.

'Yeah,' her sister agreed.

They'll have the advantage. Zeb went down the lane and past a rubbish bin. A rat darted across the road and disappeared in the darkness.

'Our approach is good,' Meghan briefed them. 'No floor on that building can see this road. We won't be visible until we enter the site.'

'They probably know how we operate,' Broker whispered. 'They'll be aware of our drones.'

'Yeah. They won't take sniping positions. That will give them away.'

Misha and Nazyr. They'll be pretending to be asleep. Both of them on the same floor or they might split up.

Zeb weighed it over as he picked his way through the lane.

They'll be on different floors! He was sure of it. *They can cover each other if they are together, but they want to kill me. They want to eliminate us. Splitting up gives them the best chances.*

'This is a taller building. Twenty floors. But there are fewer people sleeping in it. Only the first four floors are occupied and that too, only four or five people on each one,' Meghan said.

'How many apartments on each floor?' Roger asked.

'Four, but none of them are constructed. Their walls haven't gone up. All the sleepers are in the central passages.'

Zeb entered the construction site.

His mind emptied automatically.

He became one with the night as he moved in its darkness and headed towards death.

CHAPTER 68

Misha hugged his blanket and adjusted his position on the hard floor.

A man snored loudly nearby. He thought of kicking the sleeper to silence him but refrained. He confirmed that his AK74 was close to his hand and that his blade was near his left palm. He had several spare magazines and plate armor beneath his thick jacket.

He was ready.

'Remember,' he whispered in his collar mic. 'Wait for them to get close. If there are two or more of them, don't attack. Go for it if there's only one American. But even then, be careful. They will be covered. You need to kill quickly and then jump off the floor.'

'Yes,' Nazyr replied impatiently. 'I haven't forgotten. How will we know it is Carter unless he gets close?'

'I told you.' Misha gritted his teeth. 'We take out whoever we can. If it is Carter, that's great, but the rest of his team need to die, too. That's why it doesn't matter who you kill tonight. We'll get other chances. Do you remember the escape route?'

'Da. How many times are you going to ask the same questions? I'll jump to the ground, climb over the wall and get into the temple. The Americans can't cut it off because the approach to my landing is blocked off by those trucks, the diggers and equipment. I'll run to the building to its right, and from there I can either go to the bus stop outside—'

'There is a late night line there always. We checked that. You can blend in there but before that you have to get rid of your weapons and remove your balaclava. I'll be taking the same escape route.'

'I know. Why am I on the fourth floor and you on the third?'

'It doesn't matter. Be quiet and stay alert.'

It did matter, though.

I want to be the first to get to Carter.

He looked out through his eyeholes and confirmed the passage was empty. The floor ended behind him, with the drop to the ground and the night beyond it.

In front of him was the central walkway and in the gloom, he could make out the landing where the stairs joined it.

Carter will come from there.

ZEB WAITED AT THE LANDING OF THE FIRST FLOOR, crouching, checking out the left and right flanks. Meghan and Bwana behind him, lying down the steps, their heads to the floor, surveying the floor too.

Bear, Chloe, Broker and Beth outside, on the ground. They hadn't been able to circle the building because of the sand trucks and diggers at the rear.

They'll cover the front. They'll warn us if any sleeper rises.

He motioned with his hand and went down to the left. He ignored the crunch of gravel. Hands on his HK, no effort to hide it.

Because I want Misha and Nazyr to see it. I want them to attack.

It was a high-risk move, painting himself to be the target, but it was the only way to flush out the killers.

'Our armor is good but is not very effective against knife attacks,' Beth reminded him. 'You should have worn a helmet.'

No. I want them to see me.

He went down the floor and waited near the two sleepers. Neither of them stirred. They continued breathing softly, their bodies relaxed.

Nope, they aren't hostile. They aren't faking their sleep.

He returned to the landing, went past it to check out the three shapes on its right.

Their faces were uncovered. Two women, one bearded man who was clearly not Russian or Chechen.

'First floor, clear.'

'Copy that,' Beth acknowledged.

The second floor had four sleepers, three on one side of the landing and the last one on the other. A mother and her young son beneath a blanket, the child dragging down the sheet to reveal them. The two other shapes didn't move when he went near them. The last sleeper was uncovered as well. Not a hostile.

Third floor.

Two sleepers each, on either side of the landing.

Zeb went down the left.

The first shape snored with a whistling sound.

I'm sure that can't be faked.

The second one had a dark blanket that he couldn't make out clearly in the gloom. The person didn't stir, however and soft breathing came to him.

Zeb turned his back on the sleeper. Took one step towards the landing. Another one.

Heard the faintest rustle.

He dropped to a crouch before Bwana's *HOSTILE* roar echoed in his earpiece.

He spun on his heel to bring up his HK, which deflected the plunging blade.

First impressions registered instantly.

Tall broad man. Mask over his face, eyes glittering through the holes.

He isn't the Crawford Market shooter. This man is bigger.

No sounds, no curses or swearing as the attacker smoothly changed his move to catch and yank his HK forward, dragging Zeb along with it. The killer pulled his hand back to deliver another thrust.

Zeb turned his head back. Felt the blade slice through air a breath away. He rolled with his move, jerking his head sideways to catch the man's chin and let his body fall on the attacker's, which got the killer to step back.

Zeb slammed his fist into a hard belly, heard the man's breath leave in a grunt and thrust the HK at his face.

Can't shoot. My finger's nowhere near the trigger. Got to use it like a spear.

'DOWN!' Meghan yelled.

He threw himself to the floor.

The attacker read their intentions. He released the HK, slashed wildly in the air with his knife and jumped out of the floor just as rounds from the American operators punched the air.

'Missed,' Bwana said in disgust. 'He guessed we would fire.'

Zeb crawled forward cautiously and snatched a glance, ready to fire instantly. He saw the shapes of the equipment on the ground but didn't spot the attacker.

'He's down.'

'Copy that,' Broker responded calmly. 'He'll be at the back. We'll search for him. Is there a second man?'

A body fell through the air.

Zeb rolled across the passage as two shots burned the air.

'Unharmed. The bullets went wide,' Meghan said before he could ask.

'Second killer is down too,' he announced.

'I can't see either of them,' Beth said. 'They're either wearing thermal camouflage or are still hiding.'

'We'll search for them,' Roger confirmed.

Zeb searched the night for movement as he felt Bwana and Meghan come up from behind.

'We don't have a good view.' He cursed. 'That digger, those trucks, they could be hiding behind them. See that boundary wall over there? They can scale it and go across to the temple.'

'Thought of that,' Chloe said. 'Bear and I will check that getaway route.'

Zeb rolled onto his back and caught Bwana's outthrust hand to get to his feet. He went to the attacker's blanket and lifted it.

'AK74.' He picked up the rifle, examined it swiftly, removed a plastic pouch from his pocket and slipped it over the weapon to protect any prints on it.

'Why didn't he shoot?' Bwana asked.

'He couldn't, not when he was on the floor. Sure, he would have got me, but you and Meg would have killed him. He had to rise to attack, and must have figured the knife was quieter.'

'Hum police hain.' He went past the operators to the sleeper who had been snoring, who had propped himself on an elbow and was staring at them, perplexed. 'Who admi kaun tha jo idhar so raha tha?'

We are the police. Who was that man who was sleeping here?

'Pata nahin, saab. Woh so raha tha jab hum idhar aaye.'

Don't know, sir. He was sleeping when we arrived.

'Tum log building ke mazoor ho?'

Are you construction workers?

'Nahin, saab. Ek aadmi humme paise diya idhar aake sone keliye.'

No sir. One man gave us money to come and sleep here.

'Uska chehra dekha kya?'

Did you see his face?

'Nahin. Kuch to pehna tha chupane keliye.'

No. He wore something to hide it.

'He must have been masked,' Meghan murmured.

'Kitne baje mila tumko?' she asked.

What time did he meet you?

The man scratched his head. 'Shyam ke saat baje honge.'

It must have been seven pm.

'That was after Suman's press conference. They fell into our trap.'

'Yeah.' Zeb went to the stairs and bobbed his head towards the upper floor. 'Let's check out the rest of the floors, to be safe.'

CHAPTER 69

'Cover me,' Broker whispered as he went to the equipment at the back of the building.

'Don't,' Roger warned him. 'See how those vehicles are arranged to block entry to the back? They must be surrounding concrete bags to keep them safe from thieves. You'll be exposed to the other side as you climb. The killers could take you out from their cover. Beth, any sign of them?'

'Nope. Bear, Chloe?'

'We are nearing the temple's entrance. No one here that we can see,' the petite operative answered.

Broker thought about it for a moment. Roger was behind him and to his right. No sounds from behind the equipment. He looked up. The building loomed over him. He could make out its floors but couldn't see Zeb or the other operators.

'I'll sneak a look.'

'Don't,' Roger objected.

Broker ignored him. He clambered over the digger, his HK held in his right hand and looked over the barricade of equipment.

Concrete bags, piled high on the ground. Wheelbarrows, shovels, bricks and steel girders.

'Get back!' the Texan whispered harshly.

Broker jumped to the ground, on the other side of the digger.

The shadow came up from behind a pile of iron rods. Masked. His gun coming up, leaping across the air.

Broker dove at him and flung his left hand up to slap away the rifle. Bullets punctured the night over his head. He brought up his HK and was tightening his finger on the trigger when he was yanked back. His rounds went wide. He lost his grip on his rifle, which clanked to the ground. He managed to whirl around and saw the slashing blade and fell back but not far enough, as it cut a thin line across his neck.

Fury surged through him.

Instead of retreating, he thrust himself up with his right heel, blocked the return strike with his left arm and clawed at the attacker's face with his right.

The killer seemed to laugh.

The second man is behind me!

Broker felt arms wrap around his chest. He heard Roger shout in warning and heard him climb.

His fingers were stuck in the attacker's mask, which peeled away when the man shook his head.

Broker stared in shock at his face, kicked out wildly at the approaching blade, heard a round kick dirt, then the knife cut into him, and another blow knocked him out.

CHAPTER 70

Roger fired a long burst at the two men who had dropped Broker to the ground. His first few shots went into the ground. He thought he saw one of the men jerk but they ducked and weaved quickly to throw themselves behind concrete bags. He saw their heads bob and fired at them but they disappeared out of sight.

'I have them. Attend to Broker,' Beth said tightly. 'Bear, Chloe, they are going over the sidewall. Not to the temple.'

'Copy that.'

Roger went to his friend. He clamped down at his rising fear as he bent over him.

Running steps behind him.

Beth. 'I've called Vikram and Meera. EMTs are coming.'

They brought out their emergency gear and got to work.

ZEB WAS ON THE FOURTH FLOOR WHEN HE HEARD THE SHOTS. He, Meghan and Bwana were checking out the last sleeper when the younger twin called out.

'ZEB!'

He spun on his feet. Saw his expression of concern reflected on Meghan's face. She raced for the stairs with him and Bwana following.

They went down the steps, taking them two at a time. Megan slipped. Zeb caught her elbow, Bwana held the other, and they propelled her forward until she regained her balance.

Later, much later, he would look back and shake his head and think, *we were easy targets as we ran down those stairs.*

He wasn't thinking of later. It was the tone in Beth's voice that filled his mind until they reached the ground.

They rushed to the sounds of his friends. He was the first to vault over the digger. He landed on his feet and stood still, staring at the dark shape on the ground with Roger and Beth bending over it.

'Broker,' Beth said without looking up. 'He's not dead.'

No relief swept through him.

He knew what it meant.

His friend was in bad shape.

CHAPTER 71

Zeb wasn't conscious of time. He heard Roger and Beth's explanation. He was dimly aware of Bear and Chloe joining them.

'We lost them.'

The petite operator's words registered, but had no meaning.

'Punctured lung, for sure.' He heard an EMT tell Meghan. 'We'll have to examine him. The head injury looks bad. The first aid your team gave him helped.'

He watched his friend get loaded into the ambulance, which went out of the construction site and disappeared from view. He didn't move.

He was still there when Kohli and Meera spoke to him. He didn't know if he responded. They went away after a while.

DAWN BROKE. THE CONSTRUCTION SITE HAD BEEN SEALED OFF. Mumbai Police maintained a perimeter while JTF teams questioned the sleepers, the building company and residents in the surrounding buildings.

'Remember when he was like this?' Beth whispered to her sister.

'Yeah. When Broker was attacked by the Baseball Bat Killer.'

'His injuries are similar to what he sustained then. Traumatic brain injury. Ruptured lung. He wasn't in a coma then, though. Then, Zeb didn't leave the hospital for several days.'

The older twin nodded. She eyed their friend, who stood as if carved from rock, paying no attention to what was going on around him. He had been almost motionless for an hour as police officers, JTF agents and the Agency operators swirled around him. He had shaken his head at offers of coffee and answered in monosyllables. He had handed over the AK74 to Meera wordlessly and had ignored her questions.

Meghan took over. She briefed their RAW friends who had since left, but the Agency operators remained.

Zeb and Broker go way back. They were Clare's first recruits.

She looked over at her sister, whose face was pinched as she gnawed her lip and kept checking her phone for hospital updates. Bear and Chloe were conversing softly while Bwana and Roger stood a distance away, their faces granite-hard.

We haven't lost a team member in all the years we've been together.

That statistic amazed her whenever she thought of it. They took on lethal assignments in the world's deadliest hotspots as they pursued terrorists and threats to national security.

We have been hit. We have broken our fingers, dislocated our shoulders. Beth's got a boyfriend, Broker has his girlfriend, Bwana and Roger have their partners ... in all that, our team has remained intact.

She shivered and prayed mentally that Broker would recover. *And get back to his old self.*

'Any news?'

Her hand shook at the voice. Coffee from her paper cup spilled on her wrist and burned it, but she didn't feel it.

Zeb! He's snapped out of it.

'He was operated on.' Her voice shook and then steadied. 'Remember New York? Back when—'

'Similar injuries?'

'Worse. He was knifed twice. Both in the lungs. The blade

missed his heart by millimeters. The second piercing was when he was unconscious as far as the medics can tell. They hit him as well. He's in an induced coma. Stable.'

'He should recover,' Beth said fiercely.

'Do you know what happened?' Bwana asked.

Zeb nodded.

'I told him not to go over the digger,' Roger growled. 'He didn't listen. Why did he do that?'

Zeb squeezed the Texan's shoulder. A gesture to say that it wasn't Roger's fault. His friend gripped his palm and returned the squeeze in acknowledgment.

'He wanted to prove himself.'

'Prove himself? To whom?' Bear reared back in astonishment, staring at Zeb.

'To us. He knows he's older than all of us. I've noticed he's become more conscious of it in the last few years.'

'THERE'S NOTHING TO PROVE!' Chloe exclaimed, unshed tears in her eyes.

'I know that.' Zeb nodded. 'Every one of us is aware of that, except him. He thinks he has to show us he still has it, that his age isn't slowing him down.'

'It isn't! And even if it did, our missions have so many roles that he can take on. Does he think we are going to replace him with someone younger? Does he think we are going to leave him back in New York, to sit at a desk and answer the phones? This is Broker! He's got more experience and judgment in his little finger than I have in all of me.'

Beth laugh-sobbed and hugged her tight.

'I'm going to punch sense into him when he recovers,' Bear growled.

Zeb bumped fists with him at his choice of words. *When, not if.*

He balled up his worry and buried it deep inside. His fury was smoldering, ready to explode, but he controlled it, too. Anger had its uses. There was a time to call on it. It wasn't then.

He felt his friends' eyes on him.

'I'm okay. Let's visit Broker.'

CHAPTER 72

St. Elizabeth's Hospital was less than half an hour away from the construction site.

'We got lucky there,' Meghan said as they approached it. 'It's one of the city's best multispecialty treatment centers. Vikram made a call and there was a medical team there to receive Broker.'

She led the way into the tiled lobby where a JTF agent directed them to Broker's room on the second floor.

Zeb brushed past the armed police presence and watched his friend through the glass window of his recovery room. A monitor in a corner, with dials, digits and a graph running across its screen. A tube going from his friend's face to another machine to help him breathe. His head was bandaged, his chest was covered by a sheet, his face, though gaunt, looked peaceful.

Zeb's fists curled when the darkness inside him broke the tight band of his control. It filled him and dimmed his vision momentarily. He breathed harshly, rapidly, until the rage abated, leaving behind a cold fury.

'Misha and Nazyr.' He could barely recognize his own voice.

'They are dead men walking,' Meghan said bleakly.

. . .

MISHA WATCHED THE AMERICANS EMERGE FROM THE HOSPITAL. He lowered his binos casually when a police cruiser drove past and pretended to check his phone.

'We shouldn't be here.' Nazyr fidgeted nervously from the backseat. Their rented Toyota's rear windows were tinted, making it hard for the Chechen to be seen from outside.

'We need to know if Broker recognized me and told Carter.'

'There is nothing on the news about you or us.'

'There won't be. You know how RAW and JTF work. They haven't even published your sketch. We need to know if Broker talked.'

He reached between his legs, drew out the dark-hair wig and put it over his head. He inserted black contacts in his eyes and examined himself in the driver's mirror.

He ignored Nazyr's protest and got out of the car and crossed the road confidently. He entered the lobby and went to the reception.

'What happened? Why are there so many police officers?'

'I can't tell you, sir. Do you have a doctor's appointment? Are you visiting a patient?'

'A patient. I am waiting for his family.'

'Please wait in the seating area, sir. As you can see, we are very busy today.'

He smiled at her polite brush-off and drifted away. He followed an attendant who was rolling a trolley and went with him to the men's bathroom.

He went to the sink and washed his hands while the attendant went into one of the stalls to clean it.

'Is he okay? That JTF agent who was brought in? I heard the police talking about him.' Misha asked as he was leaving.

The man wiped his sweat and raised his head.

'He is alive. He is in a coma, though. He hasn't spoken since he was brought to the hospital.'

'Will he live?'

'Who knows? I heard the doctors saying he was in a serious condition.'

Misha thanked him and went out of the restroom.

'We are safe for now,' he told Nazyr as he fired up the Toyota and drove away. 'But we'll have to visit the hospital regularly to see if Broker lives or dies.'

'Whatever happens to him, the Americans are down by one. That's a win.'

'Da. I should have emptied my AK at Carter, but I had a very small window to attack in and the knife was the best.'

They have my weapons and mask, but they will be useless. No one has my prints.

He grinned when he remembered how the American agents had cried in horror when Broker had fallen.

I would have liked to see Carter's face when he got to his friend's body.

His sneer turned into a cold smile.

One down, seven more to go.

CHAPTER 73

Eleven am. JTF's office in Nariman Point.

The conference room was filled with the Agency operators and JTF agents.

The room fell silent when Bose entered with Suman Shekhawat.

'We are okay.' Zeb forestalled their questions. 'We checked in at the hospital before coming here.'

His tone was flat, empty. It didn't encourage conversation.

'Did you see them?' Bose asked.

'He was masked when he attacked me. His eyes were shining, but I don't know if that was because they caught the light. I couldn't make out their color. Broker unmasked him but...'

'Yes, I understand. The second shooter?'

'We saw him falling,' Meghan replied. 'But none of us got close to him.'

'I thought one of my rounds got the second man in the leg,' Roger offered and shrugged. 'It didn't slow either of them down, though.'

'Our people didn't get anywhere.' Meera flicked her hair back in frustration. She used the remote to bring up Malabar Hill's map on the wall. She zoomed into the construction site.

'They must have hidden beneath trucks or cars and must have escaped when the coast was clear. They didn't enter any building. No traces of blood, either. If Roger shot that man, it must have been a graze or a very slight wound.'

'They were counting on us not following them.' Bear cracked a knuckle, the sound loud in the room. 'They were correct.'

'It was the right thing to do,' Bose told him. 'They could have had more shooters. Remember the CST attack? They hired killers to come after you.'

'Prints?' Zeb asked.

'The mask, knife and AK are with our lab. We should get the results any moment now,' Kohli said. 'I am guessing there won't be a match.'

'Yes. These two are pros. That man wouldn't have given up his rifle so easily if he knew his identity could be blown.'

He felt Suman's gaze and smiled briefly. 'No, ma'am,' he answered her unasked question. 'This isn't how we expected our plan to go down.'

He turned to the RAW officers. 'Anything from the ISIS cell?'

'They weren't talking at first. We questioned them again.' Meera smiled briefly to convey it was code for aggressive interrogation. 'They denied involvement. They *were* planning attacks but weren't responsible for the Mumbai explosions.'

'They would say that,' Kohli growled.

'Yes.' Bose straightened and glanced at his watch. 'We still think they are responsible, but we need confessions.'

'Praveen Kumar?' Suman asked.

'If the ISIS cell doesn't break in a day or two, we'll bring him in.'

Zeb jammed his hands in his pockets. He knew what their taut faces meant.

Riots, when Kumar is arrested, and an escalation between Pakistan and India.

CHAPTER 74

Nawaz Khan wasn't idle. After sending his family to a safe house in Peshawar, he began hunting down who had been behind Salim.

He briefed the prime minister first, who told him to leave no stone unturned in his pursuit. The ISI chief had been meaning to do that in any case, but having political backing never hurt.

He interrogated his entire CPO team. Hostile interrogation in a hot, dark room which stank of urine and human misery.

Several hours later, he was convinced the rest of his men and protection team weren't involved.

He got Salim's family brought in. Elderly parents, a sister, and a brother.

He didn't have to go the hard route on them. His harsh voice was enough to break them, but they too didn't have anything for him. None of them believed Salim would have attempted to kill his boss. He had never spoken bitterly about Khan and, in fact, had praised the ISI chief.

Khan let them go. He investigated Salim's bank accounts. Nothing suspicious about the transactions. Incoming salary, outgoing expenses, money sent to family.

He looked into the man's travel and there were two visits to

Lahore in the month before the attack. A city he hadn't ever been to.

'What's there?' he barked at his agents. 'It can't be for tourism. Both times, he stayed just one night. Does he have a girlfriend there? A friend? FIND OUT!'

His agents scrambled while another team questioned the golf club members and reported back that none of them were involved in the attack.

The Lahore team found out that Salim had been to a five-star hotel both nights.

'There is no record of his staying there, sir.'

'It might have been erased.'

'Yes, sir. Our tech team is looking into that.'

'You have nothing else?'

'Sir, the doorman remembers his meeting someone in the bar.'

'Bar? Salim didn't drink.'

'Yes, sir, but he was there. We have a photo of this man.'

Khan leaned forward with interest as his agent showed him a picture on his phone.

'The doorman was taking a selfie and the camera caught Salim and this man. There is no other record of their being present in that hotel. CCTV feed has nothing.'

'It has been erased.'

'Yes, sir. We found this man's identity. Hidayat Ahmed. He is a shady character. He has a carpet export business in Lahore, he has an office, but there don't seem to be any employees.'

'So what? Plenty of businesses have no staff.'

'Yes, sir, but we looked into his tax records and if we believe them, he is exporting millions of dollars' worth of carpets all over the world.'

'US dollars?'

'Yes, sir. The Lahore Chamber of Commerce hasn't heard of him.'

'Bring him in.'

And so, while Broker was being attacked in Mumbai, an ISI team broke into an upscale residence in Lahore, knocked out the woman on the bed, bundled up the man and carried him to a waiting car.

When Zeb was in St. Elizabeth's Hospital, Hidayat Khan was tied to a chair in an empty factory on the outskirts of Karachi.

Nawaz Khan, in an immaculate white shirt tucked into a pair of razor-sharp creased blue trousers, gleaming shoes and a belt buckle with ISI's logo on it, approached him.

He held out his hand and an agent put a knife in his palm.

The ISI chief plunged the blade in Ahmed's shoulder without any warning.

'Why did you meet Salim?' he asked conversationally after the man's screaming had died down.

Ahmed didn't break quickly. It took close to an hour, aided by slashes across his chest, burning coal applied to his groin and an eyelid to be torn off before he admitted he knew Salim.

It turned out that the bodyguard had a gambling addiction. He bet money on cricket matches and usually lost his wagers. He borrowed from loan sharks and his debt had reached unsustainable levels.

'How did you find out about his gambling?'

'The lending brokers were my people,' Ahmed gasped.

'You promised to pay off the debts if Salim killed me,' Khan guessed.

The carpet trader shrieked and jerked when an agent applied hot coal to an open wound.

'Yes,' he sobbed.

'Why? I don't know you. ISI has never harassed you. Why did you want me dead?'

'I was told to.'

'By whom?'

Ahmed resisted.

It got an ISI operator plunging a blade in his groin to break the man.

He mentioned a name and then Nawaz Khan understood what was going on.

'Where can I find him?'

'I don't know. We have never met. We speak on the internet. We use a real-estate agent's website to leave messages.'

Khan knew how that worked. Ahmed posed as a customer and enquired about properties. The mastermind decoded his questions and replied back.

He looked at the carpet trader dispassionately.

He's telling the truth.

'Keep him alive,' he told his agents. 'He could be useful later on. No one should know he's here.'

He got his driver to take him to the airport and took the ISIS aircraft to Islamabad.

He met the prime minister and briefed him.

'Find this man,' the country's leader ordered. 'Quickly and quietly. Do you need other agencies—'

'No, sir. We don't know whom to trust.'

'I agree.'

'I will replace your protection with my hand-picked team. Do we tell India, sir?'

'No. It's none of their business. Besides, they are the ones threatening a nuclear war with us.'

Khan's heart warmed. The prime minister was a man cut from the same cloth as he.

He left the office and returned to the airport.

The ISI chief was a cold, emotionless, ruthless man who manipulated every opportunity to promote his own interests.

He thought briefly of Carter. He fingered his phone.

He owed nothing to the American. That the Agency man had saved his daughter and his life meant nothing.

Nevertheless, he sent a message.

CHAPTER 75

Zeb was looking out of the window of the JTF office that evening. The sun was still beating down brightly over a city in which traffic had resumed, and while there was still a restriction on movement at night, daytime normalcy had returned.

Like other world cities, Mumbai was resilient.

It will bounce back. Like Broker will.

He turned when the door opened. Kohli and Meera. Wooden expressions on their faces.

'No luck with prints?' he guessed.

'Yes.' Kohli slammed his palm on a desk. 'Your agencies, Interpol, none of them have anything on those prints. That balaclava mask has no label on it. It's made of cotton. It could have been bought in millions of shops around the world. The AK has its serial number filed off. It is a used weapon but again, no link to any attacks or kills around the world.'

'He was tall,' Zeb mused. 'About an inch more than me. He was broad too, but moved very fast. He is definitely an experienced operator. He could be Spetsnaz.'

'He could be the Chechen, a Kadyrovtsy,' Meghan interjected.

'The Russians thought those killers, the Kadyrovtsy, would be a force multiplier in Ukraine. Look how that's turned out,' Roger scoffed.

'Don't write them off,' Zeb said. 'There are individual fighters in that group who are exceptional.'

'They are Chechnya's president's private militia, aren't they?' Meera asked.

'Yeah. They are part of the National Guard Service. That country is a Russian republic. It isn't a sovereign country. Its leader was installed by the Russian government and after his death, his son has taken over as president. He offers the Kadyrovtsy fighters to the Russians whenever they ask for reinforcements. Yeah.' He looked at Meghan. 'He could be the Chechen, but I have a hunch it was the Russian. Misha. Nazyr is likely the shooter in Crawford Market.'

'We sent those names to all our allied agencies, even the Russians. No results.'

'Would the Russians acknowledge one of their trained killers is in India?' Bwana sneered.

'They would, to us. Our relationship with that country is different from most of the West's.'

History. Zeb looked out of the window again to watch the sun, a giant reddish-orange ball, lower towards the Arabian Sea. *After India's independence, Russia made the effort to build a relationship with it.*

It was a strategic move to counter American influence and since then, the ties between the two countries had grown, with Russia backing India on various United Nations Security Council resolutions.

That's why the Indian government will not criticize Russia outright for its Ukraine invasion.

'There might be two people who know those names,' he said. 'Grigor and Petrov.'

'Grigor Andropov,' he explained at Kohli and Meera's

confused looks. 'A friend of ours in Moscow. He's well-connected. And Sergei Petrov. He's here in Mumbai.'

The RAW deputy's forehead creased. 'We know of one Petrov here. He's a philanthropist. He runs schools—'

'He used to be an SVR agent. He was very active in Afghanistan several years ago. No,' he said quickly at the RAW officers' expressions. 'He is retired. He isn't in that life anymore. He's dedicated to his charities. He is no threat to India. You have our word.'

'We'll take it,' Kohli laughed mirthlessly. 'We have enough on our plate right now. But you should tell us about him some time.'

'When this is over.'

'You'll ask him about Misha and Nazyr?' The setting sun's rays hit Meera, making her glossy hair shine.

'We will. Later today.'

Zeb patted his pocket and brought out his phone. He had powered it off when Bose and Suman had entered the room. He turned it on and scanned his messages quickly.

One from Nawaz Khan stood out.

Don't forget Azhar Mirza.

He stared at it for a second.

Why's Khan reminding me of him? I looked him up. He's not relevant to what's happening here. Kohli and Meera too don't think anything of him.

He shook his head and pocketed his phone.

Khan's problems weren't of any interest to him.

He can deal with his threats himself.

CHAPTER 76

'We can't attack him here, in the school,' Nazyr said. He looked up and down P.D. Mello Road and then at the yellow-colored building to their right.

'Where do you think we should take him?' Misha asked him sarcastically. 'In the Dharavi school, which is in an even more crowded location? In his apartment building? Did you see the security on it? If we got past the guards, the elevators require biometric identification. There will be cameras. We don't have time to hack into them. No. His Wadala school is best. We will wait for it to be over and then question him.'

'He might not be alone.'

'I know he won't be. He's got two men with him, Viktor and Dmitri. Both of them worked with him in Afghanistan. Old agents. They help with his schools.'

'We kill them?'

'We have to. But only after finding out why Petrov is asking about us.'

'How did you know he is?'

Misha shrugged. 'I know people who know people, who know others. There are message boards, forums, websites in the dark internet. You know how it works. The SVR man in the

Mumbai Consul is an old hand too. He circulated the sketch. That ended up on one of the chat groups I monitor.'

'It wasn't Petrov who asked, then?'

'It was. The kot wants to know, was the request.'

'Kot,' Nazyr mused. 'That was Petrov's nickname when he was in the game.'

'Da. Cat. He survived so many attacks and missions, that's why they called him that. He has nine lives too.'

'They end tonight.'

The killers waited in their rented Toyota as they watched Mumbai go about its business. Misha tuned to the radio and followed the news. Nothing on Broker.

The JTF is still keeping it quiet.

Did Broker recognize me?

He thought about it.

Broker had seemed to freeze when his mask came away.

Was that because Nazyr came from behind him or he knew who I was?

Even if he did and he lives to tell Carter, it won't matter. We'll have to be more careful, that's all. The JTF and police have Nazyr's sketch, but no one has recognized him.

He snorted in amusement, turned down the volume and looked towards the school again.

'MISHA AND NAZYR?' ANDROPOV THOUGHT ALOUD. 'THAT first name is common. There could be hundreds of Russian soldiers with that name. Nazyr ... nyet. I can't think of anyone in our world with those names. Those who have a grudge against you. How are things in Mumbai?'

Zeb hesitated. They were still in the JTF's office, in a smaller meeting room. He was at a table with the Russian spymaster on a video call. His friends were ranged around him.

'What is it?' Andropov asked sharply when he didn't respond.

'They attacked Broker,' Bwana said flatly. 'He's in the hospital.'

'Svolochs,' the Russian cursed. 'How bad?'

'Bad. He's in an induced coma.'

'I'll ask around. I will lean on everyone I know. I'll get my agents to go through every record we have. If there is a Misha and Nazyr somewhere who have an interest in you, I will find out.'

'Thank you.'

'Ach. It is no problem. Find them. Find them fast.'

'We will,' Zeb promised and ended the call.

He sat unmoving for a long time and stirred when Meera and Kohli entered the room.

'Any luck?'

'Not yet.'

'We heard from the hospital. No change to Broker's condition.'

'Yeah, we're in touch with the medics too. He can't recover, though.'

Everyone stared at him, shocked.

'Yes, you heard what I said. Broker has to die.'

CHAPTER 77

'They are still inside.' Nazyr fidgeted.

'It might be a charity, but it's still a business,' Misha reasoned.

'It's nine pm! The school shut down long ago. How complicated could their business be? And, shouldn't we be inside the school's compound?'

'We will go. As soon as it becomes quieter.'

'They might come out by then.'

'If they do, we'll follow them.'

'I thought you wanted to question them in the school.'

'Da. Be quiet. We will go as soon as the traffic reduces. Be patient.'

Misha grinned at Nazyr's grumble. He patted his cargo pants' pockets to confirm he had spare magazines for his replacement AK74. A new knife was in a sheath strapped to his thigh. Plate armor underneath his jacket.

At a few minutes past ten pm, he opened the door and got out casually. Nazyr exited the passenger side and the two men crossed the road.

They entered the school's compound.

The main building was dark. No sounds.

Nazyr nudged his shoulder to point out the lights in the administration office.

'I saw,' Misha whispered irritably. 'Go and block the entrance.'

'How? There is no gate.'

'See those barrels at the wall? Let's line them up to block the entry road.'

'Petrov might come out of his office.'

'That's why we need to do this quickly, you fool. It will slow them down if they try to escape.'

'What if someone comes in and raises the alarm?'

Misha cuffed him on the shoulder. 'This is a school! Also, one for poor children. The only other people who come here are the students and the teachers. They are long gone.'

They hurried to the wall and found that the barrels were empty.

They must be used for some play activities.

He and Nazyr lifted them carefully and lined them inside the compound. They dusted their hands and Misha led the way to the office. He climbed its two steps and nodded approvingly when Nazyr stayed behind in the shadows.

He went inside the door.

Petrov was at a table, typing into a computer with Viktor and Dmitri opposite him, idly chatting.

'Sergei Petrov?'

The three men turned to him.

'Who's asking?' Dmitri spat the toothpick.

'The man the Kot was enquiring about.'

CHAPTER 78

Viktor leapt out of his chair before Misha had finished. He grabbed a glass paperweight and hurled it towards the door.

Misha ducked, sneeringly. He moved wide as Dmitri and Viktor circled him.

'You are the Crawford Market shooter?' Petrov asked. He had moved only to push his chair back from the table. He hadn't risen. He had a half-smile, as if he was utterly confident of Dmitri and Viktor's abilities.

'I heard you were asking for me.'

Misha didn't reach for his AK, which was strapped to his chest.

I won't use my gun if they don't.

He stepped back in the room to make space for himself and drew out his knife when the two attackers brought out theirs.

Dmitri and Viktor approached, making lazy weaves in their air with their knives.

They'll back me in a corner where I won't have room to go for my gun.

Misha lunged towards Viktor who stabbed defensively and at the last minute, pivoted, ducking low and cutting towards

Dmitri's belly, who shimmied back with a grunt and brought an elbow down on his back.

The killer jumped back as the two men closed in on him.

'You thought it would be so easy?' Dmitri chuckled as his blade nicked Misha's forearm. 'You could walk in here and take out the three of us?'

'Da.' Nazyr stepped into the room and blew away his head with a single shot.

CHAPTER 79

Misha pounced in the split-second of hesitation that followed.

Dmitri's body fell to the ground.

Viktor whirled at his approach but his reaction was a fraction slow.

Misha's knife sank into his throat. The killer drew it out, plunged it again, shoved the body to Nazyr and dove at Petrov, who was jumping out of his chair while clawing at a drawer.

Misha kicked at the desk, slamming it against the former spy, who stumbled back and lost his grip on the Glock. It fell to the floor.

Petrov roared in anger. He reached behind for his chair, caught it and swung it around single-handedly.

The missile smashed into Misha's shoulder.

The spy crashed into him, punching and kicking savagely.

'I can take him,' Nazyr called out.

'He's mine,' Misha said with gritted teeth. He reared back to escape Petrov's eye gouge and with a furious yell, went into the blows, absorbing the punishment, kicked out with his leg to render the man off-balance and cut him in the belly.

'Why were you asking for us?'

. . .

'BROKER HAS TO DIE,' ZEB REPEATED. 'MAKE A PRESS RELEASE. Announce that one of the American agents who was part of the JTF died in hospital.'

He got to his feet and put on his jacket.

'How will that help? Where are you going?' Kohli asked.

'It will reassure Misha and Nazyr that he died without talking. They won't disguise themselves ... assuming they weren't in the first place. They won't need to lie low.'

'It will be harder for us to find them if they go to ground,' Meghan agreed. 'Where are you going, however?'

'Petrov's school in Wadala. To see if he's found anything on these men.'

'You can call him,' Meera objected. 'Will he be still there? It's nine pm.'

'He'll be there. He's old school. He doesn't trust me. He'll talk more freely when I am in front of him.'

He went out of the JTF office before they could respond.

MEGHAN LOOKED AT HER FRIENDS.

'He's gone into that mode where he's trying to protect us. He'll insist on going alone everywhere.'

'We aren't having that, are we?' Bwana growled.

'Nope. You, me, and Beth will follow him. Let him take the lead. We'll back him up.'

Too many of us will be noticeable. She glanced at Bear, who winked in understanding.

Meghan went to the parking lot and approached it cautiously.

'He's gone,' she called out, at which her sister and Bwana joined her.

She climbed into her Range Rover, fired it up and drove out.

CHAPTER 80

Zeb drove swiftly through the light traffic. He glanced at his rear-view mirror to see if he could spot a second Range Rover.

They'll follow. Either Meg and Beth, or all of them.

He tried the school's number.

He got a dead line.

That was the land number. Why would that be disconnected?

He punched the gas and overtook a cab.

A sense of foreboding filled him as he threaded through Mumbai towards Wadala.

He came up to P.D. Mello Road twenty minutes later and parked his Range Rover half a kilometer away from the school. He walked towards it casually, checking out various vehicles on the road. None of them looked suspicious.

He got closer to the entrance and spotted the barrels inside.

Petrov's in trouble!

Zeb ran back to the nearest vehicles and confirmed they were empty.

He returned to the school and scaled its wall. A passing vehicle illuminated him briefly and for a moment, he wondered if the driver would slow down to shout at him.

The car went past.

He dropped into the school's compound lightly and listened.

No lights except for a single one in the office.

No sounds, either.

He cocked his head as a faint noise reached him.

Was that a groan?

He cursed himself for leaving in a hurry.

I've only my Glock and Spyderco with me.

They would have to do.

He scanned the office building.

No sentries that he could see.

He crouched-ran, picking his way over the ground. He climbed onto the porch and bellied to the ground as he crawled swiftly to the door.

The sounds were unmistakable as he got closer.

Repeated moans. Another voice speaking in a lower tone.

Zeb neared the door jamb. Light spilled out from the open door, illuminating a long rectangle of porch. No shadows, which meant there was no one near the entrance.

He brought out his phone and turned on its camera and angled it cautiously around the corner.

Upturned desk and chair. He thrust the phone deeper to get a wider field of view.

He could see legs. A body crouching over the fallen man, who groaned and thrashed.

'Tell me. You are brave, strong, but you know you want this pain to go away. Tell me who contacted you and I will end it.'

The speaker crooned in Russian and did something with his right hand, which made the victim wail and thrash.

Nazyr, at the crouching man's right shoulder. A thin smile on his face as he held an AK74 casually.

Two bodies beyond him, Viktor and Dmitri.

They must have heard of Petrov's enquiries.

Zeb ran it in his mind.

He would take out Nazyr. Kill shots to the chest and head.

He's less than fifteen meters away and well-lit.

He would have to get to his feet, crouch at the door, have a fraction of a second to train his Glock on the killer and fire.

It was doable.

Misha might dive to the floor, roll away and bring up his gun.

Need him alive.

Which meant leg shots, since those were the safest.

That too was doable.

Zeb withdrew his hand and left his phone at the door. Pocketing it would waste time.

He got to his feet.

Removed his Glock.

Crouched-walked to the door.

He turned his gun instantly on Nazyr, who felt his presence and reacted by throwing himself back and away and firing at the ceiling.

The lights went out.

CHAPTER 81

D*idn't expect that!*

Zeb dove to the floor and kicked with his feet rapidly to crawl along the wall, triggering his Glock in a long burst at Nazyr, who was firing in his direction.

The office had white walls which reflected the ambient light sufficiently for him to see Misha spring away from Petrov, roll on the floor and shoot at him as well.

Zeb scrambled to the corner.

This is why I shouldn't have come alone, he swore at himself as a bullet spat into the wall above him, showering him with concrete chips.

He couldn't shoot at both men. He had to pick one. He chose Nazyr.

Need Misha alive.

The Russian wasn't showing any mercy, however. He too, was moving continually on the floor, twisting and turning to get his aim better.

I can't survive this.

And then Nazyr's gun clicked on empty.

Zeb threw his Glock at the man and kicked out at the wall,

using it to lever himself in the air. He bounded across the room in a long lunge, feeling a round tug at his heel, sensing Misha change his aim and Nazyr whirling towards him, and then he was on the killer.

He grunted when the shooter's AK74 smashed into his side. He caught the barrel on its reverse, yanked it towards himself and punched a one-two at the man's throat.

He felt Misha rise and spun Nazyr quickly to use him as a shield.

'FINISH HIM!' the Russian yelled and then he was out of the door and Nazyr was punching back, quick short jabs that Zeb parried and blocked.

He danced on his feet at a leg sweep, blocked a raised knee and clubbed at an incoming fist; he slipped on a fallen weapon which gave Nazyr the opening to stab him in the throat with three fingers.

Zeb's vision blurred. He stumbled. He felt the killer reach down, saw the glint of light on a knife and gritted his teeth as he trapped the incoming wrist with both hands. He lashed out at Nazyr's feet and reversed his leg strike when Nazyr danced back, using the move to connect his toes with the killer's groin while holding on to the knife hand.

Nazyr howled.

His knife slipped.

Zeb caught it by the blade, tossed it in the air, snatched it by the handle and stabbed the killer, feeling the shock of knife meeting plate armor. He reached down and jammed the blade in the killer's thigh, withdrew it with blinding speed and knifed him in the second thigh. He ignored the rain of punches, head-butted Nazyr and flung him to the floor.

Zeb kicked the AK74 away, kicked Nazyr in the groin again and searched him swiftly. No other weapon.

He picked up his Glock and fast-changed its magazine, and went to the door where he snatched a glance.

No Misha in sight.

He could be anywhere. He could be in the darkness waiting for me to come out.

Zeb felt the move behind him.

He threw himself to the floor just as a chair crashed into the door. He rolled onto his shoulder, grunting heavily when Nazyr landed on top of him, and turned his head just enough for the blade clasped between the man's hands to slide past his neck.

'I'LL FINISH YOU! I'll—'

Zeb broke the man's teeth with a savage slash of his Glock's barrel. He struck the man again in the temple and with a massive heave, threw him away.

Nazyr couldn't move because of his injured thighs. He could only rear up and stab wildly with his knife, which Zeb evaded easily and with a chop, broke his wrist.

He dropped the Glock and grasped the knife and thrust it at Nazyr, intending to deflect it away from his neck at the last moment.

The killer didn't duck.

He leaned forward to thrust his throat at the blade, which sank into his flesh, cutting through cords and tendons as if they were butter.

'NO!' Zeb yelled.

Nazyr bared his lips in a bloodied grin, held onto his wrist and twisted and turned his head, preventing Zeb from withdrawing the knife and held on with his dying strength until his body shuddered and went limp.

Zeb stared at his dimming eyes in shock.

He heard pounding steps, let go of the man and picked up his Glock and dove towards the wall.

'DON'T SHOOT!'

Meghan entered the door. She scanned the room swiftly.

'Clear!' she spoke into her collar mic, at which Beth and Bwana entered the room with flashlights.

'Did you search the compound?' Zeb asked them.

'Yeah. No hostiles.'

Misha got away!

He bent over Nazyr.

'He killed himself.' He swore in disappointment.

'Killed himself?'

'He didn't escape from my knife. I'll explain later.'

He checked Viktor and Dmitri. Both were dead.

He hurried to Petrov and grimaced at the Russian's injuries. His belly was torn up, his guts were lying on the floor, and his chest was punctured in several places.

But he was still alive.

His eyes flickered and he reached up to grab Zeb's hand, breathing harshly.

'Dmitri ...' he whispered.

'He's dead. I checked.'

Petrov's grasp tightened. He shook his head. His eyes bored holes into Zeb.

'Dmitri ...' He breathed faintly, fell back and didn't speak any more.

Zeb knelt next to him for several moments and then sighed heavily.

He took Bwana's outstretched hand and hauled himself to his feet.

'Did you see Misha's face?'

'No,' he said bitterly. 'His back was to me when I entered the office and then Nazyr blew out the lights.'

He laid it out quickly for them and took the bottle of water Beth gave him. He drank gratefully and wiped his lips.

'Why did Petrov mention Dmitri?' Bear entered the room.

'All of you are here?' Zeb couldn't help the rueful grin.

'Yeah. We were the back up to Beth, Meg and Bwana.'

'I don't know what Petrov meant.'

He cocked his head at a vibrating sound. He felt his pockets and remembered he had left his phone at the door.

He retrieved it and accepted the call.

'Grigor,' he said and turned on the speaker.

'Zeb, about Misha—'

'He got away. I was this close to catching him.'

'He might be the most dangerous man you have come across.'

'You found out who he is?'

'Da. He's Dmitri Ruslan's twin. Nazyr is their adopted brother.'

CHAPTER 82

Zeb rocked back on his heels in shock. Chloe sucked in her breath sharply while Bear growled beneath his breath.

'Come again!'

'You heard me correctly the first time,' Andropov said without inflection. 'Dmitri's mother separated from her husband soon after the birth of the twins. She took Misha with her and went to her family in the Ural Mountains. She adopted Nazyr, a Chechen boy, when he was three years old. His folks had some family in the Urals too and they migrated from Grozny to join them. However, his parents died on that long, cold trek, leaving the young boy all by himself. Ruslan's mom brought him up as her own child.'

'How—'

'I am getting to that.' The Russian spymaster spoke over Beth. 'Dmitri reconnected with his mother when he joined the SVR. He found out about his twin and Nazyr and accepted them as his siblings. The three of them became very close ... but he deliberately didn't enter their details in any of his family records. We'll never know why. There are some rumors that he didn't want either of them to join the military or enter any of Russia's secret agencies. His plan worked only partly. The two men joined Kadyrovtsy and became elite killers in that organization. They kept their second names as Ruslan, but because they served in Chechnya, no one connected them to the Russian.'

'Dmitri Ruslan must have told them about us,' Zeb thought aloud. 'And when I killed him, they started their revenge mission.'

'Da. Once I knew who to look for, I could track them. They arrived in Moscow after you made off with Gorshky. They spent several weeks in the city. They must have been piecing together what happened.'

'They tracked our Lear and came to Mumbai.'

'Da. He looks similar to Dmitri, which is why he was masked. I guess his plan was to reveal himself once he had you.'

Makes sense.

'He must have heard of Petrov's enquiries—'

'Sergei?' Andropov asked sharply. 'Is he okay?'

'He's dead,' Zeb said heavily. 'His friends, too. Misha was torturing Petrov in his school when I arrived.'

'They got away?'

'Misha did. I killed Nazyr.'

'Tell me everything.'

Zeb broke it down for his friend.

'Sergei Petrov, Viktor and Dmitri did good. They tried to atone for their pasts.'

'Yeah.' Meghan nodded. 'They were committed to their charities.'

'Petrov took Ruslan's name when he was dying.' Zeb looked down at the man's body. 'Misha must have revealed his identity while he was torturing him.'

'Or, Sergei recognized him. Don't forget, he had connections everywhere.'

'How did you find out?'

'From a retired SVR agent. Dmitri Ruslan was his mentee. He went with him to the Urals once and that's where he met the twin and adopted sibling. He too never mentioned it to anyone and once he quit the agency, he wanted nothing to do with it anymore.'

'Zeb. Misha Ruslan is reputed to be one of the best Kadyrovtsy killers.'

And he's out there, alone, looking for revenge.

CHAPTER 83

'Nazyr Ruslan,' Bose said in satisfaction the next day, after Kohli and Meera had briefed the JTF team. 'We are getting there. We are nailing down the perps.'

'We don't know if he and Misha had anything to do with the bombings,' Zeb cautioned.

'They seem to have connected with the terrorists. That's obvious from their presence in Pingleshwar. And they sent those killers to attack you near CST. For us in Mumbai, they are involved as much as the bombers.'

He looked at the wall where Beth projected Dmitri Ruslan's photograph. 'Shall we circulate that to every TV station?'

'No. Let him think we still don't know who he is.'

'He could take you out with a long gun.'

'Several people have tried that.'

Zeb shifted on his feet as he looked at the image.

I was wrong about him and Nazyr. I thought they were sent by some agency to take us out. What else could I be wrong about?

The thought stayed with him after the meeting broke up and he and his team researched escape routes Misha could have taken.

It didn't leave his mind throughout the day. It nagged at him over lunch and when they reconvened in the conference room in the evening for another update.

'We need to check if the bombs are still in place,' Khalid told the leader.

'Why?'

'The JTF could have discovered them and are covering it up?'

'Why?' his boss repeated.

'So that we could walk into a trap.'

'What trap? These men will go to Dharavi on the fifteenth and trigger the bombs with a mobile phone.' He cocked his head at the silent killers in the room.

'I still think we need to make sure the explosives are still in place. Dharavi has been searched by the police several times.'

The leader drummed his fingers on the table as he looked at the TV.

'All right.' He nodded at Khalid. 'But, you go. These men cannot be seen.'

CHAPTER 84

The TV was on mute as usual during the briefing. Zeb glanced at it casually. His brow furrowed when images of the Indian and Pakistani prime ministers came up.

Threat of War, was the banner.

He read the subtitles for a few seconds and the nagging doubt in his mind surfaced.

'We will arrest Praveen Kumar today,' Bose was saying, with Suman Shekhawat nodding her head.

'Don't.'

Everyone turned to look at him.

'He was set up.'

He stood up so quickly that his chair toppled behind him. He didn't set it upright. Someone did that for him, but he didn't turn to see who it was.

It's so clear now. Why didn't I see it earlier?

'Set up?' Bose looked angrily at him. 'It's his name on the account. He hasn't hidden he's a member of Hindus For India.'

'I read his file. He's smart. Why would an intelligent person leave his prints on the bombing so obviously? He would have known that you would track down Hadi Asadi's rent payments.'

'What are you getting at?' Suman asked impatiently. 'Who set him up?'

'Azhar Mirza.'

CHAPTER 85

Everyone gaped at him.

'Azhar Mirza?' Kohli asked incredulously. 'He's not in Pakistan's army anymore. His own government is hunting—'

Bose cut him off with a raised hand. His face sharpened.

'Let Zeb explain. I want to hear this.'

'Nawaz Khan mentioned his name to me when I met him.'

'Khan? The ISI chief? When did you meet him?' Suman Shekhawat asked, astonished.

'In Karachi, ma'am. The ISIS cell tip came from him.'

'You didn't mention this.' She whirled on Bose.

'The fewer people who know, the better. You can see how it would go down politically ... that ISI had to help us.'

Her face cleared rapidly. 'Yes, I agree. Continue.'

'I didn't pay it any attention. He sent me a text yesterday, reminding me of Mirza. I didn't know why he sent it to me, then. Now, I do. Think of it. Mirza tried to mount a coup and failed. He's still there, however. In Pakistan. He is enormously wealthy and I have no doubt several factions in their military support him.'

'They do,' Bose confirmed.

'When he was active in the army, he waged not only a verbal war with India but also ordered their troops to shell your borders.'

'He didn't stop at that. We suspect he got their army to infiltrate our territory a few times. We pushed them back. He's got motive. He wants India destroyed. He has never hidden his hatred for us.'

'But why now?' Suman asked.

'He's preparing for another coup.'

CHAPTER 86

Bose's words rang in the room.

'That's a big leap,' Suman interjected.

'No, ma'am,' Zeb replied. 'I came to the same conclusion.'

'Explain.'

Meghan and Beth's hands shot up at the same time.

Bose smiled. 'I was wondering when either of you would speak.'

'Zeb's right, ma'am.' Beth grinned. 'It all makes sense. Mirza sets off these attacks in India. I bet he started the internet rumors too, about Hindu extremists. He set Praveen Kumar up. With his military intelligence connections and wealth, that wouldn't have been hard. He's got India and Pakistan close to war. The Pakistani prime minister's position is weak, politically. He isn't an elected leader. He was appointed to his role after the last PM lost the no-confidence motion against him. The current leader, while he is in the majority party, was seen as the most acceptable person and that's why he was chosen.'

'Mirza will come out of hiding,' Meghan took over. 'He'll mount his coup when tensions between the two countries rise further.'

'As if they aren't high enough,' Meera said somberly.

'Yeah. He'll declare himself to be the only person who can keep Pakistan safe from the evil neighbor.'

'And once he's in power, things are going to get worse between us and them.'

'Yes, ma'am,' the older twin agreed with the NIA head.

'It sounds plausible,' Suman said. 'But what about the terrorists? Who are they?'

'A kill team. He would have access to several such terrorists from his time in military intelligence.'

'The ISIS cell?'

'I think you'll find they had nothing to do with the bombings.'

'It isn't enough, however. A coup needs a critical point. What we have between India and Pakistan ... we have been here before. After Mumbai 2008 and a few times before that.'

'There will be at least one more bombing,' Zeb said softly. 'That will be the trigger.'

His words had a chilling effect. Suman crossed her arms as if to brace herself. 'All this is guess work.'

'Yes, ma'am. But I am sure that's how these events will play out.'

'In that case, when will the next bombing be?'

'On Fifteenth August. India's Independence Day. The target will be another Muslim majority residential area in Mumbai.'

CHAPTER 87

Khalid wasn't bothered that the hotel they were staying in had security cameras.

His cover was perfect. There was no reason for anyone to suspect him. Heck, he had met the shooters in Horniman Circle and no law enforcement agency had shown any interest in him or the leader.

He didn't disguise himself.

He went out through the lobby and flagged a taxi.

'Dharavi,' he told the driver.

'WHY WILL BOMBINGS IN MUMBAI STRENGTHEN MIRZA'S position?' Suman asked and then answered her own question. 'It is the day that matters, isn't it? On Independence Day, his internet army will say Hindu extremists want to eradicate Muslims from India. Those social media posts will influence our two governments. They might go to war on that day itself.'

'Yes, ma'am.'

'Call Khan,' she told Bose.

Most of the JTF agents left the room when the RAW chief

gestured at them, leaving only the Agency operators, Meera, Kohli and Suman with him.

He went to the speakerphone and asked to be connected to ISI's headquarters. The operator came back shortly and put him through.

'This is Aditya Bose, the chief of India's Research and Analysis Wing,' he said firmly in English. 'I want to speak to Lieutenant General Nawaz Khan.'

The operator overcame her surprise. 'He is not available, sir. Can I take a message?'

'If you don't put me through in the next second, you will be responsible for the India-Pakistan war.'

'Really, Aditya!' Suman whispered. 'That poor woman is just following her protocol.'

The operator connected him before he could reply.

'Bose,' Khan said curtly. 'What can I do for you?'

'Can you share everything you have on Azhar Mirza?'

'No.'

Bose's lips thinned. 'You messaged Carter about him. We worked out—'

'Get your army to back off from our borders. Tell your government to stop making threats and false accusations. *Then* we'll talk.'

'Khan, this is Suman Shekhawat. I am sure you know or have guessed what Mirza is planning. It affects both our countries—'

'Shekhawat.' Khan didn't use a prefix. 'You heard what I said. This call is over. Don't bother me again until your country makes progress.'

He hung up.

'That basta—' Bear began and bit his lip when Chloe glowered at him.

'Yes.' Bose smiled briefly. 'He is an ego-centric man.'

Zeb got to his feet.

'You have feet on the ground in Islamabad?'

'Yes.' Bose narrowed his eyes. 'Why?'

'Can you find out where Khan will be later in the evening?'

'Yes, we track the movements of all senior Pakistani ... but why?'

'I'll get the intel from Khan.'

'You're going to Pakistan?' Beth burst out.

'Yeah. Do any of you know a better or quicker way of getting the dirt on Mirza?'

None of them did.

'What of Misha Ruslan?' Chloe asked. 'He's still out there. He'll want revenge.'

'Finding these terrorists and defusing their bombs takes priority.'

CHAPTER 88

Khalid smiled as he stepped around a woman washing her child in a Dharavi alley. He ducked beneath washing lines and went past homes where women were cooking.

He crossed to Sule's office and heard the man's voice from within. He didn't stop or pause until he came to his target location.

'I am with the electricity company.' He showed his badge to the woman who was in the office. 'We got some complaints that your power was going off intermittently.'

She frowned as she took him in, in his blue shirt and trousers and carrying an equipment bag. 'No. It's working fine. Who made that call?'

'There must have been some mix-up in that case.' He laughed. 'I got my orders to check this out and fix it. Since I am here, why don't I inspect your fuse board and wiring?'

'Will you be turning off the power?'

'No. I will take a quick look and be out of your way.'

'Go ahead then.'

Khalid flashed a smile and went to the utility room where he knew the fuse board was. He confirmed no one was watching him or was anywhere in the vicinity. He went to the tables in the far corner on which cartons were stacked. They were dusty.

That's good. No one has touched them.

He raised one corner of a table with difficulty, unscrewed a leg, and looked inside.

It was packed with C4.

He knew that all the tables were coated with a chemical that prevented explosive experts and sniffer dogs from detecting it.

I did that myself. I also inserted the detonators and phone deep inside.

He screwed the leg back, tapped the rest of the supports and got back a solid sound.

Someone might see my prints on the table and might wonder.

He thought about it for a moment. There was no way he could cover his smudges with dust without attracting suspicion.

He shrugged.

No one comes to this room. Even if they do, the occupants of this place will not know what those smudges mean.

He wiped his hands on his pants and went to the office.

'Everything is in good condition.'

The woman nodded without looking up from the book she was writing in.

'That's good,' she said distractedly.

Khalid whistled as he left the place.

From surrounding rooms, the sounds of children playing or reciting came to him.

His eyes fell on a calendar nailed to the wall.

It was the thirteenth.

In two more days, there won't be anyone playing here.

CHAPTER 89

Zeb landed in Islamabad at nine pm.

He used his diplomatic passport to get through immigration.

'Pakistan Golf Club,' he told the taxi driver.

RAW's intel said that was where Nawaz Khan was dining.

The club was located in the Margala Hills, a scenic neighborhood in the capital city. Luxury cars on the patio, a turbaned doorman and several armed men who checked the identities of the arriving visitors.

The guards flicked through Zeb's diplomatic passport and waved him inside.

'I am meeting a friend in the dining room,' he told the receptionist, handing her his fake credentials. 'I'll find him.'

'Sir, you need to sign in. I can't see your name in the visitor list. What's your friend's name? Is he a member?'

'It's Lieutenant General Nawaz Khan.'

She glanced at the soldier in the lobby, who stared back impassively. She licked her lips and handed back his passport.

'You know where to find him?'

I don't, but the armed guard presence will guide me.

'Yeah,' he said confidently.

He went past the soldier and checked out the dining room. No sign of Khan.

He won't be in the open. He'll be in a private room.

Zeb searched the corridors until he came to a couple of armed guards blocking the route to a hallway that had just one door behind them.

'No entry. Go back,' one soldier told him brusquely.

Zeb didn't negotiate.

He charged at them, feinted at the last minute, snatched the weapon from the left sentry's hand, knocked out the second man with it and pointed it at the guard.

That was easier than I expected. They weren't expecting someone to run at them.

'STEP BACK!'

He back-walked until he came to the door, turned its handle, yanked it open and slammed it shut behind him.

Khan, in a meeting with two men, seated around a small table. A trolley with used dishes nearby. All three men whirling in surprise at his entrance.

Zeb pointed the rifle at the only sentry inside the room. 'Don't shoot.'

He turned to the men with Khan. 'OUT!'

'WHO ARE YOU?' one of them yelled.

'SIR, THIS MAN—' The guards burst through the door, aiming their guns at him.

'I know him,' Khan said expressionlessly. 'Leave the room,' he told his companions and his CPO.

'Sir, but—'

'I am not asking.'

The men glared at Zeb as they went out. The guards looked uncertain and then at Khan's nod, left and shut the door.

'How did you find me? Why are you here?'

Zeb took a long step, caught the ISI chief by his collar and flung him against a wall.

The door opened instantly at the crashing sound. The two

guards aimed their rifles at Zeb as they stared in disbelief at their boss, who picked himself up from the floor, straightened his clothing and turned to them.

'It's all right. Leave us alone.'

Zeb would have laughed at their expressions if it hadn't been for their taut fingers on their triggers.

'SUNA NAHI KYA? JAO!'

Didn't you hear? Go!

The guards reluctantly backed out and shut the door again.

'You came this close to dying,' Khan snarled at Zeb.

'Yes, but I would have killed you first. Where is Azhar Mirza? What do you know about him? I am aware of the coup he's planning. He's behind the Mumbai blasts. He has stoked up the tension between India and Pakistan. WHERE IS HE?'

'Sir, are you okay?' a guard yelled from outside.

'Yes. Don't disturb us.'

The ISI chief turned to Zeb. 'I have nothing to tell you. I gave you his name. I don't know anything about a coup—'

'He was behind your assassination attempt, wasn't he? He got Salim to go after you.'

'Were you with Bose and Shekhawat when they called me? You heard what I told them?'

Zeb took in his hard expression. He smiled.

'Within the next hour, every newspaper and TV station will know who Zeba is. They will know that the cover you made for her is a false identity. Social media will pick that up. Before the night is over, the entire world will know Nawaz Khan's daughter is working in a law firm in LA. Your enemies will know, too.'

'YOU ARE THREATENING MY DAUGHTER?' Khan lunged across the table with his hands outstretched.

Zeb slapped him, a hard blow that threw the man back into his chair.

'Yes. Because you are playing with the lives of hundreds of millions of people. If you don't tell me about Mirza, all bets are off.'

Khan's face worked in anger. He cursed Zeb and his hands twitched.

'We don't know where he is,' he said coldly when he had regained control. 'We think he's hiding somewhere in the Hindu Kush Mountains. We suspect he's got a base there.'

'He's planning a coup?'

'Yes.'

'He's behind the Mumbai attacks?'

'His people are.'

'Why didn't you share that with India?'

'Why should I?' Khan sneered. 'Are you forgetting they are our enemy?'

Zeb thought about arguing with him and then gave up.

He's a hard-liner. No amount of debate will convince him.

'Do you know who his men in Mumbai are?'

The ISI man didn't move.

Zeb brought out his phone. 'Zeba.'

Khan swore at him and went to the door.

'Riyaz!'

One of the men ran up.

'Come inside, shut the door.'

The man did his bidding.

'Show this man the photographs of Mirza's Mumbai men.'

'Sir?'

'Show him.'

Riyaz nodded hastily, unlocked his phone and showed Zeb two images.

'Junaid Mahar and Khalid Gul.'

'Who are they?'

'Tell him,' Khan ordered.

'Mahar was a Lieutenant Colonel in the army, Gul was a captain. They are close associates of Mirza. Like his right-hand men. They planned his first coup.'

'They are in Mumbai, right now?'

'That's what we believe. They have dropped out of sight. We don't think they are in Pakistan.'

'They set off the bombs?'

'Mahar executes Mirza's vision,' Khan said reluctantly. 'He won't get his hands dirty, however. That's Gul's job. Looks like they outsourced some of the bombing to third parties, going by Hadi Asadi. But yes, those two are key.'

'Do you know where they are holed up?'

'No.'

'Do you know what else they are planning?'

The ISI chief hesitated.

'They will carry out a devastating attack on Mumbai on India's Independence, which will make Mirza come out of hiding and mount his coup.'

'He has enough support for that?'

'The most powerful generals are with him. He has promised them cabinet positions.'

'Your prime minister knows?'

Khan dismissed Riyaz and, when the man had left, shook his head. 'Not yet. I came to know only today. We have been interrogating Mirza's associates and piecing together the picture.'

'Send me Mahar and Gul's photographs and files.'

'Both of them have diplomatic passports.'

'They are using their own identities?'

'No, otherwise we would have found out where they are staying. But they will use those passports to escape.'

'Are they like you?'

'What do you mean?'

'Hard-liners. Do they hate India?'

'They share Azhar Mirza's views. That India's destruction is the only solution for Pakistan's well-being.'

'Don't you believe that too?'

'I want India humiliated, not destroyed.'

Zeb didn't debate geo-politics with him.

'Share everything that you have, not just on Mazhar and Gul but on Mirza too. You know what's at stake.'

'Yes,' Khan said savagely. 'The hundreds of millions of Indians.'

'Yes. But Zeba, too,'

CHAPTER 90

Ten am in the JTF office the next day.

'You would have done that?' Meera asked wonderingly when Zeb had briefed them on his meeting. 'You would have leaked Zeba Khan's identity?'

'No.' He grinned. 'I would have beaten the intel out of him, but using her name was quicker and scarier for him.'

'Circulate those photographs to every police station in the city and every agency in the country,' Bose commanded to Rahul.

'They have to be discreet,' Zeb told him. 'If Mahar or Gul find out they are made, they might set off the explosions.'

'There are thousands of officers in Mumbai,' Chloe murmured. 'Can they—'

'They *will* make quiet enquiries,' Bose completed grimly. 'Suman and I will personally visit every agency's office in Mumbai and brief their chiefs. Good work.'

He squeezed Zeb's shoulder and left the room with the NIA head.

'They will be disguised.' Beth frowned as she read through the men's files rapidly. 'They might stay in a hotel, either together or separately.'

'Together,' Meghan insisted. 'They will want to minimize being out there in the open.'

'Yes, that's my guess too.' Meera nodded. 'We'll organize calling teams. We'll run their photographs through our facial recognition software. We have cameras at the airport.'

'Not just there. We installed several all over the city,' Kohli added. 'In Muslim majority areas, at traffic junctions. We have got a much wider coverage than we did several weeks ago.'

Zeb and his crew followed the RAW officers out of the office to a lower floor where they briefed a roomful of agents, who dispersed and went to rows of desks and began calling.

RAW's tech team were in a separate office. Large screens on the wall showed live footage from various parts of the city. A wall of servers hummed softly. Aircon turned to full blast. One of the women in a crisp white shirt and blue jeans nodded at Kohli's instructions, took the photographs and went back to her seat.

'What about Dharavi?' Zeb frowned at the wall. 'I don't see any feed from there.'

'That's down to Sule!' Kohli made a face. 'He got his men to take down our cameras. He said he doesn't trust us.'

'But—'

'He said Dharavi can protect itself. We reached a compromise. He allowed us to cover some of the entrances, but not all. I'll be going there later today to convince him to install cameras at the remaining ones, too. This isn't the time for ego games.'

Zeb nodded and cocked his head when Meghan came to him.

'We'll take their live feed and run it through Werner too,' she said under her breath.

'Our facial recognition is better than theirs?'

'I don't know. Kohli and Meera are tightlipped about their software. But it won't hurt.'

He squeezed her shoulder and went to the window. He felt restless. *There's nothing I can do here. It will be down to the software and RAW's callers.*

'I'm going to the hospital,' he told the twins.

They gave him a thumbs-up without looking up.

'I'll come with you.' Bwana, hard-faced.

'Me too,' Bear said.

'We'll stay here.' Roger met his eyes. Chloe nodded too.

Zeb went out and put on his shades. He surveyed the busy street for several moments before stepping into the sunlight with Bwana ahead of him.

'You don't need to do that.'

'Like hell I don't,' the African-American growled. 'Misha might be out there in a car with a long gun.'

'He won't be. He'll know there are cameras around this building. In any case, taking a shot from Mumbai's streets isn't a good idea. The traffic will prevent his getaway.'

His friend didn't reply. He opened the door to their Range Rover and bowed courteously for Zeb, who shook his head and got behind the wheel.

MISHA DIDN'T KNOW THAT ZEB HAD GUESSED CORRECTLY.

The killer wasn't near the JTF office. He was hanging out at the hospital.

He was dressed in a khaki outfit and sat in a taxi, behind an ambulance from across the entrance. He had paid the driver generously and had borrowed the man's vehicle for the day.

A perspiring man approached him.

'Off duty,' he said in Hindi.

He felt cold and emotionless.

He had spent the previous day raging and grieving at Nazyr's death. That was behind him.

He didn't move or react when he spotted the dark Range Rover. Only his eyes moved as he tracked its turn into the hospital's driveway. He saw Carter's silhouette for a fleeting second, and then the vehicle was out of sight.

He waited.

Killing time would be soon.

CHAPTER 91

'No change,' a white-coated doctor said. 'He's stable, that's all we can say at the moment.'

Zeb thanked him and went to Broker's room. He and his friends looked through the observation window for a long while until he sighed.

'Let's go.'

'Back to JTF?' Bear asked.

'Nope. We won't be of much help there. Dharavi. I want to talk to some of the residents again. Some of them may remember Nazyr and which direction he went. That could give us a clue to where Misha might be holed up.'

'No one remembered the last time we asked.'

'Won't hurt if we try again.'

'WE GOT a HIT!'

Zeb winced at Beth's shout in his earpiece. He raised a hand apologetically when a driver honked angrily at his sudden swerve.

'WE GOT TWO MEN LOOKING LIKE MAHAR AND GUL. BOTH OF THEM DISGUISED—'

'We got several hits,' Meghan said, tempering her sister's

excitement. 'Different men. None of them looking like our suspects, but their builds match. They must be disguised.'

'Yeah, several of them,' the younger twin agreed. 'But we have something to go on, now. Some of them are staying in downtown hotels, a few mid-town or north in the city.'

'Focus on the downtown ones,' Zeb told her. 'Especially those where the men are staying in the same joint.'

'Yeah, and Kohli and Meera are on top of that, too. Their callers are ringing those hotels—'

'They have false identities?'

'Indian businessmen,' she answered Bear's question. 'All of them. You know how facial recognition works. Werner can see through prosthetics, but simple changes, contact lenses and dyed hair, are still hard to detect.'

Zeb nodded absently. *Low-tech still beats high-tech.*

'None of those men are in their hotels?'

'No. We're cross-checking if they visited the previous blast sites or the other possible neighborhoods.'

Zeb reached Dharavi. He parked near a police vehicle and entered the settlement. He and his friends went past the leather factories and neared Sule's office.

'Mrs. DeSouza—'

'How can they do this? Why will they send a man for no reason?'

He slowed at the sight of the philanthropist in the corridor. A middle-aged, bespectacled woman in a sari accosted him.

'You are here again?' Sule growled at them. 'I told Kohli I will not allow any more cameras.'

'Take it up with him.' Zeb raised his hands defensively. 'We aren't here for that.'

'Are they with the electricity company?' The woman turned sharply and sized them up. 'They can't be. They don't look Indian, but if that organization can send a man and lie about it, I won't put it beyond them—'

'Mrs. DeSouza, I told you. I called the company up myself.

They said they hadn't sent anyone. There's nothing in their records about any call from us.'

'Why did that man say that, then? Why would he waste his time?'

'I don't know. I am sure it's a mistake.'

This has nothing to do with us.

Zeb made to step around them when the woman blocked his way and glared at him.

'Are you going to my school too to check on the fuse board?'

'Ma'am?' he asked, startled.

'Carter,' Sule said with barely restrained patience. 'Meet Mrs. DeSouza, our school principal. An electrician came yesterday to check out the wiring, but there was no reason to do so—'

'Yeah, I heard. Ma'am, I am not going to your school.'

She glowered at him and reluctantly stepped out of his way.

Zeb went down the hallway, shaking his head in amusement. The sounds of children reciting their lessons came to him.

His steps faltered.

Dharavi. About thirty percent of its residents are Muslim. It's not a majority.

He stopped.

'What?' Bwana looked at him curiously.

He held a hand up as he thought swiftly.

It would make for a great story, though. Muslims in a slum killed by Hindu extremists.

No, there are other targets.

Mumbra, Kurla, Haji Ali, Crawford Market ... the major ones have already been targeted.

He looked back.

Mrs. DeSouza was still arguing with Sule. She was quivering with righteous anger. Her time was valuable. How dare an electrician waste it? Didn't he value *his* time?

'Ma'am.' He went to them quickly. 'This man came yesterday?'

'Zeb,' Bear whispered from behind. 'What's up?'

'Yes,' the principal said angrily. 'I was busy with my examination marking, otherwise I would have taken him to task then and there.'

'What exactly did he say?'

'That we had reported a fault. We were having power failures. We had nothing of the sort—'

Zeb held his hand up to stop her.

'Was he my height?'

'No, about an inch shorter.'

'Can you describe him?'

'Yes, of course. I will never forget that time-waster. He had black hair. Slick, in some fancy style.'

'Beard, mustache?'

'No, clean-shaven.'

'We might have him on camera.'

Zeb whirled on Sule. 'I thought you didn't allow Kohli to mount them.'

'I didn't. I let them install a few at the entrances.' The philanthropist smirked. 'But I got my people to set them up inside Dharavi, at various points. There is one right here, hidden in that light.'

He pointed to the ceiling.

'This is the only way to get to the school. My camera would have spotted him.'

'Show us.'

Mrs. DeSouza looked curiously at Zeb. She made to speak, but something in his tone and on his face made her stop.

Sule took them inside his office, where he got Nilu to bring up the camera feed.

'That's him!' the principal said triumphantly, pointing at the screen. 'See how lazy he is. He isn't walking quickly.'

Zeb took in the lean, wiry man.

His head snapped up. He met Bwana and Bear's eyes.

That could be Gul.

They nodded silently.

'Can you show me where he went, ma'am?'

'Yes, of course.'

Mrs. DeSouza was eager. Someone was taking an interest in her issue. She swept down the hallway without waiting to see if they followed her.

'Carter, what's this?' Sule hissed angrily. 'Why are you wasting everyone's time?'

'Bwana,' Zeb ignored him. 'Call it in.'

'I was sitting there.' Mrs. DeSouza pointed at the table in the main classroom where a teacher was reading aloud from a book, while a bunch of students repeated after her.

They stopped and looked curiously at the arrivals.

Mrs. DeSouza waved imperiously at them to continue. 'He came in,' she spoke above their voices, 'talked to me and went to the back where the fuse board is.'

'Show me.'

She led them to the utility room.

Zeb scanned it swiftly from the door.

Brooms, dust bins, books and various school equipment on shelves, and the fuse board on the wall.

He went to it.

Doesn't look like he touched it. There's dust on it.

He took a second look around, noticing the film of dirt on every surface.

'No one comes here?'

'Only the cleaner, but she uses the broom and the wash bucket. She doesn't touch anything else.'

Bear nudged him from behind.

Zeb followed his friend's eyes to the table where a carton looked askew. He looked at it closely and crouched when he saw the marks on its legs.

'Sule, clear the school.'

'What? Why? Carter, are you out of your mind—'

'Sule, clear the school. There could be a bomb here.'

CHAPTER 92

Arjun Sule gawked at him. Mrs. DeSouza gasped in surprise from the doorway, her hand flying to her mouth.

'Bomb?' the former criminal asked. 'Do you know—'

Zeb caught his shoulder and pushed him out of the room with the school principal moving back hastily.

'CLEAR. THE. SCHOOL. NOW!'

Sule recovered.

'NILU! PADMA!' he roared.

His aide and daughter rushed up.

'Wait,' Zeb told him before he issued commands. 'This has to be done quietly without arousing suspicion.'

'Why? You said there could be a bomb.'

'Those who have planted it might be watching. If they know we have found it, they could set it off.'

'MY GOD!' The philanthropist's face turned ashen. His face trembled.

'ARJUN!' Mrs. DeSouza waggled her finger at him. 'This is not the time to panic. You clear out Dharavi. Padma and I will deal with my children.'

She huffed angrily at his fear, caught his daughter by the elbow and went inside the classroom.

'Children,' she began.

'Ma'am,' Zeb interrupted her. He was conscious of the urgency, of the need to move fast and yet couldn't help grinning at the way she had taken charge.

The teacher and the students broke away from their lesson. They eyed him curiously. The kids whispered among themselves and giggled.

Beth and Meg would have had a field day, here.

'You will have to do this without arousing suspicion,' he told the principal. 'People might wonder why the school is closing early.'

She looked at him. She turned to the students. 'Reena, go and get Shirin.'

A girl got up, went out of the room towards another class and returned with an older student.

'This is Shirin. She manages our school's Twitter account.'

Twitter account?

Zeb took in the girl who was in uniform like the rest of the students. Her glossy hair was pulled back in a tight braid. She regarded the Americans calmly.

'How old are you?'

'Ten,' she answered.

'And you manage the school's social media account?'

'Yes. I post videos on YouTube, design the website—'

'She does everything,' Mrs. DeSouza said proudly.

Zeb shook his head in bemusement and then straightened in urgency.

'You need to make an announcement, something that won't raise suspicion. A reason for the school to close and the students to leave.'

'Water.' Shirin's eyes gleamed. 'We have closed down a few times because the main pipe burst. That will be believable. Why do we need to do this, though?'

'I'll explain later.' Mrs. DeSouza took her by the elbow. 'Come along. Padma, you organize the rest of the school.'

Zeb turned to Sule who was in the hallway with his aide.

'We can't empty Dharavi,' he said softly. 'It's too big. It will draw attention. Clear this part. Move everyone to the farthest section.'

'That will be the leather factories, as you enter.'

'Do it. No one should know why, however. And monitor all the entrances. Get your people to rig up cameras and hook them to your computer. Warn everyone entering that there is no water. Limit the number of people who come in.'

'Shouldn't we block all the entrances?'

'No. The terrorists might suspect we discovered the bomb. That's why I want the cameras. We'll know who's coming in. But, get your people to watch all the arrivals. Can you do that?'

'This is my territory.' Sule stiffened. 'People listen to me. Yes, I'll organize this.'

'The students' parents can collect them from the entrances.'

'That's not needed. All of them are from Dharavi. My people are escorting them home.'

'Do we still need the social media announcement in that case?' Bwana asked.

'Let Shirin go ahead with it. Gul and Mahar might have informers here. That post will help.'

'Kohli and Meera are on the way,' Bear whispered when the philanthropist left with his aide. 'With a bomb-disposal squad. There'll be plain-clothes teams to surround Dharavi.'

'To watch out for Gul.' Zeb nodded.

'Yeah. We took the camera feed from Nilu and have sent it to Beth and Meg. They'll work with the JTF teams to work out where he's staying.'

Mahar could be there too, in the same hotel.

Zeb flattened himself against the wall when students rushed out of their classrooms and filled the corridor. People streamed out of their homes and the factories and went towards the factories.

'Water pipe burst.'

'Gas leak,' someone argued. 'It has to be that.'

Yes, that's a better explanation. Zeb watched the residents move in a coordinated manner, with Sule's men directing them.

Half an hour later the school and its immediate vicinity were quiet.

The philanthropist hurried to them. His face shone with perspiration.

'Shouldn't you leave, too?'

'We'll wait for the JTF.'

'But the bombs?'

'We have time.'

'Time for what?'

'They're set to explode tomorrow.'

'Are you sure of that?'

'No. That's why we got you to clear this part of Dharavi.'

Approaching footsteps. Meera, Kohli, the rest of his team and several civilians.

Zeb took in the plain-clothes people and frowned.

'They are?'

'JTF. Bomb-disposal experts. Medics. Special officers.'

'What about their gear?' Zeb moved out to the central hallway to make way for the entrants.

'There.' Meera bobbed her head towards another corridor where a couple of men were wheeling in a trolley.

CAUTION! GAS CYLINDERS

A fire-hazard sign was emblazoned next to the label.

'Millennium Hotel,' Beth told him.

'What's there ... Gul?' He whipped around to her.

'Yeah.' She fist-bumped him. 'And in the neighboring room, a man who we think is Mahar. The same build and height.'

'We got them,' Meera exulted. 'We have our people watching

the hotel. One team is disguised as hotel staff. They'll alert us if they leave.'

'They both are posing as Indian businessmen,' Meghan briefed him rapidly as the bomb squad donned their gear and got a motorized robot to enter the school.

The JTF and American teams moved farther away and watched from a safe distance.

'They have great covers,' the older twin continued. 'I called their offices. Receptionists answered, took my details, told me someone from the marketing teams would get back to me. The companies have real offices, have tax filings.'

'They're likely to be Pakistan Military Intelligence's outfits,' Kohli snarled. 'They weren't on our radar.'

It was stifling hot, but none of them left the hallway. The RAW officers were in continual radio contact with the rest of their personnel. Someone handed a bottle of water to Zeb. He drank it without taking his eyes away from the door to the main classroom. He was conscious of the twins whispering to the rest of his friends, but he didn't join in.

Was my guess right?

Ninety minutes later, a bomb squad officer came out into the hallway. He removed his helmet and wiped his head with a towel.

And gave them a thumbs-up.

A cheer erupted from the JTF team.

Zeb stumbled at Bwana's thump on his back.

'Cell-phone operated, sir,' the officer answered Kohli's question. 'C4 in the legs. The lab will have to analyze it, but it looks similar to the explosive at the other locations.'

'Can it be detonated any other way?' Meera asked.

'No, ma'am. We have defused the bomb completely. Someone would have to come in, insert a detonator and trigger it for it to explode.'

She high-fived the twins and whirled on Kohli, her face shining. 'Let's arrest them.'

'No,' Zeb said.

'What? Why?'

'Remember Hadi Asadi. Gul and Mahar might have a back-up team that we don't know of.'

'We'll sweat that out of them.'

'They're experienced operators. They won't give in so quickly We know where they are. We can track them. Wait till tomorrow. See what they do and then arrest them.'

Kohli and Meera exchanged glances. The Special Agent called Bose and conferred briefly.

He nodded and hung up.

'Aditya agrees with you. We wait till tomorrow.'

MISHA RUSLAN STOOD WITH THE CROWD NEAR THE LEATHER factory. He had his head turned away from the camera on the ceiling.

He had followed Carter inside Dharavi and when he had heard about the gas leak and water shortage, had stayed inside.

He had seen Sule's men mount the camera and suspected there was more to the story being circulated.

The truth didn't bother him.

Carter and his team were his sole focus.

He stayed in Dharavi, a hunter patiently waiting for his prey.

CHAPTER 93

Independence Day dawned on India just like any other day.

Hot. At five am, a touch of smog in Mumbai that obscured the sun.

Zeb was up early. He didn't go for his run. He was in his Range Rover at five-thirty, quickly joined by the twins. He raised his eyes to the rear-view mirror in an unconscious gesture towards the empty seat which Broker normally occupied.

A honk from behind. Bear in the second vehicle.

They drove to Dharavi.

GUL FRESHENED UP, KNOCKED ON MAHAR'S ROOM AND entered.

'Khalid,' the leader greeted him expansively and offered him a glass of juice.

'You are looking happy.'

'I am. Today is when India gets destroyed.'

Gul looked at the four killers who were watching the TV. Red Fort in Delhi, where the Indian prime minister would unfurl the country's flag and address the nation.

'Go.' Mahar embraced each of the killers. 'Make Pakistan proud. Remember—'

'Yes,' the team leader said expressionlessly. 'We should make sure we are seen near Dharavi. It should look like we aren't casual people. We'll call the number at just past seven-thirty am, when the prime minister is making his speech.'

'Correct, and after the explosions you will go to Mumbai Airport and fly to Islamabad where you will trigger more bombs there.'

Mahar patted them on the back and watched them go.

'Come.' He turned to Gul.

'Where?'

'Let's follow them.'

'Why? I thought we agreed—'

'Yes. But I want to see this myself. We'll go in separate cars. In any case, you should be there if something goes wrong.'

'Nothing will,' Gul said confidently. 'There was a gas leak and water shortage yesterday at Dharavi, but it's sorted now.'

DOWNTOWN MUMBAI TO DHARAVI TOOK TWENTY MINUTES that early in the morning. Zeb drove swiftly in the thin traffic. There were flags and bunting on light posts and posters of various Indian and state leaders hung from walls.

It's a national holiday.

Perfect timing for Mirza to strike at India.

'Leather factory entrance?' Bear asked in his earpiece.

'Yeah. That's the closest. We'll be on Tilak Road.'

He side-eyed Meghan. 'Meera and Kohli?'

'They have flooded the neighborhood with plain-clothes officers. Snipers on rooftops.'

'Yes,' the deputy drawled in his earpiece. 'Development that you may not be aware of. The four men that we identified ... they have set off from Mahar and Gul's hotel.'

'Any luck with their identities?' Zeb asked.

They must be part of Mirza's outfit. There's no other reason for them to visit Mahar's room so often.

'No luck. They too have Indian passports. Good covers.'

'They must be covert operatives that Mirza worked with in the past.'

'That's our guess too.'

'But why are they there?' Roger asked. 'Gul is likely to trigger the bombs with a call.'

'They could be the protection team.'

Zeb didn't reply.

He continued driving as he laid out the jigsaw puzzle in his mind and considered it. Something was off, but he didn't know what it was.

He swallowed his frustration.

'Another development.' Meera again. 'Both Mahar and Gul have left the hotel. Separate cars. Driving towards Dharavi.'

Zeb punched the gas.

GUL PARKED BY THE SIDE OF TILAK ROAD. HE SEARCHED THE neighborhood for police presence. Didn't spot any.

A truck drove past, a bullhorn on its cab playing patriotic songs. The Indian prime minister's banner on its side ruffled in the wind.

He got out of his car, went to a tea-cart and ordered a beverage.

'We are here,' the team leader said in his earpiece.

Gul sipped his tea and looked around casually. He spotted the white Honda and made out the shadows inside. He raised his cup imperceptibly.

'I am here, too,' Mahar announced.

THE LEADER SAT BACK IN HIS LEATHER SEAT AND TURNED ON the air conditioning. He could see Gul in the distance.

He fired off a message to Azhar Mirza.

Keep watching India's celebrations.

I am, came the instant reply. *We'll celebrate too.*

At seven-twenty am, the killers got out of their Honda. They stretched, pretended to yawn, and at a signal from the team leader, began crossing Tilak Road.

'See them?' Meera asked tautly.

'Yeah,' Zeb replied. He searched for her among the cars, but couldn't find her.

He and his team had ditched their Range Rovers and had climbed into an empty tourist bus that Kohli had arranged. Its dark windows and curtains gave them an unrestricted view.

At seven-thirty am, the radio in Gul's car began playing the national anthem. He had returned to it after his tea, from where he watched the killers cross the road.

A twenty-one-gun salute followed. A pause, and then the Indian prime minister started his speech.

'Now!' Gul spoke in his collar mic and called the detonator's number.

He waited.

Nothing happened.

He tried again.

No result.

Sweat broke out on his forehead.

'What happened?' Mahar yelled.

'I DON'T KNOW! IT'S NOT WORKING.'

'DID THE INDIANS FIND OUT ABOUT THE BOMBS?'

'THERE WAS NOTHING ON THE NEWS.'

'Shall we go inside Dharavi and shoot people up?' the team leader asked casually.

'NO!' Mahar screamed. 'KHALID YOU GO INSIDE AND CHECK THE BOMB. QUICKLY. THE SPEECH WILL BE OVER IN A FEW MINUTES. THE FOUR OF YOU, STAY THERE. DO YOU HAVE GUNS?'

'Yes, in our car.'

Gul crossed the road.

He made out the four killers a hundred meters away, to his right. A taxi swept past. The entrance to the leather factories was right ahead. The smell of Dharavi enveloped him.

'TAKE HIM,' KOHLI SAID LACONICALLY.

GUL FALTERED WHEN THE TEA-VENDOR WHO HAD SERVED HIM shoved his cart away and brought out an HK. Men and women in civilian clothing burst out of taxis and from beneath trucks and buses, all of them pointing their guns at him.

'STOP!' someone yelled at him.

A woman, in a white shirt and jeans.

She too had a gun on him as she ran up Tilak Road.

'STOP. RAISE YOUR HANDS.'

Gul's left hand flashed to his other pocket. He pressed the dial button on the burner phone in it. His right hand streaked to his waist and came out with a handgun.

'You'll have to do it without me,' he spoke into his mic. 'I'll buy you time.'

He fired at the woman, a long burst that missed when she dove to the ground. He shot at the approaching men.

A car rocked in an explosion. A van blew up in flames. More loud sounds followed and smoke enveloped Tilak Road, but Gul wasn't registering them.

His body jerked and shuddered with the impact of rounds.

He fell to the ground.

. . .

'WHERE ARE YOU?' MAHAR YELLED AS HE PEERED through the smoke.

'We got away,' the team leader said emotionlessly. 'The explosions gave us time. We shot three police officers and escaped. We are going towards Mahim Junction.'

'DON'T RUN. YOU'LL BE NOTICED.'

'We aren't. This isn't our first operation. Shall we come back to help you?'

'NO! GO TO THE AIRPORT. FLY OUT. STICK TO YOUR MISSION. YOU HAVE A VERY SMALL WINDOW BEFORE THE POLICE SEND OUT YOUR DETAILS TO MUMBAI AIRPORT.'

He was getting out of his car when he saw a woman running towards him with her gun, followed by several men.

'JUNAID MAHAR!' she yelled at him.

'Lieutenant Colonel,' he corrected her coldly, showing no fear of the guns on him. 'I am a diplomat with the Pakistan High Commission. Why are you—'

She decked him.

'CAN YOU SEE THOSE MEN?' ZEB ASKED.

'No.' Meghan jammed her face against the window. 'The smoke is too thick.'

He swore, reached down and picked up his HK and hustled out of the bus. His team spread out as they crossed Tilak Road.

'We're going inside Dharavi.'

'We see you,' a voice announced. 'Those green markings on your chests, backs and shoulders are visible.'

That must be one of the snipers.

He burst through the narrow passage.

'STAY INSIDE!' he shouted at residents who were crowding the entrance curiously. 'DID ANYONE COME HERE?'

'Nahin,' someone replied as the people fell back.

No.

Zeb went down the corridor.

If they came here, they would have started shooting if that's what they were planning.

There were no gunshots, no screaming. Only sirens wailing from Tilak Road.

He came to a central hallway and gestured for his team to split.

CHLOE LED THE TWINS TO THE SCHOOL.

'MUMBAI POLICE!' she yelled at a boy who ducked inside his house. A woman looked curiously out of a window and disappeared from sight.

The school was deserted. The hallways were empty.

Got to be sure.

She held her hand up to slow down the twins behind her and entered the main classroom.

Empty.

As were the others.

She went to the utility room.

The upturned table. Its legs on the floor. Plastic sheets and cable pieces. No trace of any explosives.

'No one's here,' Beth said from behind.

She nodded but went deeper, looked at the cartons and boxes, shrugged her shoulder and turned to the door.

The scrape of a heel.

She threw herself sideways as a hail of bullets stitched the wall. She caught sight of a man firing from behind a stack of boxes. His face partially exposed.

'MISHA RUSLAN!'

She wasn't aware she had yelled aloud.

Saw him throw his hand up.

Something flew in the air.

'GRENADE!' she screamed and felt something tug at her, and then there was darkness.

CHAPTER 94

'She's okay!'

Zeb sighed in relief at Beth's shout. He looked over her and Meghan's shoulders at Chloe, who groaned and sat up, rubbing her head.

'What happened? I saw the grenade—'

'Meg and I pulled you out of the room just in time. But you caught some of the blast wave and cracked your head against the wall. That knocked you out.'

'Misha!'

'He's gone,' Zeb said bitterly. 'He was hiding in that room all night long. We need to check how he got into Dharavi, but he rigged another explosion that knocked out a rear wall and escaped.'

'You haven't found him?'

'No. JTF teams are hunting him, but my guess is he's gone.'

He stepped back when she got to her feet and was enveloped by Bear. He smoothed her hair and kissed her on the forehead.

His friend's face was tight when he turned to Zeb.

'This is his plan. He'll try to pick us off one by one.'

'I know.'

Meera and Kohli came up.

'No signs of him,' the deputy said.

We can't think of him. Not until these terrorists are captured.

'Those four killers?'

'They got away too. Looks like Gul rigged several vehicles on the road as a precaution.'

JTF didn't search the street, Zeb thought. *That would have given the game away to Gul and Mahar, who would have activated their plan B.*

'Mahar?'

'He isn't talking. He's claiming diplomatic immunity. He wants us to deport him.'

Deport. Airport.

'LET'S GO!' Zeb yelled.

'Go where?' Bwana shouted back.

'TO THE AIRPORT. I KNOW WHERE THOSE MEN ARE GOING.'

CHAPTER 95

'Mirza, or Mahar and Gul, who were behind the plan ... they wanted us to see those men. Those killers. That's why they had those Indian identities. The story would be the same. Hindu extremists targeting Muslims.'

Zeb explained rapidly as he drove to Mumbai International Airport.

'Makes sense,' Kohli replied in his earpiece after a while. 'But why do you think they are going to the airport? Why wouldn't they hide in the city?'

'Because they'll fly to Pakistan and explode another set of bombs there. Tomorrow. On Pakistan's Independence Day!'

The shocked silence was broken by Bose's curse.

'Of course!' the RAW chief said. 'Pakistan would have blamed not just Hindu extremists but Indian aggression. They would claim this was an invasion of their country. Going by the current tensions, the two countries would have possibly launched airstrikes, and that would play into Azhar Mirza's hand. Vikram, alert the airport! Those men cannot—'

'They have gone, sir.' Meera cut in. 'I got off the phone with the airport just now. A flight left for Islamabad fifteen minutes ago. It is out of our airspace.'

Bose swore loudly. 'Suman and I will brief our Home Minister. They will take it up—'

'You won't get anywhere, sir.'

'Why do you say that, Zeb?' the NIA head asked him sharply.

'Because their government won't be receptive. It has been turned hostile to India by Mirza's plan. You should call Nawaz Khan too, but I don't trust him.'

'Why not? Capturing those men is in his interests too.'

Zeb recalled the ISI chief's words and expressions. 'He's a hard-liner too. He might let the bombs explode and only then apprehend those men. He won't mind a few innocents dying. He will enjoy the accusations piled on India—'

'You are saying Mirza has succeeded even after all this?'

'No, ma'am. He hasn't. You should publicize Mirza's plan. Parade Mahar in front of the TV cameras. Get your story out there, first. And most importantly, please convince the prime minister not to strike first.'

'We can do that.'

'That's why you are going to the airport,' Kohli said wonderingly. 'Your team can move faster than we could mobilize a strike team. Those killers are flying commercial. Your Lear can make up for the time advantage they have. You'll take those men out in Islamabad.'

'Yeah. I hope I have read Khan wrong. That he gets those men arrested as soon as they step off the plane.'

'There's a risk in your going there. Pakistani security forces might shoot you in the airport. In the heat of battle, they might not stop to ask for identification.'

'I am aware of that.'

'We'll warn their police and security forces.'

'Do that, but if I guess right, Nawaz Khan will play a hand there, too. He will slow down their response. He hates me for threatening his daughter. Once he knows I am coming, he'll let us do the dirty work and then take credit for it.'

'You saved her life.'

'Nawaz Khan is a man who thinks the world owes him favors.'

CHAPTER 96

Meghan opened a map of Islamabad Airport once they were airborne.

'This is the international arrivals terminal.' She pointed. 'Those men have Indian passports. That will slow down their entry to the country. Border control and all that. That will help us catch up.'

'They won't be armed,' Roger mused.

'Not in the aircraft,' Zeb agreed. 'But we don't know if Mirza has arranged weapons for them in the airport. We don't know if the security over there is on his side. We should not rule anything out.'

'How do we do this? We can't carry weapons.'

'We go physical. There are eight of us and only four of them. We take them down as soon as they enter the arrivals.'

'Eight of us?' Chloe reminded him.

The memory hit him like a blow to the gut.

Broker would have cracked some joke. He would have talked of going to the golf club while we are in Islamabad.

Zeb got to his feet abruptly and hugged her hard.

'We will get him,' he said against her hair.

I will get Misha Ruslan.

'As soon as this is over.'

'I know.' She squeezed him in return and kissed his cheek.

He dropped back to his seat and squinted at the map. Worked it out in his mind.

We can take those men out if they aren't armed.

I'm worried Khan might order the security men to fire on us. He'll claim it was a misunderstanding.

They had to anticipate that.

'Where are the fire alarms?' he asked the twins.

CHAPTER 97

They landed at Islamabad International Airport at six pm with the sun shining, briefly bathing their Lear in gold and orange.

'They too have landed. Fifteen minutes ago. We didn't make as much time as we'd hoped. The wind was against us,' Meghan said tightly.

'But we hacked into the airport's security system. We are tracking the cameras. We'll find them. We know where the guards are,' her sister said.

They hustled out of the aircraft swiftly in their civilian clothing with nothing but their US diplomatic passports.

'You're visiting Pakistan often, sir.' The Border Control officer scanned Zeb's document and noted the previous entries.

'Yeah,' he drawled, fighting to keep the impatience from his voice. 'You know the state of the world. My government is working closely with yours to address grain shortages in Pakistan.'

The man nodded absently, stamped his passport and waved him through.

'Guards to our three o'clock,' Bwana said beneath his breath when they entered the arrivals lounge.

The terminal was crowded with passengers. Family members greeting arrivals, travelers towing luggage, continual airport announcements over the loudspeakers.

Zeb checked out the armed men. *Some kind of elite unit*, he gauged from their uniforms. They were alert, gripped their HKs as they watched the flow of arrivals in the lounge. He met one of the guard's eyes, who didn't react.

Didn't he recognize us? Didn't Khan warn them?

There were more armed guards and soldiers around the lounge, scattered at vantage points.

'Where are the men?'

'They have cleared immigration,' Beth looked up from her screen. 'But I lost them in the arrival hallway. They had their heads down and were in a bunch of other travelers.'

'Did they leave the terminal?'

'No,' she replied confidently. 'We're tracking the outside cameras. No one matches their build. They're still in the terminal.'

They split up. The twins at the mouth of the arrival hallway, on their screens, Bear and Chloe to check out the newsstands, while Bwana and Roger went to inspect the cafés and restaurants.

Zeb drifted towards the restrooms.

He didn't go far when a man emerged.

That's Chandan Ramani! He recognized the killer from the Mumbai hotel images. *And there, the rest of them, behind him.*

'Got them. On my eleven. In front of the men's bathroom.'

The men didn't have any luggage. They wore loose jackets, however, and were holding their arms close to their chests.

'Looks like they're armed. I can see lines beneath their clothing.'

They must have weaponed up in the bathroom.

The men hadn't spotted him.

Would they know me? Did Mahar and Gul warn them about us?

We'll have to assume they do.

The killers spread out as if they didn't know each other and started towards the exit.

Zeb angled to cut them off. A guard near the sliding door, watching him.

'Roger?'

'On it. Count down to five.'

On Zeb's fifth step, the fire alarms rang out. Their sirens drowned out every other noise in the terminal.

The guard looked up and around.

'Every guard is distracted,' Bwana said.

Zeb felt him approach behind him.

Chandan Ramani snatched his head up as well.

He looked at Zeb.

Recognition flared in his eyes.

His mouth opened to yell a warning.

His hand flashed beneath his jacket.

Zeb dove at him.

He barreled into the man just as his AK74 came up. He caught the gun hand and jerked it towards the ceiling as they fell to the floor.

He felt something sail through the air and in his peripheral vision saw a large suitcase crash into another man. Another piece of luggage slammed into the remaining men.

He heard Bear shout. Chloe yell out in warning.

He wrestled with Ramani for the gun but couldn't stop a round that flew at the ceiling.

Its crack was audible over the sirens.

Someone screamed.

Zeb gritted his teeth against the flurry of punches Ramani threw at him. He kept twisting and ducking his head to avoid the eye and throat jabs. The tiled floor was slippery. He didn't have sufficient purchase. His hand kept slipping from the killer's gun wrist, but he held on and with a muttered oath when a blow to his ribs stunned him, reared up and dug his right elbow in the terrorist's sternum.

He took a blow to his throat and gasped but crashed his elbow in the man's jaw and felt his teeth break, and kept grinding it down until the man gave out a muffled howl and his AK slipped to the floor. Then Zeb let go of the gun hand and chopped his neck brutally.

'DON'T MOVE!'

He looked up cautiously to see the guard pointing his gun at him.

Bear, Bwana and Roger were on top of the other killers, but they too were surrounded by security men.

'These men are terrorists,' he said in Urdu. 'They bombed Mumbai and fled to Pakistan.'

'DON'T MOVE. DON'T TALK. DON'T TOUCH THAT GUN.'

'It's not my gun.'

The guard snarled, reversed his HK and clubbed his head.

CHAPTER 98

A small holding cell in the security complex at Islamabad International Airport.

A table. A jug of water, a few glasses. Two chairs.

None of the Agency operators sat on them.

Zeb felt his temple and examined the swelling with his fingers. *No cut. I have suffered worse injuries.*

He compartmentalized the throbbing and glanced at his watch.

'We've been here half an hour,' Bear growled.

Bwana went to the dark glass on one wall and pounded at it.

'YOU KNOW WE HAVE US DIPLOMATIC PASSPORTS?' he yelled at the people behind the one-way mirror. 'DID YOU MISS WHERE WE TOOK DOWN FOUR TERRORISTS WHILE YOUR GUARDS WATCHED? DO YOU WANT TO KNOW WHAT THE HEADLINES WILL BE TOMORROW?'

'Carter.'

Zeb looked up when Nawaz Khan entered the room. He was in uniform, a gun holstered at his waist. He straightened a chair, dropped into it, and looked at them with a superior smile.

'It took you long enough,' Roger snarled at him.

'The security forces thought you were terrorists. They assumed your US passports were forgeries.'

'Bose warned you,' Chloe burst out. 'He sent you everything on Ramani and the rest of the killers. He told you which flight they were on ... and did you follow the news? Gul was killed in Mumbai, Mahar is in custody and Azhar Mirza's name is splashed all over the media.'

'I have been busy.' Khan continued, smiling smugly. 'I haven't kept on top of what's happening in India.'

He'll make us sweat for a day or two, Zeb figured. *He's probably already told the story his way. That ISI intel and his team worked with the airport security guards to take down the terrorists. The travelers at the airport won't know any better.*

'Why are you holding us?' he asked.

'Me? I am not doing anything. It's the airport police. They arrested you. They want to investigate who you are. Your passports are false. They know you aren't diplomats. They aren't sure if you are colluding with the terrorists. I had to pull a lot of strings to get to see you.'

Meghan snorted.

She straightened.

'Beth and I, we recorded everything that happened in the lounge. We uploaded the video to various social media sites.'

She glanced at her watch.

'Those videos will be published in the next fifteen minutes if you don't release us. I'm sure the story you've put out is that ISI captured Ramani and his team. Those videos will show you are lying. The world will see Pakistan's guards did nothing. Along with those videos, Bose's messages to you and other agencies will be released as well. They will make clear that you had been informed of these terrorists' flight. Those social media posts along with the breaking news from India ... I don't think they're going to portray you in a good light. If you still don't release us, President Morgan will call your prime minister. You can imagine how that conversation will go. He might even accuse you and your agency of being involved in the Mumbai bombings. ISI has history, there.'

'And,' Beth chuckled before Khan could respond. 'At about the same time as those posts, another one will go out with Zeba's details. Of course, you don't have to believe us. Wait and see what comes up on the social media platforms.'

Bear cocked his head at the glass. 'You should get over there and tell them to stop recording and erase whatever they have on tape so far.'

Khan's face twisted in fury. He shot up from his chair. He went to the door and hurled it open.

'GO! GET OUT OF MY COUNTRY.'

IT TOOK ANOTHER HOUR FOR THEM TO RETRIEVE THEIR phones and passports and for their Lear to be released.

Zeb buckled in while the aircraft taxied and watched curiously as the twins and Chloe huddled over their phones.

'What?'

'Broker is awake.'

Beth's straight-faced response didn't register initially.

And then she smiled and whooped.

SIX AM WHEN THEY LANDED IN MUMBAI.

Kohli and Meera were there to receive them. Both RAW officers grinned broadly and hugged each of them.

'Aditya and Suman said whatever you want is yours,' the Special Agent said.

'We want to get to the hospital.'

'Yes, Zeb. I'll arrange two vehicles for you.'

'Our Range Rovers are—'

'You'll be jet-lagged. I'll get someone to collect your rides and drive them to your hotel. Go in our cars.'

Zeb didn't argue.

He shook Kohli's and Meera's hands and got into an armored van with his team.

Forty minutes to the downtown hospital.

Five minutes to show their identification to the security team on Broker's floor and then they were outside his room.

'Lungs will heal.'

'Stable.'

'No apparent head or brain injury.'

'Some more scans.'

He didn't pay attention to the twins and Chloe conferring with the doctor. He watched his friend on the bed.

Broker seemed to feel the weight of their gazes.

He stirred and opened his eyes.

He gestured weakly, at which Beth yelped in delight and burst inside his room.

Zeb followed and stood at the foot of his bed while his team surrounded his friend.

'Took you long enough,' Roger growled.

'This was the only way to get y'all to do some work. I was doing all the heavy lifting.'

Zeb chuckled.

'It was Dmitri Ruslan. That confused me and gave him the opening to injure me. How could it be, though? Dmitri is dead.'

'He is. It was his twin. Misha Ruslan. Nazyr was their adopted sibling.'

'Was?'

'Yeah.'

'Twin?'

'Yeah. Long story. We'll brief you later.'

It was also not the time to ask Broker why he made his move on his own.

'We'll get Misha.' He squeezed his friend's arm.

'I know you will.'

CHAPTER 99

One month later

Zeb crouch-climbed the flights of stairs to the sixth floor. Armed JTF operators on every landing.

His team behind him.

The building was in Juhu, a fancy neighborhood in the western suburbs of Mumbai where celebrities lived.

JTF had released Misha Ruslan's photograph and details to the media. That got the citizens to call in. Most of the sightings were false leads, but after weeks of investigation and leaning on every criminal outfit in the city, they had arrived at the apartment building in Juhu.

Plainclothes operatives infiltrated it during the day. Drone surveillance confirmed there was a single male occupant in the third flat on the sixth floor. Video footage showed it was Misha Ruslan.

'He's ours,' Zeb told Kohli and Meera.

They didn't argue.

'We'll support you,' the deputy said, which was how the operators were lined up on the landings and the single entrance was covered as well.

His bedroom overlooks the rear street. A steep drop to ground level. There's no chance he can escape that way.

Still, JTF had covered both mouths of the street.

It was mid-day when Zeb took to the stairs. A deliberate move.

Misha will expect any attack to be at night. He'll be prepared for that. He won't expect us to come in broad daylight.

'He's in the living room, watching TV,' Beth, in his earpiece.

Zeb tapped his mic in acknowledgment and kept climbing. Bwana, Bear and Roger behind him. Meghan and Chloe bringing up the rear.

'All clear,' the guard on the fifth-floor landing told him. 'No resident has come out of their flat. No alarms have been raised.'

Sixth floor landing.

Zeb crawled to the door and inched it open.

Marble tiles. Dim lighting in the ceiling. Brass elevator doors. Soft music piped through hidden speakers.

'Is this how Bollywood actors live?' Bwana asked.

'Nope,' Chloe retorted. 'These are B- and C-list celebrities and business people.'

Will Misha have cameras mounted in the hallway?

Zeb peered at the ceiling but didn't spot any.

Every apartment door in the building not only had a peephole, but also a security camera.

That's at eye-level, though.

He signaled that he was going through and crawled onto the marble floor. He hoped no resident opened their door and squawked in surprise, but even if they did, their GO wouldn't change.

He reached Misha's door. The camera was above him.

He reached down to his pocket and brought out the explosive. Stuck it to the door. Wedged a detonator in it. Hooked it to his phone and crawled back to the landing door from where he made the call.

He sprang up at the explosion, which was loud and powerful enough to rip apart the door and remove a section of the holding wall.

Zeb shot through the opening.

Misha on the couch, twisting his head to the door.

'POLICE!'

The Russian reacted as if the blast's shock wave hadn't hit him.

He shouted in anger, reached forward, picked up the coffee table with one hand and flung it towards the opening.

Zeb ducked from the missile.

He raised his HK.

He slipped on a concrete shard and his single shot went wide.

He cursed at Misha disappearing down the hallway and followed him carefully, prepared for an ambush.

No attack came.

The Russian went straight to his bedroom and threw himself out of the glass window.

What?

Zeb raced to the shattered window to see the killer leap wide and clutch at a lamppost four meters away and slide down it. A wedding procession was on the street, below them.

Where did that come from?

He didn't bother to ask in his comms.

He climbed to the sill and dove into the air.

If he can do it, so can I.

CHAPTER 100

Zeb's outstretched hands clawed at empty air and then curled around the smooth metal of the post. His body crashed against it as he slid down.

His eyes tracked Misha, who looked up at him and then dove into the procession.

Zeb jumped the last few meters to the ground, regained his balance, and shoved through the crowd.

A loud band playing. A bunch of men and women dancing at the head. A decorated umbrella beneath which was the groom in a colorful outfit.

The sights and sounds registered on him as he pushed and shoved his way through the revelers.

Can't allow him to take hostages.

He caught sight of Misha ahead of him and then he disappeared from sight.

Someone screamed and Zeb jumped back just in time for the knife, which appeared from behind a woman, to slash blindly.

She stumbled onto him, shouting wildly.

She's not injured.

He checked her out automatically as he pushed her onto other celebrants and followed the Russian deeper.

Behind the groom now, who was unaware of the lethal chase. A firework exploded. The band strengthened in volume. Red mist in the air.

Blood!

No! That's gulal.

Colored powder, usually red, that was used in Indian festivals and celebrations.

Three men surged onto him.

Pushed by Misha who growled and chopped at him with his knife.

Zeb shoved the men away hastily. They shouted in anger and fear and then the blade sliced his jacket and scraped off his armor.

He clubbed Misha in the face.

The Russian's nose broke, but he kept attacking. He reversed the knife to sweep at the throat.

Zeb didn't have room to move. Only the immediate people around him were aware of the fight and they were shouting and trying to get away, but the band drowned out their yells and the revelers were jammed tight.

He blocked the knife arm with his left hand and yanked it back quickly when Misha grinned savagely and turned the blade swiftly to follow his palm.

The killer's right hand reached beneath his shirt. It came out with a Glock.

The red mist descended on Zeb.

He leaned into the attack instead of getting away. He ignored the gun, which was still rising, and caught the knife wrist with both hands, twisting brutally to break it and grasping the falling blade. He slashed at the gun hand and then his hand moved in a blur as he plunged the blade repeatedly in Misha's chest and throat, punched him to the ground and kept him down as the crowd finally realized what was happening and screamed and scattered, but the band still kept playing on until it too died away, leaving Zeb with his knee to Misha's chest. The Russian shuddered and his blood leaked onto the street and gulal rained on them.

Zeb felt a hand on his shoulder. He took several breaths to clear the rage and lifted his head.

Kohli, behind whom were his friends.

'I thought you wanted him alive.'

'You thought wrong.'

CHAPTER 101

Neelam Gaikwad sighed as she opened her apartment door and dumped her bag on the dining table.

She went to the bathroom, took a long shower and dressed in a fresh sari in front of her mirror.

Her hair was gray. Her face had more lines in it than a month ago. The apartment was quiet when normally it would have Nisha chattering away as she did her school work. The TV would have blared loudly.

Now, there was nothing but silence.

The mother studied herself in the mirror.

She had cried just that once in the hospital and then hadn't given in to her grief. It was there, within her. She could feel it within herself, but it was walled tight behind invisible bands that prevented her from sobbing.

'You should cry,' her friends told her.

'You should let it out,' they advised.

She knew they were right, but she couldn't.

Her sobs wouldn't come.

She went about her life monotonously.

One dull day after another, teaching in her school, returning to her empty apartment since her husband had passed away long before, leaving her with the family home that she had lived in along with Nisha, but which now felt hollow and empty and enormously large.

Neelam Gaikwad went to the kitchen and arranged flowers and fruit on a wicker tray and left the apartment to walk the short distance to Prabhadevi Temple.

It was evening. Still hot. Cars honked as traffic flowed past her. Someone called her name, but she didn't respond.

Going to the temple had become an empty ritual, and she wanted to finish it as quickly as possible and return to the empty apartment.

Wind ruffled her sari. The sun behind the gathered dark clouds.

She joined the crowd of worshippers at the temple, left her footwear at the steps and climbed them.

She rang the brass bell and when it was her turn to approach the idol, she placed her fruit and flower offering at its feet and bowed her head.

Her mind was empty.

In other times she and Nisha would have chanted prayers. Those days were gone.

She straightened, adjusted her sari and went down the steps.

She frowned when she saw the box wedged in her footwear.

She looked around.

No one paid her any attention. Worshippers went inside and came out.

A drop of rain fell on her head.

She bent down and picked up the box.

It was wrapped in fine paper. The folds were neat and crisp. She shook it. Felt something move inside.

She drew it to her nose. She didn't know why, but something about the red wrapping made her smell it.

Jasmine and coconut. Her mind flashed to when she used to apply oil to Nisha's hair and braid it with flowers.

She forced the memories away.

Some more rain drops fell on her.

She didn't register them as she opened the wrapping and stared at the wooden box. It was deep brown and had a metal clasp.

She opened it and gasped at its contents.

A wooden flute on a bed of red velvet.

She removed it with shaking fingers.

It was heavy. It was used, going by the marks on it, but it was polished and had a certain heft and feel to it.

Neelam Gaikwad didn't know anything of flutes, but she knew instinctively that the instrument she held wasn't an ordinary one. It wasn't one that could be bought in stores.

It looked like it had been crafted by hand by a highly skilled artisan and had been lovingly cared for.

Her fingers shook as she stroked its fine polish, feeling the wood's grain.

She felt the dam inside her creak when she brought it to her mouth and blew, and then it broke and her tears came just as the heavens parted and the rain poured on her.

Someone came to her and shouted to seek shelter. She ignored the woman and kept blowing on the flute as she sobbed and the shower intensified and then lessened, and the sun came out from behind the clouds and lit Mumbai with a rainbow.

Neelam Gaikwad didn't know that the flute had belonged to one of the country's most renowned musicians who had received a call late at night, had listened quietly and agreed, and had packed his favorite instrument and had shipped it to Mumbai, where a man had collected it and placed it in her footwear.

She didn't know of an American named Zeb Carter, who had called on every little goodwill he had to reach out to the flautist.

She knew the men behind the Crawford Market explosions were dead and that many terrorists had been killed or arrested.

Neelam Gaikwad sat on the steps, crying and playing the flute and when she was out of breath and when the rainbow too disappeared, she placed the instrument back in its box and put it in her handbag.

She got to her feet, but instead of returning home, went up the steps again, inside the temple and bowed her head to the deity.

This time, the prayers came.

MORE BOOKS

Click here to download The Watcher, a novella exclusive to Ty Patterson's newsletter subscribers

Check out Cordite here, the next Cutter Grogan thriller

Check out Moscow here, the previous Zeb Carter thriller

Join Ty Patterson's Facebook group of readers, here

BONUS CHAPTER FROM CORDITE

'Cutter Grogan?'

He turned casually to take in the elderly woman who was in a flowered shirt and dark trousers. She clutched her handbag and smiled tightly at him, but there was no humor in it. Her eyes had no spark in them.

'Yeah?'

'I am Jenna Gutierrez. I saw you on TV a few times. I searched for your address and came here.'

He looked beyond her. It was closing time. The neighboring offices had shut. The weekend was starting; he had friends waiting for him.

'Something I can help you with, ma'am?'

'You can find who raped and killed my daughter.'

He blinked.

There was no anger in the woman's tone. It was flat, as if all emotion had been wrung out of her.

'That's something for the cops, ma'am.'

'I have been to them. They aren't of any help. They said the investigation is ongoing, but I know there won't be a result.'

'Why not?'

'Because the animals who did this are powerful and are well-connected. You really think cops in this country are going to go against them? Where the victim was a Hispanic woman, daughter of a Mexican immigrant? Are you aware of the world we live in, Mr. Grogan?'

I am.

'Not every officer is like that, ma'am. I have good friends in the NYPD. I can direct you to them.'

'This didn't happen in New York. She was killed in California.'

'I know a few officers there, too. In any case, this is not the kind of case I take on.'

'Yeah. I watched some of your TV interviews. I read up on you. The Speaker's daughter. Some billionaire's kid. I am sorry for wasting your time, Mr. Grogan.'

She turned away, went to the elevator and jabbed the button.

Cutter watched her.

A slight figure who still clutched her bag tightly. She didn't give any indication she was aware of his gaze.

This isn't my kind of case, he told himself firmly, even though her words had stung. *There are good cops. They can help her.*

Zeb and his crew were waiting for him in a mid-town bar.

I haven't met them since Moscow and Mumbai.

Jenna Gutierrez went inside the elevator and disappeared from sight.

The bar was in Columbus Circle. It was crowded and noisy, but where his friends were sitting was an oasis of calm.

Cutter hugged Zeb hard. He inspected Broker carefully, who winked and grinned at him.

'I won't break. I am fully recovered.'

He shook the older operator's hand, winced at Bwana and Bear's hugs, fist-bumped Roger and sat next to Meghan. Beth and Chloe high-fived him and the younger twin slid a glass of juice over to him.

'We ordered for you. Zeb and you.' She wrinkled her nose. 'What is that concoction?'

'It's good for the soul,' he said expansively. 'You wouldn't know.'

'I don't want to know,' she sneered.

He let the conversation flow, responding automatically until Meghan tugged his sleeve.

'What's it? You aren't with us?'

He told her about Jenna Gutierrez.

'She isn't wrong, is she?' Beth slurped her drink loudly. 'Lately you seem to be taking rich or celebrity folks' cases.'

'Is that how you see me?'

'Nope. But that's how those who don't know you, will judge you.'

'This is a police investigation.'

'When has that stopped you?' Chloe retorted.

'Are you worried about her fees?' Meghan taunted.

He flushed. 'That's a low blow. You know I rarely take fees.'

'Hear her out. Make some calls. What do you lose in that?' Zeb told him. 'What she said ... that's exactly the kind of case you take. That's who you are.'

Jenna Gutierrez signed out from work the next day. She deposited her coat in the locker and went out onto the street.

She blinked at the sight of Cutter Grogan lounging against a fire hydrant.

'I have a table for us, over there.' He cocked his head at an outdoor café down the street.

'You will take my case?' Hope bloomed in her chest.

'I will hear you out,' he told her.

'That's good enough for me. Have you heard of Paul Kastelli?'

'The senator?'

'Yeah. It was his son who raped and murdered my daughter.'

AUTHOR'S MESSAGE

Thank you for taking the time to read *Mumbai*. If you enjoyed it, please consider telling your friends and posting a short review.

Sign up to Ty Patterson's mailing list and get *The Watcher*, a Zeb Carter novella, exclusive to newsletter subscribers. Join Ty Patterson's Facebook Readers Group, here.

BOOKS BY TY PATTERSON:

ZEB CARTER SERIES

Ten books in the series and counting

Cutter Grogan Series (Zeb Carter Universe)

Six books in the series and counting

Zeb Carter Short Stories

Three books and counting

Warriors Series (Zeb Carter Universe)

Twelve books in the series

Gemini Series (Zeb Carter Universe)

Four thrillers in the series

Warriors Series Shorts (Zeb Carter Universe)

Six novellas in the series

Cade Stryker Series

Two military sci-fi thrillers

ABOUT THE AUTHOR

Ty has been a trench digger, loose tea vendor, leather goods salesman, marine lubricants salesman, diesel engine mechanic, and is now an action thriller author.

Ty is privileged that thriller readers love his books. 'Unputdownable,' 'Turbocharged,' 'Ty sets the standard in thriller writing,' are some of the reviews for his books.

Ty lives with his wife and son, who humor his ridiculous belief that he's in charge.

Made in the USA
Columbia, SC
16 July 2022